RECKLESS

RECKLESS

Sarah Jackson

CHAMELEON

in association with
Granada Television

Acknowledgements

Thanks to my agent Robert Kirby and editors Deborah Waight and Nicky Paris. Thanks especially to Liz Counihan for the medical advice, and of course, to the usual suspects: Andy Lane, Tina Anghelatos, Ben Jeapes, Gus Smith, Molly Brown and Chris Amies; Alex Stewart; Jane Killick; Barbara and Peter Morris; Martin Weaver; the students and staff of Clarion 89; Kurt Roth, Devon Monk, Cindy and Lee Zender, Judy and Dan Tucker, and other friends in e-space too numerous to mention.

First published in Great Britain in 1997 by
Chameleon Books
106 Great Russell Street
London WC1B 3LJ

Text © Sarah Jackson 1997
The right of Sarah Jackson to be identified as the author of this work
has been asserted by her in accordance with the Copyright,
Designs and Patents Act, 1988

Reckless © Granada Television Productions

Adapted from scripts by Paul Abbott

Front cover photograph shows
Robson Green as *Owen Springer* and
Francesca Annis as *Anna Fairley*.

CIP data for this title is available
from the British Library

ISBN 0 223 99124 7

Typeset by Falcon Oast Graphic Art
Printed in Great Britain by
WBC, Bridgend

Chapter 1

Owen Springer was late. His father was comatose, and he was late.

His feet pounded out the rhythm of his thoughts as he sprinted through the hospital grounds: out of the gate, traffic was pouring down the high road and there was no taxi in sight.

He was very late. His father's breath growing fainter and his lips more cyanotic. In Manchester, while Owen was here in poxy London.

Into the taxi, the blessed, blessed taxi and to Euston Station. He finally got to the ticket office. His breath rasped in his chest as he bought his ticket.

He found the platform and collapsed into the first seat he came to.

And then he realized that he should have phoned from the station to see how the old man was doing. He started to get up but saw, rather than felt, the train gliding away from the station.

Okay. There was nothing he could do now so he settled back into his seat.

He'll be all right, the insistent rhythm of the train seemed to say: he has to be, he has to be.

Owen reached into his holdall for a paper and the crossword: anything to pass the time. But he hadn't bought one.

Food then, he thought. He jounced his way back

down the carriage, through the next one, to the buffet car. He bought himself a cheese and pickle sandwich and a coffee. While he was waiting for his change, he noticed a sign: *phonecards sold here*.

'What's this?' he said to the buffet attendant. 'Anything to increase people's frustration levels?' The attendant frowned. 'I mean if you're wanting to make a phone call...'

'There's one over there,' the attendant said, gesturing toward the wall. He handed over Owen's change.

There is a God, Owen thought. He sorted two pound coins out of his change. 'Give us a card, then.'

'Sorry, sir. Sold out.'

Then again, Owen thought, maybe not. He let out a sigh of frustration.

He grabbed his sandwich and started back to his seat. A man in a chalk-stripe suit was just putting his mobile phone away.

It had to be worth a try. ' 'Scuse me,' Owen said. 'They've no phonecards left at the buffet car. Do you mind if I...' The man's glare told Owen his answer, but he finished anyway. 'use your phone?'

'Yes,' said the man. 'I do mind.'

'Charmed I'm sure,' Owen said. He walked on, balancing himself against the jouncing of the train. Now he was looking for phones and he could see quite a few. A woman with a baby had one out on the table in front of her, as she flipped through her address book.

' 'Scuse me? Could I use your phone, please?'

She looked up. Owen realized she was older than he'd taken her for. 'Absolutely not,' she said.

Owen caught the eye of the man opposite. There was a bulge in his jeans-jacket pocket. 'Look, I have got money...'

'Sorry,' the man said. 'I'm expecting a call.'

Owen felt his jaw clench in annoyance. 'Please,' he said, trying to get exactly the right note of desperation – not too much, not too little – into his voice. 'It's an emergency.'

'I've heard that one before.' The man grinned, showing a row of uneven teeth. He had muscles like a builder's mate.

Funny boy, Owen thought as he backed off.

Plebs, he thought, heading back toward the buffet car. Maybe he'd have better luck there.

But he didn't. He'd tried four more people when an expensively dressed woman said, 'Here. Use mine.'

She held out her phone. Owen registered auburn hair and dark brown eyes as he took it. More class than the rest put together, he thought as he moved away and dialled his father's number.

Irma, his father's home-help, answered. It took only moments for Owen to discover that his father was still unconscious and that the doctor hadn't yet arrived. He strove to sound calm. 'Irma, listen to me,' he said. 'You get on the phone now and ask him what he thinks "emergency" means. If he's not there in fifteen minutes, you phone an ambulance – go straight to Casualty with him, right?'

'I don't know, Owen...'

'*Right?*' Owen insisted, too loudly. He realized that the phone's owner was listening. So were most of the other passengers. Well good for them. Maybe now they'd realize he'd been serious all along. That should help them sleep better at night. He said goodbye, and closed the phone.

He went to give it back. One of the City businessmen who'd refused to help him caught his eye, then glanced away.

3

Owen handed the phone back to the woman. 'Appreciate it,' he said. 'Thanks.'

She smiled and despite his worries, Owen found himself smiling back.

Definitely more class than the rest of them, he thought as he went back to his seat.

The damn key wouldn't turn in the lock. Owen jiggled it a bit harder, and it finally gave. He lugged his bags inside and dumped them down. There was a light on in the kitchen.

'Hiya, Owen,' came Irma's voice. 'Doctor's up there with him now.'

Owen sprinted up the stairs three at a time. The door to his father's room was standing slightly ajar so he went in without knocking. Dad was lying in bed. His skin was ashen, and there were circles as dark as bruises under his eyes. The GP, Dr Pall, was standing by the bed, getting something out of his case. He looked up as Owen pushed past.

Owen ignored him and went straight to his dad's side. He picked up the old man's wrist. He found the pulse without difficulty. It was light but steady. Owen's own pulse slowed perceptibly.

'Why isn't he in hospital?' Owen said, trying not to make it sound too accusatory, and failing.

Dr Pall started to prepare a syringe. 'Because he doesn't need to be,' he said calmly.

Owen felt his jaw clench. 'I'm a doctor,' he said. He knew he didn't look like one. 'You know he's got a history of angina?'

Dr Pall never faltered in his preparations. 'I'm aware of both those things, yes.' He pressed the plunger on the syringe and a few droplets of fluid squirted into the air. 'He'll be fine.'

Maybe, Owen thought. But he wasn't taking anyone's word for it – particularly not a GP who'd taken over an hour to get there. He went to Pall's case and checked the medication phial. 'Glucagon?' he asked.

'He's hypoglycemic.'

First Owen had heard of it, but then the old man never did tell him all that much. 'Diabetic? Since when?'

'Lunchtime, I should think,' Pall said. He stared down at Owen's dad. 'See you later, Arnold.'

He started down stairs. Owen followed him. The GP went into the kitchen, as if he was expected. Sure enough, Irma had made tea. Dr Pall sat down. He took a sip of tea, then pulled out his clipboard and started to scribble his notes.

Disgruntled, Owen grabbed a mug and lounged against the door frame. He restrained himself from demanding to know what was going on; he knew Dr Pall needed to record what he'd done as accurately and quickly as possible.

Eventually, the GP looked up. 'We call it "Logan's Run",' he said. He put down his pen and took a sip of tea. 'Friday morning when they get the pension – straight out the post office to the White Lion.' Charming, Owen thought. But there was affection, rather than contempt in the other man's voice. 'Five pints of Guinness and enough Scotch to remake Whisky Galore.' He drained his mug and held it out. 'Cheers for that, Irma.' He turned back to Owen. 'He's diabetic because of the booze. His circulation's lousy on account of the fags, and his heart's usually racing faster than the horse he backed at dinner.'

Reasonable diagnosis, Owen thought. He was a surgeon, not a physician, but it sounded kosher. But that wasn't what was bothering him. 'How come I'm

5

the last to know he's diabetic?'

Irma turned back from the sink. 'I'm only allowed to tell you what he tells me to tell you. And I'm not his keeper.' She shook suds from her hands. 'I'm only meant to do four hours a day, tidying up. He had me on me hands and knees pointing his garden wall last week.'

Bloody hell, Owen thought. 'I'm sorry.' He smiled. 'Thanks. And thanks for getting in touch.'

Dr Pall got to his feet. 'Get him down to the clinic. I'll do his weight.' He picked up his bag and turned to Owen. 'He talks a lot about you.'

'Me?' Owen was startled.

'He's very proud of you.'

Owen stared at Dr Pall's retreating back. If his dad was proud of him, it was the first he'd heard of it.

If Owen's dad was proud of him, or even pleased to see him, he didn't show it much the next morning. Owen had just finished preparing a breakfast tray for him; but before he took it upstairs, he decided to empty the rubbish bin: it was overflowing. Apparently, there were some things Irma just wouldn't do.

'What the hell are you doing here?' Owen looked round. His dad was standing by the kitchen table, his dressing gown open over his pyjamas. 'Did you get an early train?'

'No, a late one. Did you know you've been asleep for sixteen hours?'

His dad looked uncomfortable. 'Yeah, well I've had a bit of this thing going around...'

Owen tugged at the bin bag. It was stuck. 'No you haven't.' He pulled harder, wary of tearing the plastic. 'You were pissed as a rat.'

6

'Pissed nothing! It's a medical condition.'

'So's suicide, if you catch it early enough.' The bag came free. 'I was here when the GP came. And guess what – you're diabetic.'

'Here we go – Dr Flossie and his tambourine.' He pointed at the tray. 'That's not for me? I have bacon and eggs.'

'No you don't, Dad – you told me you were looking after yourself.' Chance would be a fine thing, Owen thought. They both knew what Dad's priorities were – booze, fags and horses, not necessarily in that order.

'What – the virtually fat free, fish-like cardboard diet you sent us?' Dad poked at the bowl of rapidly cooling porridge with one finger and licked it clean. When he'd finished grimacing, he said, 'I gave it to Irma – I've never seen her look so poorly.'

Owen tied a knot in the bag and took it outside. Dad followed him, and took the lid off the bin before Owen could.

'I still don't understand why you sold the other house – I was round the corner,' Owen said. They'd been over it a thousand times; Owen knew exactly what his father was going to say, but it still didn't make a lot of sense to him. Dad slapped the lid back on the bin and walked off down the garden, to where a couple of scrawny chickens scratched among the grass.

'I told you – too many memories of your mum in London.' He reached into the ramshackle hen coop. 'I was born in Manchester. I should die in Manchester.'

'Oh, you'll manage that in no time.' Owen glared at him.

'You don't give up, do you?' He pulled his hand out of the coop, and held up a creamy white egg. A perfect little package of cholesterol.

'You're diabetic, Dad. You didn't tell me.' There had to be something he could say to make him see what he was doing to himself. But Dad just reached back into the coop and came out with two more eggs. Owen let out a sigh of exasperation. 'Fine.'

'Just because you're a doctor . . .' Dad cut in. He sounded like a petulant five-year-old.

Owen ignored him. 'But if you're eating like that, and you're smoking like that...'

'It doesn't give you the right to everybody's business.' Irma came down the path. Owen nodded to her. 'A bloke can't fart without it ending up in his file.' Dad turned. 'Morning, Irma,' he said, sourly.

Owen could have screamed. 'I don't know what I'm doing here.'

Dad scowled. 'Well don't look at me. I didn't send for you.' He went inside, carrying the eggs.

Irma started to follow him, but Owen caught her arm.

'I wouldn't waste your breath,' she said. 'It's midday before you can talk to him.' Owen nodded, and she went on, 'I've brought you a duvet and a few clean sheets.'

Owen glanced into the kitchen. Dad was at the cooker, breaking eggs into the frying pan. 'How much is he drinking, Irma?'

'Less than he did, but more than he should,' Irma murmured. She smiled at him sympathetically. Owen tried to smile back.

Chapter 2

An application form in triplicate; photos in duplicate; his tie knotted firmly if not altogether tidily, *and* he was on time.

Owen supposed he was as ready as he was ever going to be and he marched into the waiting area of St Gregory's Hospital. It was all potplants and leather sofas. Owen wondered idly how much they'd spent on corporate branding.

A clerical worker walked past. Owen followed her with his eyes. Cute.

'Dr Springer?' said a voice with a Scottish accent from behind him. Owen looked round. The woman speaking to him was tall and dark. Not bad, he thought. 'Mr Crane's apologies, but he's got behind.' She smiled. Cool customer, Owen thought. Bet they call her the Ice Queen. But only behind her back. 'Can you go down to Theatre 7?'

Well, it was a different approach. He nodded. 'But who do I give this to?' he asked, waving his application form with the mugshots clipped to the corner threatening to fall off.

The Ice Queen took it. 'Me,' she said. She pointed to the far door. 'Down to the right, double doors on your left, left again. Follow the red line. Look for number seven.'

As he got to the door, he saw a man coming down

the corridor. Behind him, the Ice Queen murmured, 'Ah.'

'So that would make this...'

'Owen Springer?' the other man said, before Owen could speak.

'Richard Crane?' Owen held his hand out.

'That's right.' They shook hands. Crane had a surprisingly strong grip. 'Sorry to keep you waiting.' He nodded back the way he had come. Owen fell into stride beside him, walking quickly to keep up. 'Couple of emergencies, and the whole thing grinds to a halt.' He pushed open an office door. 'You know we've already interviewed for this job, don't you?'

'Yeah,' Owen said, following him in.

'Where are you from?' Crane asked, before they'd even sat down. He had a long, bony face. He'd be a sure bet to play Sherlock Holmes, Owen thought.

He forced himself to concentrate. 'I'm from Sunderland originally, but my family moved down to London when I was fifteen.' Good so far? Owen wondered. He couldn't tell. But this was the easy part. 'I went to University College Hospital as a student, then I got taken on to Spinetti's firm.'

Crane gestured at a seat near his desk. 'Sit down,' he said. Rotten bedside manner, Owen thought. 'Is he good?' Crane asked.

It was a loaded question, Owen realized. 'He's the best,' he said. He calculated the pause exactly, and added, 'The best down there.'

'Did he teach you anything?' Crane steepled his fingers.

'He's better at surgery than he is at teaching.'

Again, the long, measuring stare. 'What's your fundamental philosophy of surgical teaching?'

It wasn't a question Owen had expected or

10

prepared for. 'I don't understand the question,' he admitted after a moment. If he couldn't act smart, at least he could act smart enough not to sound dumb.

'Well, you're working with one the country's top surgeons, in one of the top teaching hospitals in Europe.' He smiled, but there was no warmth in it. 'And you've applied to move north – grant starved, talent starved, sun starved north.' The smile widened, and now he seemed genuinely amused. But so might a crocodile, Owen reminded himself. 'It's about three degrees cooler in Manchester, you know. Questions are bound to be asked.'

Okay, Owen thought, so he want's a bit of syco-phancy. That I can do. 'I heard about you, and I thought I should spread myself about a bit.'

'Crap.' Crane spit the word out like a crocodile rejecting the inedible bits of the fish he'd just eaten.

Well, if lies wouldn't cut it, maybe the truth would just have to do. 'Yes,' Owen said. 'It's for family reasons.'

'Starting one or abandoning one?' The look in Crane's eyes could have frozen boiling oil.

'My dad's not too good. I just don't want to be that far away.' With that out of the way, Owen tried the flattery route again. 'And Professor Spinetti emphati-cally recommended that I should try your firm.'

'Well,' Crane said, 'Much as I admire your attach-ment to your father, and much as I'm flattered by Dr Spinetti's praise – I don't know the former from Adam, and the latter got the job I applied for.' There wasn't even the pretence of a smile now. 'So let's start again, shall we?' Owen could only nod. 'What's your fundamental philosophy on surgical teaching in this country at this time, Mr Springer?'

Owen sighed.

Owen wandered down the street towards his dad's house, jacket slung over one shoulder. The interview hadn't got any better. Worse if anything.

Irma was weeding the pocket handkerchief of a front garden. Dad was bloody lucky to have her, Owen thought. He hoped the old man knew it.

'Irma?' he said.

She turned, and spent a moment looking at him. 'Very smart,' she said, and grinned. 'I was saying to your dad –"I bet he's got a woman on".'

That'd be the day. 'Nah – I scare 'em all away, Irma.'

She looked at him appraisingly. 'Our Shirley'd give you a run for your money if you get stuck.'

Her Shirley was very nice but not his type. 'I never *have* any money.' That was true. The flat in Notting Hill Gate ate most of it. 'Where is he?'

Irma nodded to the top of the house. Owen went inside. Time they had a proper talk, and not just about what to have for breakfast.

There were a couple of full black rubbish bags standing on the landing. Owen poked his head into his dad's room. The old man wasn't there.

A muffled thump led him to the spare room. There was stuff everywhere – old clothes on the bed, boxes and carrier bags on the floor, the wardrobe door bursting open. Dad was piling junk into another bin bag.

'What're you doing now?' Owen asked.

'Well, you'll put your back out on that sofa.' He pointed at the bed. 'That'll do till you find some-where.' He pushed down on the rubbish in the bag. 'Assuming you get the job.'

'What job?' Owen asked, trying to sound innocent.

'St Gregory's – Surgical Registrar.' Annoyance must have appeared on Owen's face, because the old man added quickly, 'Not that I was peeping.'

'You opened the letter.' Why he was surprised, he didn't know. Dad always had opened his post when he was a kid. It had been a major source of rows.

'In error,' Dad said, with the aggrieved air of the wrongly accused. 'I couldn't find me glasses.'

'You managed to find them to know to re-seal it?' Owen shot back.

Dad abandoned the bag. He slapped a large box. 'Give us a hand with this.'

Owen recognized the distraction technique – Dad was a past master. But he decided to go with it anyway. 'Where do you want it?'

'I don't know.'

'Well, what's in it?'

'I don't know.'

Owen sighed. It was going to be a long afternoon. He was right. But a couple of hours later a flatbed truck drew up outside. A couple of heavy looking guys with crewcuts got out.

Owen watched as they started to heave the junk on to the truck. His dad stood next to him.

'It's our Gary and Mick,' Irma said as she beamed proudly at them.

They turned and stared at Owen. 'Hiya,' he said.

'He's the doctor,' Irma said.

They continued to stare. Owen got the impression they'd have been more impressed if he'd been a wrestling champion.

Owen turned away. Lose some, lose some, he thought. At least on days like today. 'How long you had the chickens, Dad?' he asked.

'I won 'em in the pub,' Dad said. He handed a carrier bag full of old newspapers to Gary. 'I was going to sell them on, but they turf out more eggs than

Asda. Pays for the odd pint.' Mick fumbled slowly with a box. 'And dull as they are, they could do a jig-saw faster than this pair.' He glared at them. 'Come on lads – you'll have it dark!' They speeded up for all of thirty seconds. Then it was back to the slow fumble. 'Think you'll get it?' Dad asked.

'The job?' Owen wondered what the old man was hoping to hear. 'Dunno. Competition's pretty hot for Registrars.'

There was a moment of silence, broken only by Gary's grunt as he heaved a bag on to the truck.

'I don't want you chasing jobs up here on my account,' Dad said.

'Your account?' Owen said, wondering if he were really that transparent. 'So everything I do is a reac-tion to what you're getting up to?'

'Well, why are you?' Dad sounded pleased.

But there was honour at stake. 'I just want to get out of London for a bit.' That sounded pretty thin. 'I've been in the same hospital since I started training. It doesn't look good.' Dad looked unconvinced. 'You'll be doing me a favour if you can just put us up for a bit, that's all.'

Dad still didn't look as if he were buying it, but Owen could tell from his expression that his honour had been satisfied. 'Right,' he said.

With that settled, Owen went to help the lads. The rate they were going, he was never going to get his tea.

Chapter 3

Another day and another office. Owen glanced up at the black glass spear of Anna Fairley Management Consultancy before he went in. He couldn't see for the life of him why he had to have another interview, and he'd said as much to Viv Reid, the Surgical Business Manager, on the phone.

'Management Assessment', she'd called it. To assess his ability at independent thinking and how he would fit into a team.

Load of rubbish, Owen called it. But he hadn't said anything. So here he was, like a good little boy.

The offices were plush enough to put the ones in St Gregory's to shame. He wondered how many hospital beds the Consultancy's fee had cost.

Too many, he decided, as he followed the directions the receptionist gave him.

He found himself in a room bare but for a table and two chairs – and the unblinking eye of a video camera. Sharp stick, that's what that thing needs, Owen thought. He smiled at it, instead. Not a lot they could do about a smile.

The door opened. The man who came in introduced himself as Brian. He was thirty-fiveish, sharp suit, slick hair and a classy briefcase. He gestured for Owen to sit down.

Owen did so, warily. This is how lambs feel in the

slaughter house, he thought. Or would if they were brighter.

But Brian was speaking and he realized he'd barely heard a word the man had said. '. . . a video camera throughout the interview.' Owen nodded as if he'd been listening. 'To help us assess your response to the questions.' He took a form out of his case and pushed it across the table to Owen. 'You understand that this interview is completely confidential to you, us and the Health Trust.'

Why no, man, I'm going to sell it to the *Sun*, Owen thought. But he grunted, 'Yes.'

'Would you mind signing the form to that effect?' Brian pushed a pen across the table.

Owen barely managed to conceal his disgust as he signed.

If anything, the interview went worse than the one with Richard Crane. At least Crane had had something approaching a sense of humour, even if it wasn't much closer than sarcasm. This guy acted as if 'funny' wasn't in his vocabulary.

'And you're fully fit?' he asked – the last in a long line of questions about Owen's eating and exercise habits.

'Butcher's dog,' Owen answered.

'Yes?'

'Yes.' As if I'm going to admit to anything else, Owen thought.

Brian ticked a box on his form off, then looked at his notes. 'Describe what sports you like to participate in.'

'Footie,' Owen said, and watched as Brian wrote it down squarely in the middle of a section clearly intended for much more. So he went on, 'Full team, five-a-side, American Football, table football. Cricket:

16

indoor cricket, outdoor cricket, bedroom cricket. Swimming: silver lifesaving, backstroke, breaststroke, butterfly and crawl.' He paused. 'Crawling's my strongest.'

If he hoped to get a reaction, he failed. Brian simply took the time he needed to write everything down, then said, 'In as many words as you think *necessary...*' Gotcha, Owen thought triumphantly, 'describe what you believe to be your personal assets.'

Oh, too easy, Owen thought. 'Young, sexy, bright, ambitious, tasty, adventurous, sexual. Put funny – I'm very funny. Touching, moving passionate, compassionate, successful, charming, smart, clean. I'm tough, Brian. Very tough.'

He was good, Owen thought. He never let his expression change once.

Anna Fairley was not amused. She watched the video monitor with growing annoyance.

'Truthful when necessary,' the young man being interviewed said. 'Born liar when necessary, open when necessary, private when necessary...'

'What's the contract?' she demanded. The guy was familiar, but she couldn't place him. Her assistant handed her an application form. St Gregory's Health Trust. Oh dear.

'Sharp, quick to learn, and quick to unlearn. And very quick to apologize...' he went on.

Owen Springer. She recognized him now – the man on the train who'd borrowed her phone. 'He's just taking the piss,' she said. She flicked his monitor off. No need, really, even to assess him formally.

Owen knocked back the last of his Coke.

He hadn't really wanted to work at St Gregory's

anyway. And his dad didn't really need him that much.

Liar, he thought to himself.

He looked through the cafe window at the street outside. A girl walked past. Nice legs, he thought. As he turned back, a movement in the wine bar opposite caught his eye: a shock of auburn hair.

For a second he wasn't sure. But the woman moved, and something in the set of her head convinced him: it was the woman from the train. He never had apologized properly.

What the hell, he thought. Just because he'd had a rotten day didn't mean he couldn't make somebody else's.

He paid at the counter, then went across to the wine bar. For a second, he thought about going straight inside, but decided that might seem pushy; besides, there was still a chance he might be wrong. So instead he tapped on the window until she looked up.

She smiled and he headed for the cafe door.

'It was you on the train,' he said. She frowned at him. 'Mobile,' he explained.

Her expression cleared. 'Oh yes,' she said. 'How is your dad?'

'He's okay,' Owen said. 'Mind if I . . .' he looked at the table. She smiled. He sat down. When the waitress came, he ordered fresh drinks for both of them.

'Thanks,' the woman from the train said. She picked up her coffee cup and made a mock toast with it. 'Cheers!'

'Least I can do,' Owen said. Besides, he was enjoying the company. And the view: her eyes really were stunning.

'You know Manchester well?'

Owen laughed. 'Ask me again in three months. I've just interviewed for a job up here.'

'Really?'

Owen couldn't stop himself from pulling a sour face. 'Well, I say interview. It was a personality assessment. Bunch of arseholes pretending to be Management Psychologists.' He found that he was holding his cup far too tightly. Definitely not the way to impress the lady. Nevertheless, he said, 'And it's a job I'm overqualified for, and considering a pay cut for.' He put the cup down in time to stop his coffee sloshing everywhere. 'And they'd be bloody lucky to have me.'

'So why bother?' she asked. Now, if they'd asked me like that in the interview, they might have got somewhere, he thought. And so might I.

'I need to be here for my dad.'

'He's the only reason you want to move jobs?' she sounded surprised, but not unsympathetic.

'Well, he's not exactly dying on his feet,' he admitted. 'He does a cracking impression most of the time, though.'

She smiled. It was like the sun coming out. 'So a doctor in the house is going to be a comfort to him.'

Owen thought of the label he'd put on Dad's hidden bottle of Scotch – *I've marked it, PTO*; and on the other side, *And I've pee'd in it.* That would really please him. 'He'd prefer a chain smoking barmaid...' Then he clocked what she'd said. 'How did you know I was a doctor?'

She looked flummoxed, just for a second. Then she said, 'You mentioned.'

'I didn't.' He was sure of it.

'You said, "new job as a doctor",' she said firmly.

'No.' Owen was equally firm. He never liked

admitting what he did: most people had a hard time believing him.

'Well,' she said, 'I don't know how that happened. Maybe you just *look* like a doctor...'

'Give us a break,' Owen cut in. 'You'd be the first woman in my entire career who thought I *looked* like a doctor.' He grinned wryly. 'Binman, more often than not.'

She grabbed her handbag. 'Look, I think I'd better get back to work.'

Damn, Owen thought. He hadn't meant to frighten her off. 'Where's work?' he said, hoping to stall her long enough to calm her down.

'Round the corner, more or less.' She still looked panicked.

'Thanks for the chat.' It sounded weak, even to him. He tried again. 'Nice talking to you.' She stared at him. Huge brown eyes, with flecks of gold. And he wasn't going to see her again. 'It's Owen, by the way.'

He stuck his hand out, hardly daring to hope that she would take it. But she did. 'Anna.' Her grasp was warm and firm. Damn; everything she did was so right. 'Thanks for the drink. And good luck.'

He watched her go. As the door swung shut behind her, he sat back down, wondering if anything else could possibly go wrong with the day.

Then he noticed her briefcase. He grabbed it and ran after her.

Too late – there was no one in sight. Damn, he thought. Then it occurred to him that if he could find some identification in the case, he could return it to her.

Clouds, he thought. Silver linings.

He squatted down and opened the case. A picture stared up at him. His own, attached to his application form for the job at St Gregory's.

'Bloody hell', he muttered. He felt his jaw go tight. No wonder she'd known he was a doctor. There was an assessment sheet slipped between the photo and the application form. His gaze fell on the last section – the one marked *recommendations*. There was only one word written in it: *No*.

It was all Owen could do to stop himself scrunching the form up into a ball; instead he made himself check the address in the heading of the recommendation sheet. He slammed the case shut.

Everything she did was so right. Except this. And this was so, so wrong.

Relief flooded through Anna when she got the message from Michelle. Someone had found her briefcase in the cafe and brought it in.

She was less relieved when she realized the someone was Owen Springer, and still less when she realized he wanted to talk about his interview. Probably, she should have stopped him when he opened the case, took out the application forms and brandished them at her.

Probably.

'Look . . .' she said.

'You saw me do that interview and you didn't tell me?' He was plainly furious.

'I'm sorry,' Anna said, though she was rapidly losing patience. 'What did you expect me to say?'

Owen waved his application form at her. 'What's all this crap? Not recommended?'

'It just means the assessment was void,' Anna said. 'Mainly because you deliberately sabotaged it.' It was a half truth: anyone who did that was hardly likely to get a recommendation. 'And this is confidential information.' She hoped it would shut him up. She was wrong.

'I'm telling you, I know most of this mob and I'm better qualified than any of them.' He brandished one of the forms at her: a blond-haired guy smiled out of his photo at her. She remembered him well – he'd been affable without crawling, yet prepared to state his opinions plainly. A good choice. 'Gordon Jones,' Owen said. 'You picked him?'

'I don't pick anyone – they're just viability percentages...' A thought occurred to her. 'You read the other files?' They really were confidential.

'Well,' Owen went on, ignoring her, 'Just pray you never need keyhole surgery from old "Shovels".'

Anna grabbed the forms from him. 'That's privately commissioned information, and I'm not prepared to discuss it.' She was flushed. She could feel it. She took a deep breath and said, as coldly as she could, 'Thank you for the bag.' He just stared at her. 'You'd better go.'

There was a moment when they just looked at each other. His eyes were quite compelling. Brian popped his head round the door, breaking the moment.

'You okay, Anna?'

'Fine, Brian,' she said. She was in the right. So she really didn't know why she was so upset.

'You want me to throw him out?'

Owen swivelled round. His face hardened. For a moment, he looked like someone else entirely. 'Well come on,' he challenged. 'You want to try it?'

Brian didn't move, but there was uncertainty in his eyes. His gaze flicked over to Anna.

'No,' she said. 'It's okay.'

Brian backed out. The door slammed.

'Well – I see you've a talent for picking the best,' Owen said. 'And I really like your style – you took a drink even when you knew you were avoiding me.'

He sounded genuinely bitter. Or maybe he was just hurt.

Don't get drawn in, Anna told herself. 'You insisted on buying me a drink to repay a favour. It had nothing to do with your interview.'

That stopped him. Again, there was silence for a moment. Some emotion she couldn't quite read flickered across his face and was gone.

'I was brilliant in there,' he said at last. 'I had nothing but good things to say about me.' So he did admit he'd been an idiot, Anna thought. But she wasn't ready for what he said next. 'You know I need that job.' He sounded desperate, almost ready to beg.

'Not when I made your assessment, I didn't,' Anna said, and was glad that it didn't sound too desperate.

'And you're that professional?'

'I am, actually.'

'Okay.' He sounded resigned, which was probably just as well. 'Just answer me one thing: without the benefit of the questionnaire – do I look like a doctor?' He smiled, and suddenly Anna could see what he would be like with all the anger stripped away.

She couldn't help smiling back. 'Not particularly,' she said. But she had to admit, he didn't look much like a binman, either.

The door clicked open. Owen considered burying his head under the duvet and pretending to be asleep, but opened one eye instead.

Dad came through the door, carrying a breakfast tray. Toast and marmalade, orange juice and tea. It was almost healthy.

Owen struggled upright. 'What do you want?' His father had never made breakfast in bed for him in his life before. Then the reason became obvious: there was a letter with the St Gregory's logo on the flap nestling behind the orange juice. He pushed it with his finger. 'I really don't feel like opening that.'

Dad sat on the bed. 'I knew you wouldn't,' he said. 'So I did.' Owen looked at him warily. 'You got the job.' Owen's mouth fell open. He shut it rapidly. Then he tried to think of something to say. 'So we'll settle at forty, then,' Dad finished.

'Forty what?' Owen asked, still trying to absorb the first piece of news.

'A week,' Dad said, as if he were speaking to a child. 'For the room.'

Chapter 4

I love the smell of antiseptic in the morning, Owen thought as he waited in the St Gregory's reception area. He loved the feel of his white coat, and the sense of purpose it gave him, too.

A sound behind him made him turn.

'Owen Springer?' said the man approaching him. 'John McGinley.'

This was the registrar Owen had been told to wait for. 'Hiya,' he said.

John headed down the corridor. Owen fell into place beside him, trying to get the measure of him. He was about Owen's own age – about right for the post he was holding, in other words, which was senior to the one Owen was taking up.

They turned a corner, went down another corridor.

'What the hell're you doing here?' John asked. He had a heavy Irish accent. 'You were working with Spinetti?'

Oh gawd, here we go, Owen thought. 'Don't say it like that,' he said. 'He's good but he's not brilliant.'

John grinned. 'What did you do? Kill a patient?'

Owen couldn't be bothered to go into the explanation about his dad. 'Crane's got a good reputation, hasn't he?'

John let out a short laugh. 'Bears are cuddly, but

they can still pull your knackers off.'

Great, Owen thought.

A moment later they came to a turning off the main corridor, with a door at the end. John opened it and ushered Owen in.

'The doctors' mess room,' he said. Owen surveyed it – a couple of chairs, a mess of coffee cups and biscuit wrappers on the low table, a pile of washing up in the sink and a bed for the doctor on call in the corner, currently occupied. Pretty standard, in other words. 'Tea, coffee and an underpowered microwave from the psychiatric block,' John went on. He raised his voice. 'Danny Glassman – Owen Springer. New Surgical Reg.'

The lump on the bed opened its eyes. 'Hello,' Danny croaked.

'That's not pharyngitis,' John said, 'That's an old plum they stuck in there at boarding school.'

Danny got up and got himself a glass of water. 'This man is a bog treading Irishman,' he said. The croak had gone, and had been replaced by a voice that would have done the Prince of Wales proud. 'This man thinks anything higher than a potato peeler's privileged.' Charming, Owen thought. 'Where are you from, Owen?'

'I'm from Sunderland, Danny,' Owen answered, thickening up his Geordie accent just a bit.

'Oh God, it's ten a penny time!' Danny said. He shoved his face under the tap, saving Owen from having to make a reply. Owen wondered if he were joking: probably not, judging by the look on John's face. Danny came out from under the tap. 'And this isn't conjunctivitis, this is overtime?'

John ignored him, and turned to Owen. 'Five nights on, five nights off. If we're understaffed, you alternate the on call with him.'

'Good,' Owen said. 'Perfect.'

John went back out into the corridor and Owen followed.

'You were second in command to Spinetti,' John said.

'I was,' Owen admitted.

'It's not going to be a problem for you – playing down?'

Owen found himself liking the other man – better by far to get it out in the open before it became a problem. 'I'm not proud, John,' he said. 'And I'm very good at taking advice.'

John looked sceptical. 'So long as you don't mind advice sounding more like instructions, we'll get on fine.' Well, that's to the point, Owen thought. John went on, 'Have they found you some accommodation?'

Owen shook his head. 'I'm sorted. My dad's up here – I'm moving in with him till I find somewhere.'

John grinned. 'I knew it!'

'What?'

'You're getting divorced. I knew you were giving off a smell.' Owen tried to get a word in, but John rattled on, 'Isn't it really amazing though – three years short of the Millenium and they can still make you feel like a pariah?' And I didn't even push his button, Owen thought. 'I look round at some of the divorced guys and wonder how the hell they do it – you know, illiterate apes with dicks this big . . .' He held his thumb and forefinger half and inch apart. 'Having the time of their bloody lives – like they just lost a tumour.' He paused. But before Owen could say anything, he went on, 'Why can't we just enjoy it, for God's sake?'

27

He finally ran down.

'I think we're a bit different,' Owen said, carefully.

'In what way?' John asked. He looked like he was expecting Moses to bring the word of God down off the mountain to enlighten him.

'I'm not getting divorced,' Owen said. 'I've never been married.'

Disappointment warred with embarrassment on John's face and embarrassment won. 'Okay,' he said.

Richard Crane was determined not to be impressed by Owen Springer, even if he did come with the highest references.

The man was a joker and a buffoon, and Richard wanted none of it.

Nevertheless, he was too professional to let that estimation get in the way during his ward round.

'We'll start with last night's emergency admissions, shall we?' he said, and let Danny Glassman lead him, Springer and McGinley to one of the beds.

'This is Francine Hartley, a forty-two-year-old secretary,' Glassman said. 'She was admitted at three a.m. with a twenty-four hour history of acute epigastric and right-sided abdominal pain, and vomiting.' He consulted her notes. 'She was tender with guarding in the upper abdomen, and had a temperature of 37.5; her haemoglobin was normal but the white cell count was elevated at 15.2; her biochemistry was normal, and so were her chest and abdominal x-rays.'

Crane absorbed this while he moved towards the bed. He smiled – he'd mastered the art early on: the smile was professional, but not so professional as to seem insincere. Yet he could put it on even when he was furious, even when he was achingly tired or fed up. For the patients, of course. His staff had to take him as they found him, and like it.

'Morning, Mrs Hartley,' he said cheerfully. 'I'm Mr Crane, the Consulting Surgeon.' He turned to indicate Springer. 'Would you mind if our new doctor, Mr Springer, gives us his opinion?' The woman looked uncertain. 'He's only new to us, by the way – not to the business.'

The woman smiled tremulously, then nodded.

'Certainly,' Owen said. He moved forward and lowered himself gently on to the edge of the bed. 'Morning. Could you show me where the pain is, Mrs Hartley?' She indicated her abdomen, without touching it. 'Is it sore to touch?' Springer asked. He was looking at her hands, not her abdomen, Crane noted. 'Would you look up for me?' She did so. 'Down?' Again, she did so. 'Do you mind if I examine your abdomen?' Springer asked. Mrs Hartley looked worried. 'I'll be as gentle as I can, I promise.' Delicately, he palped her abdomen. Crane noted with reluctant approval the way he watched her face, not her stomach.

When he was done, Springer thanked Mrs Hartley, stood up and turned to Crane. 'Signs of tenderness and guarding in the right upper quadrant. The differential diagnosis includes acute cholecystitis, acute pancreatitis, and – less likely – acute appendicitis and pelvic inflamatory disease.' He glanced at the patient. 'She seems to be slightly jaundiced, which is more in keeping with acute cholecystitis or pancreatitis.'

Again, Crane had to give his grudging approval. Springer hadn't missed a trick. But preliminary diagnosis was only half the battle. 'What would you do to confirm it?' he asked. He needed good doctors on his team; yet part of him wanted Springer to miss something.

He was disappointed. 'We need to check her serum amylase and liver function tests and she should have an urgent ultrasound scan.'

Very good, Crane thought. 'And if the scan showed a dilated common bile duct and stones in the gall bladder?'

'Check her clotting and arrange for an urgent ERCP. I would then plan to remove her gall bladder before she went home.'

'Anything else?'

'She's pyrexial with an elevated white cell count – we should check blood cultures and start intravenous antibiotics immediately.'

Crane wasn't an unfair man: he had to admit that he was impressed. 'I've got nothing to add to that, thank you.' He turned to Mrs Hartley, who still looked worried. 'I'd stick with him, if I were you.'

Anna was typing up her report for Farnhault Properties when Michelle came through the door, carrying the largest bouquet of flowers she had seen in a long time.

'These came for you,' Michelle said. She put the basket down on the desk.

'Ooh, goodness,' Anna said. She frowned at the flowers for a second, then thought to look for a card.

Thanks, it said. *The Binman.*

She took a moment to work it out. When she did, she smiled.

Nothing impressed Crane so much as ability. Whatever he'd previously thought of Springer, Crane had to admit he had ability in carloads. So Crane decided to forgive him for the runaround he'd given them all at interview.

But while they were scrubbing up for theatre, he discovered something that appalled him all over again.

'So why didn't you mention this before, Springer? You worry me, you really do,' he said, as the staff nurse tied his gown. 'I couldn't disagree more fundamentally.' Springer didn't have the good grace even to look abashed. He moved over to the sinks to scrub up, and elbowed on one of the taps. 'How can even a half-developed intelligence believe Newcastle can achieve as much as Manchester United?'

'At least we play total football,' Springer answered. Such sheer stupidity in the face of the known facts was beyond Crane.

'Total football?' he roared. 'Total crap! Two reasonable seasons, a fifteen million pound investment and you think you're there to stay.'

Danny Glassman came over to get gowned up. Now there was a man with more sense than to argue.

'You'll last about as long as that Chelsea fan we caught syphoning petty cash to pay for a season ticket.' He said it with finality, and punctuated his words with a slam of the elbow at the handle of the tap. 'It wasn't the fraud so much as the absolute bloody waste of money.'

And with that he swept into theatre, leaving Springer satisfyingly silent behind him.

Vivien Reid knew there was one place you could count on finding surgeons. No matter how many people they had cut up, they never seemed to go off their food.

So when she needed to find the new Surgical Registrar, she waited till lunchtime, then headed for the canteen.

She found him in the meal queue, with Danny Glassman and John McGinley. They were chatting about something, but she was sure they wouldn't mind her butting in when they realized it was important.

'We need to talk,' she said, without preamble. 'It'd be great in office hours, but things are a bit squeezed for the next fortnight.'

Owen smiled. Nice smile, she thought, and reminded herself not to be distracted. 'No problem,' he said. 'Let's have dinner.' He paused, apparently for effect, then said, 'Who are you?'

'Viv Reid,' McGinley butted in. 'Surgical Business Manager.'

'Vivien Reid,' she corrected. 'There's an eight per cent overspend on Surgical.' Owen looked at her as if she'd come from another planet. Typical doctor – no grasp of the practicalities. 'I'd like to tighten your leash before the 'Happy Cutters' lead us all into insolvency.' Not so much another planet, Vivien thought – now he was looking at her as if she'd crawled out from under a stone. But she ploughed on. 'Have you got a Budgets and Resources Certificate?'

'Not on me, no.'

The famous Springer wit, she thought. She'd heard all about it already. 'Well, you'll have to have one – it's only a two-day course, but its compulsory.' She punched a number into her mobile. With any luck they could fit him in this week or next. 'Carolyn,' she said, 'Is Trevor there?'

'They reckon if you xerox her arse, it comes out as a signed photo of Theresa Gorman,' McGinley said.

Vivien found herself flushing. 'Watch your step, McGinley,' she said. 'That's harrassment.' And you'd better believe I'll do you for it, Sunshine, she added silently. Just give me the chance.

'No, that's anthropology,' he contradicted. She stared at him coldly. 'And you've jumped the queue, Viv.'

Why, she thought, so I have. And didn't move.

Crane was turning out not to be such a bad bloke, Owen thought, as observed him doing an appendectomy.

Not that you'd want to cross him, mind.

'Anyway, Mr Springer,' Crane said. 'How are you settling in?'

'He's doing nicely, sir,' John cut in before Owen could answer.

That was a mistake. 'Patients do nicely,' Crane said.

'Are you making progress?' John asked.

'Yes, it's an impressive unit,' Owen said. As he watched, Crane did a neat job of removing the offending appendix.

'You're allowed negative observations,' Crane said, in a voice that suggested the exact opposite.

'I haven't got any negative observations,' Owen protested.

'So – your contract's intact, we're paying you what the job's worth, and everything's fine.' He glanced sideways at Owen.

Owen thought about it for a second. You had to be honest, especially with someone like Crane, who was as sharp as a scalpel. 'No,' he said quietly.

'Well, what is it then?'

Owen wished he'd never started, but he said, 'Okay – it feels odd having to go back to alternative night cover, sleeping in.'

Beneath his mask, Crane's face registered irritation. 'Small complaint then, on the face of things?' He turned to his nurse. 'Retract harder, please.'

'Well...'

He spoke to Owen while watching what he was doing with the patient. 'I think the best way to measure a surgeon is...' again, he turned to the nurse – 'swab please – to see what sort of decisions he makes at three in the morning with two hours sleep.' He paused while he negotiated a tricky moment in the operation. 'He doesn't forget those moments, and quite frankly, neither do I – especially if we have to bury them.' He stopped what he was doing and turned to face Owen. 'And with great respect, there is no one else to do it – so you, Mr Springer, have to.' Owen was careful to keep his expression neutral. After a moment, Crane smiled. 'References aside, you never expected to get this job, did you?'

Sharp as a scalpel, Owen thought. Damn it. 'Well, no – I didn't.'

'So it's a *very* small complaint?'

'Yeah,' Owen admitted, 'But ...'

'And we're still an impressive unit?'

'Yes,' Owen said. He'd meant it the first time. He still meant it now.

'Good.' Crane turned to McGinley. 'There,' he said.

He walked away, leaving them to close up.

So did I do all right or not? Owen wondered. He really couldn't tell.

Chapter 5

The next day, Owen woke up and realized that he just had to do something about the wallpaper in his room. It wasn't the colours as such: it was more the whole concept of multicoloured daisies the size of dinner plates.

He waited for his moment, and just before lunch he propelled his dad down the hall heading for the front door.

'Wallpaper?' Dad said, as if he'd never heard the word before.

'Fresh air'll do you good,' Owen said.

'What's wrong with the stuff I put up last year?' Dad grumbled.

They got outside. Owen thought he could hear a bus coming.

'You must've been drunk when you decorated. I keep thinking I'm falling out of bed,' Owen said.

He frowned. The bus was definitely coming so he grabbed Dad's arm and headed across the road.

'Where you off?' Dad asked.

'The bus,' Owen said. He hadn't realized the old man's hearing was that bad. It certainly wasn't when it came to catching the winners on the racing.

'We can go in the car,' Dad said.

First he had heard of a car. 'You've been on the sick five years,' he said. 'How come you can afford a car?'

In answer, Dad slid the garage doors open and in the darkness there was a beaten up old Ford Escort, more rust than metal, and probably held together with string and prayers. There was a Disabled sticker on the windscreen.

'Oh,' Owen said. It didn't rate much more.

Dubiously, he followed Dad's lead and got in.

'Right,' Dad said. He grinned maniacally. 'Let's burn some rubber.'

Owen got his wallpaper, but Dad made him pay for it – both in money, which he'd expected, and with a couple of hours standing in the bookies, watching one horse after another go down.

It was all right, though. Worth it just to be spending the time with him.

Afterwards, they went to the pub and sat outside with their beers. Owen felt more cheerful than he had in days. Job was good, Dad was good; now if he could only stop thinking about the woman from the train, he'd be getting somewhere.

He wondered idly if she'd liked the flowers. He'd half hoped she might ring him. She had the number, after all – it was on his application form.

'See that . . .' Dad said, interrupting his little fantasy, and pointing at the pile of rubble on the other side of the street. 'First club in Manchester open after midnight.' He sipped his pint. 'Jazz club.' He licked the foam from around his mouth. 'That's where I met your mother.'

Dad didn't talk about her often. Now, Owen sensed, he wanted to. 'Do you think about her, then?'

Dad nodded. A look of infinite regret passed across his face. 'You're a lot like her, you know.' He took another drink. Owen tried to think of something to say, but failed. 'I reckon we could've had a ball this time of life – you know, house paid for, no commitments.' He stared off into the distance. 'We could've really enjoyed ourselves now. If she hadn't died.'

Owen took a long slug of his beer. 'Or if she hadn't divorced you.'

Dad grinned ruefully. 'That and all, yeah.'

They finished their drinks in silence.

There were better parts of the job than inspecting haemorrhoid patients, Owen thought. At least this time he was supervising Danny.

The patient yelped.

'Be careful,' Owen said. 'You're not pot holing.' The patient looked despairingly over her shoulder at him. 'Nice and easy,' Owen said.

In truth, Danny had all the delicacy of an elephant in rut.

Owen stared out the window, unable to watch any more. Just then, a Mercedes drew up outside. Visiting a private patient, no doubt, Owen thought.

Then he realized who had got out: Anna. She was carrying a bunch of flowers, and she hurried inside.

Owen realized he was smiling. 'You're doing really well,' he lied to Danny. 'I need to vanish for ten minutes.'

As he hurried away he heard Danny say, 'That had nothing to do with you Mrs Feldman, just in case you were wondering.' Owen grimaced. Danny worked it out just about then. 'If you weren't wondering, I apologize for planting that suggestion.'

Owen broke into a run as soon as he got into the corridor. When he came to the stairwell, he looked down just in time to see Anna getting into the lift.

He belted up the stairs, up three flights, the fourth,

to the private wards. Anna was just disappearing into the Eleanor Carver Wing. He went in, and found her in one of the rooms off the ward.

He gulped air. 'Hiya,' he gasped, trying to sound casual.

Anna turned. She had been talking to the old woman in the bed. 'Hello,' she said. The old woman smiled at him.

'You got the flowers,' he asked.

'They're lovely, thank you,' the old lady said. 'But if you're going to go to that much trouble again, don't get chrysanthemums – they're a bit busy for me.'

Owen frowned at her. She stared back glassily, and he realized that wherever she thought she was, it wasn't the Eleanor Carver Wing of St Gregory's Hospital. 'I'll do me best,' he said.

There was an uncomfortable silence. Owen glanced at her notes, which were hanging on the end of her bed. Myrtle Fairley, aged eighty-two.

'Well, don't just stand there – get a chair.' Myrtle patted the edge of her bed. Owen didn't move. 'How's Barbara?'

'This is Dr Springer, mother,' Anna said.

Mother. Right, Owen thought. 'It's Owen,' he said. 'How you doing?'

Something seemed to click back into place in her eyes. 'Steadily enough, till they rammed a tube up my drainpipe and made me sing *The Rolling Hills*.' She cackled. It was the dirtiest laugh Owen had heard in a long time. But then she looked round vaguely, and it was obvious she'd forgotten why she was laughing.

'Would you mind?' Anna said to Owen. There was a wealth of pain in her voice.

He had to respect that, so he left.

Owen was waiting outside when Anna came out of

the ward. He was nursing a coffee from the machine. She went to get one.

'Alzheimer's,' she said. She was surprised how glad she was to see him. Visiting her mother always left her wanting to talk to someone. 'The only thing she's consistently remembered is that she asked me for a crossword book three weeks ago.' She punched for a coffee. 'Barbara's my sister.'

'She's looking fit enough, taking into account she's had a gall bladder whipped out,' Owen said. How did he ... Anna thought. How dare he ... ? But before she could say anything, he said, 'And if you want my advice, you're wasting your money paying for a private room. She'd get the same treatment downstairs you know – the only advantage is cable TV.'

'That's your hobby, then – reading other people's files?' Anna said coldly.

'That last bit was a joke,' he said, defensively.

Well, he certainly had something to defend. 'And who the hell asked you to make moral judgements about how people spend their money?' she went on, as if he'd not said anything. 'She's not your patient!'

It took all Owen's charm and tact to get Anna to calm down enough to agree to come for a coffee with him – a decent coffee, not the gnat's pee from the machine provided.

He studied her while he waited to be served: that hair, that mouth, and the eyes.

He took the coffee over.

'Thanks,' she said. She was still pale.

'Milk?' Owen asked.

'Black.' He filed that away for reference.

He bit his lip. 'I'm really sorry, okay?'

She nodded. Sighed. He decided he was forgiven.

And realized he wanted to remember everything about her – the way she spoke, her facial expressions, the way she leaned forward with her elbows on the table, cradling her coffee cup.

'Your father's obviously very important to you?' she asked. Owen shrugged. It wasn't really something he'd given a lot of thought to. Dad just . . . was. 'That's where we came in – you were traveling north to be with him because he was sick.'

Owen made a derisive noise in his throat. 'That was a false alarm.'

But Anna persisted. 'Presumably you dropped everything? You'd have come here at any cost?'

He realized that she was measuring herself against him in some obscure fashion. It made him uncomfortable. 'I guess. . . yes.' But it doesn't make me a better person than you, he thought. 'So . . .'

But Anna was barely paying him any attention. 'It's different at the moment, because she needed an operation,' she said, as if she were talking to herself. 'Before that she was in a nursing home. The best we could buy.'

We. The world came crashing in on Owen. Reflexively, he glanced at her left hand, at her ring finger, which was bare.

So could *we* be her and her sister? Somehow, he doubted it. His luck was just never that good.

'Constructive care, Monday to Friday,' she went on, softly. 'Fantasy tea parties where we would rig the questions so the responses made sense.' She studied his face, as if she could find all the answers she would ever need written there. It sent shivers down his spine. 'You've made me feel a bit odd about it.'

Owen laughed, not that it was funny. Anything to lighten the mood. 'Me? Why?' She didn't answer, so he went on, 'It's completely different. See, my dad –

40

he could drink the pair of us under the table, he'd run the pair of us both round the block and *still* have the stamina for an all-nighter.'

But apparently it didn't make her feel any better. 'So you came just because you knew he missed you?'

Owen shrugged.

'I pay four hundred pounds a week to see the back of her because she soils the sheets.'

Owen couldn't think of anything to say. Not for a moment.

It was amazing how his bedside manner failed when he was involved with someone personally.

Involved with someone. He filed that insight away to examine later.

But she was waiting for him to say something.

'I'm no Geriatrician but I've treated a few Alzheimer's patients. I'll be honest with you – I'd do exactly the same thing.' He said it with as much conviction as he could manage, but he couldn't help thinking of his dad, with his booze and his fags and his horses. What would I do, Dad? He wondered. What would I do if you ended up like that – confused and only happy because you didn't know what was going on. Stick you in a private ward and see you once a week if you were lucky?

Well, he'd seen him less than that while he'd been in London. At least it would be different now.

Anna shook her head. 'I would,' he said earnestly.

She laughed.

'What?' Owen said. He smiled, just to see her happier.

'You sound just like a doctor.'

'I am a doctor,' he protested. And to prove it, his bleeper went off. He stood up. 'You know, I wouldn't knock her lifestyle. That's the good thing about cable

41

TV and short-term memory – she can watch the same film three times a day and still be in for a surprise ending.'

She smiled: a real smile, and one that he had put on her face. He walked away, taking the memory of it with him.

He was still thinking of her smile that afternoon, when he did his rounds, and on the way home that evening.

And he was definitely thinking about it while he was in the shower. At least, he was till his dad passed him a can of beer. Owen took a long swig. He stared at Dad, waiting for him to go, but he didn't.

'I've worked it out,' Dad said. 'If I can lay off the drink Monday to Wednesday, ease myself into Thurday with – what – three pints?'

Owen balanced the beer on the shower tray and finished lathering himself. 'Over how long?'

'Five hour period,' Dad said, with the air of a mathematician who has just worked out the value of pi to fifty decimal places.

'Two pints,' Owen said firmly.

'*Two* pints,' Dad said, sounding only a bit disappointed. 'Then I'm off it again, Friday and Saturday – so I should be entitled to get absolutely off me face every Sunday.' Nice try, Dad, Owen thought. He shook his head. 'You see – that's where you lot fall down,' Dad grumbled. 'You never offer anything – you just take things away.' He pulled a properly disgusted face. 'No booze, no fags, no women. Dig, dig, dig.'

'How're you doing on the fags score?' It wasn't often Dad opened up this kind of conversation. Owen reckoned he ought to make the most of it.

'Down to five a day,' Dad said. 'Maybe six.'

Owen reached past Dad for the towel. 'And women?' Now why the hell did I ask him that? He wondered.

Dad pulled a wry face. 'One every ten years. Maybe twelve. You?'

'Nobody,' Owen said.

But he could see in his dad's face that he'd given himself away.

Chapter 6

The phone rang. Anna picked it up.

'It's the Binman,' said the voice on the other end.

Anna frowned. Then she realized who it was. 'Owen?'

'You busy?'

Anna looked at the piles of paperwork on her desk. 'I'm at work. Of course I'm busy.'

'Can't you get a cold or something?'

'What?' It was a ridiculous remark, yet he sounded deadly serious.

'Look out the window,' he commanded. Curious, Anna moved across the room till she could see the street outside. There was nothing there. 'Left a bit,' Owen said. 'Left... a bit more.'

Then Anna spotted it: a beaten up old rustbucket of a car, with her mother sitting in the back seat.

She bolted out of the office leaving a bewildered Michelle staring after her.

It was worse than she thought. Her mother was all dressed up for a day out. Nicely dressed, and with her make-up done just right – pink lipstick and blusher, a touch of blue eyeshadow – she looked as if there was nothing in the world wrong with her. Owen was leaning against the passenger door, looking just a little bit smug.

'What are you doing?' Anna demanded.

'They were sending her off for occupational ther-apy, so I volunteered,' he said. He sounded like a cat who'd not only got the cream, but found the dairy. 'It's okay,' he said soothingly. 'She's insured. Get in.'

Anna leaned down to the window. 'Mum, are you all right?' She must be so scared, not knowing what was going on or who Owen was.

Mum beamed at her. 'I'm fine.' She even seemed to know where she was.

Anna said, 'This is outrageous!'

She'd directed it to Owen, but her mother said, 'I know – I feel like I'm wearing someone else's knickers.'

Anna stood up. She glared at Owen, wondering how one man could make her so furious so often in such a short space of time. 'You take her back.'

'Look,' he said.

Anna didn't want to hear his excuses and evasions. 'Take her back.' But as she said it, she caught sight of her mother's face: such disappointment. Then she thought of her watching the same film on cable three times a day. 'I'll come with you,' she said at last.

Mum smiled. 'We're going to the Lakes, aren't we?'

Anna looked at Owen. 'What's she talking about?'

He grinned. 'Get your stuff and I'll explain on the way.'

She did. But she made Owen take the Mercedes, for comfort's sake. Not that he needed much persua-sion, especially not when she said she was happy for him to drive.

They drove in silence for a while, until they were out of the city. As they cruised down the M6, Owen said, 'Did you know you were conceived in a hotel in Ullswater?'

Anna blushed. 'She told you that?'

He didn't answer directly, for which Anna was grateful. 'If you try interrogating her short-term memory, you'd die of exhaustion.'

'Me?' Mum asked from the back.

'No,' Owen said. 'But if you go back far enough, she remembers everything. Ask her.'

'Me?'

'Yes. Where we off, Myrtle?'

'Ullswater,' Mum said. She sounded very sure of herself. Anna scowled.

'Whereabouts?' Owen asked.

'Sanderson hotel.' Mum peered at her in the rearview mirror. She giggled. 'Oh, straighten your face – if the wind changes, you've had it.' She turned to Owen. 'What've you brought her for?'

Well, Anna thought – at least that was the Mum she knew and understood.

Sometime later, Owen turned into a winding lane. Deep-green hedges stretched up on either side of them, but because the hills were so steep they had a good view of the valley below.

'Here we go,' Mum said. 'We're warm – we're getting there.'

Owen craned round. 'You sure it's the Sanderson?' He turned back in time to avoid a disaster.

Mum stared at him vaguely. 'I'm nearly sure it's the Sanderson – Charles proposed.'

Owen grinned. That grin, Anna thought. It could turn Atilla the Hun into a humanitarian. 'Before or after?' he asked.

Mum gripped the back of Owen's seat. She had become very quiet and serious. 'Oh, before. He gave me the ring in the garden so we could pretend we were already married.' It sounded plausible enough, Anna supposed. She knew for a fact she'd been born a scant nine months after the wedding. And yet, she really didn't believe her mother was capable of remembering so much. 'Oh yes – I recognize all this!' Owen shot Anna a triumphant look. Maybe, she thought. Maybe . . .

'This is so exciting,' Mum said. 'Turn right.' Owen did so. The broad silvery expanse of the Ullswater spread out before them. Mum gasped. 'Would you look at that – they've flooded it.'

Damn, Anna thought. Oh damn. She felt tears prick her eyes. 'They haven't flooded it, it's a lake.' Mum looked upset. 'It's been there forever.'

'Oh,' Mum said softly.

Owen swung a sharp left. 'Yes!' he crowed. 'Yes, yes, yes.'

The gates of the Sanderson Hotel stood before them. They drove through, and soon they were looking at the building itself, in all its faded glory.

Owen parked the car, and they got out. The hotel grounds went right down to the lake's edge, but Mum stood looking up at the hotel. It was creamy white, and in the afternoon sun it was easy to ignore the peeling paint on the shutters, and the slightly unkempt look of the garden.

'Yes,' Mum said. 'It was just here.' She turned for a moment and looked at the water. A couple of ducks paddled near the shore. 'We were right by the water. I said, "Charles, I'm frightened – they'll see straight through us".' She smiled, and it was as if the sun had come out on a cloudy day. '"No," he said. "They'll look for a ring, and here it is".' Anna swallowed hard, imagining the hotel in its heyday, with uniformed staff and the gardens clipped and formal, and tables on the lawn for drinks before dinner. And her mother, so young and scared. And beautiful. 'And he produced it, laughing,' Mum said. It was clear that she was seeing some other, better time. 'But his hands were shaking. 'Marry me, Myrtle,' he said.' She gazed up at the hotel. At one window, in particular. 'I loved him so much it hurt. He smelled of sandalwood. That wasn't him, it was something he'd bought – for my benefit, I suppose.' She swayed slightly. 'I'd never seen a man before.' Her fingers stroked the lace on the neck of her dress. 'I knew it was dangerous: I might get pregnant. But I didn't care.' She sounded defiant, now. 'It would just speed things up as far as I was concerned. I just knew I wanted him for the rest of my life.'

Anna's throat was so tight she couldn't bear it, couldn't breath. She knew she was crying and that Owen would see. Somehow, it didn't matter. She went over to her mum, and put her arm round her. All this time, it had been locked up inside her, waiting to get out. Waiting for someone to have the wit to ask her. To bring her here, and let her remember.

And she'd left her in that nursing home, with her pretend tea parties and her cable-television-same-movie-three-times-a-day life... it didn't bear thinking about.

'Anna,' Mum said. Anna turned to her, but realized that her mother wasn't speaking to her. She was still remembering, still lost in that other world. 'Anna was beautiful. Everybody said she was a mixture of the two of us, but she wasn't. She was the spit of him.' She stroked Anna's hair. '*Spit* of him.' She hadn't taken her eyes off the bedroom window. 'We brought her back here on her first birthday.'

'Oh Mum,' Anna murmured.

Apart from that, there was nothing else to say. Not even when they went inside and had tea, and tired sandwiches made with bread that was curling at the

48

edges, and cakes that were slightly stale.

Afterwards, they went back outside, to the car.

'It's a long drive back,' Anna said. 'Are you sure you're all right?'

Mum stared round at the hotel. At the silver sheet of the lake. At the bedroom window. 'Lovely,' she said.

Owen came over to Anna. 'Are *you* all right?' He was standing so close they were almost touching. He put his hand out, and for a moment she thought he would pat her arm. Or something. But instead he shoved his hands into his pockets.

'I'm fine,' Anna said. She sounded uncertain, even to herself. 'Fine,' she repeated, and this time managed to make it more definite.

'Are you mad at me?' Owen asked.

Anna smiled. 'No,' she said, wondering how she'd managed to get him to the point where he thought she might be, when he'd done such a lovely thing for her. And for Mum, of course. 'Thanks, Owen.'

The sound of footsteps on gravel made her turn. Mum was wandering off towards the car. Her skirt had got caught up in her knickers. Anna dived after her. She stopped her gently, and unhooked the skirt.

'That could have been embarrassing,' Mum said. 'Bless you, nurse.' She smiled sweetly at Anna.

Anna sat in the back on the way home. Mum curled up in her arms and slept. Absently, Anna stroked her hair. Mum had done that to her when she was a child. To let you know I'm there, even when you're asleep, she used to say.

Anna glanced up. She looked into the rearview mirror, and saw that Owen was watching her.

Their eyes caught, just for an instant. Then he was looking at the road again. The moment had passed.

Chapter 7

They'd guessed or Owen had somehow let them know. He'd been mooning around like a teenager, and Danny and John had chivied it out of him. Now they wanted to know all about it.

So here they were in the staff canteen, and they weren't going to stop till he told them. Which was all right with him, because he was bursting to tell someone.

'Staff?' Danny asked, sitting down next to him. He put his beer on the table.

'Real person,' Owen said. Just because he wanted to tell them didn't mean he had to make it easy for them.

'But she's married?' John asked. He seemed less enthusiastic about it than Owen had hoped he'd be.

'No ring,' Owen said. He was pinning his hopes on that.

'Divorced?' John insisted.

'No evidence either way,' Owen said patiently. 'Which, presumably, is a good sign.'

'Whoa, whoa,' Danny said. 'You work in a hospital which has the highest ratio of tasty single females. And you get hooked on a second-hand thyroid.' Owen looked at him with distaste. If that was how going to a single sex boarding school taught you to view women, he was even even happier than usual that he'd gone to the local comprehensive. 'Now,' Danny continued, 'That's like working in a car factory and cycling to work.'

'And what would a privileged eejit like you know about working in a car factory?' John asked. As ever, his Irish accent got stronger the more excited he got.

'More than you'd know about married women,' Danny said sulkily. 'His wife bombed him out for a consultant,' he explained to Owen. 'She took the house, took the furniture – and then she took his job.' He seemed quite gleeful about it, so Owen wasn't surprised when John sloshed his drink over him. 'Come on!' Danny said.

While Danny was wiping himself down, John turned to Owen. 'Look – be very careful how you answer,' he said in an undertone. 'Is the second letter of her first name "N"?'

'Yeah,' Owen said. He couldn't for the life of him see what the problem was.

'Were you talking to her in the canteen last Thursday?'

'So?' Owen asked. His intrigue was rapidly turning to irritation. 'How do you know her?'

John didn't answer. Instead, he turned to Danny. 'Glassman – scram.'

Danny was still wiping himself down. 'Look at me – this is a Paul Smith, you bastard!'

John didn't bother to answer. 'Mr Whittaker on D1 needs his pustules draining.'

'Yeah, well tough shit,' Danny snarled. 'I'll be having cornflakes on Paediatrics.' He slammed off.

When he'd gone, John leaned across the table. 'Look, I'm telling you – forget it. That woman is carrying a health warning.'

Owen had had it with the cloak and dagger stuff.

But he needed to know. 'How do you know her?'

'You won't like me for this.'

Owen sighed. 'Just tell me . . .'

'You know who she's married to?'

John was right. Owen didn't like what he had to say.

Just because he was over forty didn't mean he was past it. Richard Crane dribbled the ball past the Junior Staff defense. Only the goalie now, he thought.

Five-a-side football. Nothing like it. Unless you counted a good game of squash.

And they weren't going to stop him. Not these young dogs. No strategy, that was their problem. He wasn't even winded, and there was the goal ahead of him.

Something careened into the back of him. His legs went out from under him and the ball flew off into the distance.

A second later, there was another thump.

The ref's whistle shrieked.

Richard started to clamber to his feet, and found himself looking up into his assailant's triumphant face.

It was Owen Springer.

Now what the hell was all that about, Richard wondered as he limped heavily away.

It was pouring with rain. Just my luck, Anna thought. She pulled her brolly out of her bag and extended it.

The wind whipped the rain into her face. Horrible day, she thought. She wished she'd brought lunch in with her, but if she wanted to eat there was nothing for it but a trip to the shop.

She thought she heard someone call her name. Surely not, she thought; but then she heard it again.

'Anna!'

She turned. Owen Springer was standing there. 'Oh, hello,' she said. She walked back to him. 'Why didn't you call if you were . . .'

'Why didn't you tell me who you were married to?'

The question startled Anna. 'I beg your pardon?'

'Why didn't you say?' The rain plastered his hair to his head and ran down his face into his eyes but he didn't seem to care.

'Why should I?' Anna asked. It obviously mattered to him, but she couldn't see that it was anything to do with him.

'Because you let me hijack a surgical patient,' he said, as if the trip had been her idea, not his. 'My boss's surgical patient, who just happens to be his bloody mother-in-law.' He swiped the water out of his eyes. 'Well, that's my job gone if he ever finds out.'

'He won't,' Anna said. She tried to sound reassuring, but she was cold and wet, and she wanted her lunch.

'What if he does?' Owen persisted.

'Well,' she said, 'I won't tell him, and my mother can't remember – and that only leaves you.'

For a second she thought he would leave it at that. But then he said, 'Why don't you wear a ring?'

'That's none of your business,' she said. She had really had quite enough of this.

'You're still married?'

Anna thought about just walking away, but there was an edge of desperation in the question. 'Yes,' she said.

'So why don't you use his name?'

That did it. 'What the hell's that got to do with you?'

He stared at her. His jaw worked independently of his brain. 'Because I think I'm in love with you.'

No, she thought. She'd known from the minute

he'd started asking her about her ring or even before that. But when? She couldn't say.

'I have to go.' She turned. Walked away. Tried not to think about him, about those eyes. The gentleness of him, when he'd spoken to Mum.

'Mrs Crane!' he called. She turned. She couldn't do anything else. 'I am. Definitely. I'm in love with you.'

He was looking at her with those eyes, and she couldn't look away. She had never been more scared of anything in her life than she was of him at that moment.

Chapter 8

Richard brought his car to a screaming halt in the drive outside his house. He leapt out, just in time to see his next-door neighbour, Phyllis, taking a tray of elaborately garnished hors d'ouevres inside. It was damned useful for Anna, having a neighbour who was a professional caterer. It took a big load off her.

'Phyllis.' He nodded to her, trying to act as if he weren't outrageously late.

He went in, only to encounter the last person he wanted to see – Anna. She was looking flustered, carrying cutlery into the dining room.

'Sorry!' he said. 'Okay?' He knew it wasn't: not when this dinner party meant so much to her. But tell that to a man with a strangulated hernia.

'He looks helpful,' Phyllis said, cutting between him and Anna.

He started up the stairs. 'That's it, is it?' Anna called after him. 'You just go and have a shower now.'

Richard ran back down. He darted into the dining room – he had to admit it looked splendid, what with the snowy linen table cloth offset by the stark crimson arrangement of gladioli and... something else he couldn't identify. He put his hands on Anna's shoulders and kissed her gently on the cheek.

Then he went and took his shower.

Anna came into the bedroom while he was changing.

'Tell me about them,' he said.

She smiled. It made the sun come out for him, that smile. 'Gillies and Fiona,' she said. 'They're Scots, and it's business, so we won't be talking about the weather.'

'Yes,' Richard said. He arched his eyebrows at her to tell her to carry on.

'Their interests are plastic injection moulding, and they're about to employ about 200 managers across the UK, whom – with any luck – they will refer to me for assessment.' She grinned, but this time sardonically. 'So we won't be talking about *you* much.'

Richard grinned back, although the barb stung just a little. 'I know.'

'OK.'

Blip! Owen clicked the button on the TV remote. Meg Ryan, Tom Hanks going gooey eyed all over each other.

Blip. Something set in – of all places – a hospital: girl gives guy the heave-ho.

Blip. Courtroom drama. Owen didn't wait to find out if it was a divorce case, but he'd have laid odds.

He couldn't settle. He couldn't get the memory of Anna's face out of his mind. Her eyes, when he'd said he loved her. Shock. Fear.

Not at all what he'd hoped for.

Why should he have to feel ashamed of the way he felt? Of the way it made her feel?

Why was he here watching telly on a Friday night, when by rights he ought to be exploring Manchester's thrilling nightlife.

Blip!

But he didn't wait to see what was on. He got up. Dad started to wave him out the way of the television.

'Dad,' Owen said, 'Can I borrow the car?'

Dad pulled a sour face. 'Car when you need it, skip when you don't?'

'Dad...' Owen just wasn't in the mood.

Dad pulled the keys out of his pocket and chucked them to Owen. 'That front off-side tyre needs some air.' He leaned over to get the remote. 'And if the oil light flickers, stick a bit of multigrade in.'

Owen nodded and left. As he went, he heard Dad mutter, 'And the tank's nearly empty.'

The Macreadys – Gillies and Fiona both – were crashing bores. Worse still, Gillies *wanted* to talk about Richard's work. Apparently, he had stunning insights to share that he was sure Richard and Anna hadn't heard before.

'I just can't imagine what it must be like to sit there looking at people, knowing more about their insides than they do.' Richard forced a smile. Out of the corner of his eye, he could see Anna doing her best poker face. 'I mean it's just about as far down the line as you get.'

'It is,' Richard agreed. There was no stopping the flow of incisive perceptions the man was capable of.

'You know,' Gillies went on. 'Life or death "within these hands of mine". What a skill.' He brandished his knife, apparently unaware of the irony. 'What a *skill!*'

There was no way out but to get involved, Richard decided. 'You're trying to avoid the phrase, "cutting edge" for fear of sounding trite,' – if not bloody ridiculous, given the context, Richard thought; but Gillies seemed not to notice. 'But I'm sure it's what you mean, Gillies.'

'Absolutely.'

Richard speared a morsel of poached salmon. 'Well,

it's that old existentialist joke about where the philosopher would be without enough moving targets to construct a theory.'

'Quite,' Gillies said, looking blank.

Richard caught Anna looking at him. He'd known her for long enough to realize that if Gillies caught on that he'd had the piss taken out of him, there'd be big trouble.

Time to be good, he thought. 'We all contribute to each other's success and you seem to be underplaying the huge importance of plastic injection moulding.' Gillies smiled and Anna relaxed visibly. 'Why assume for one minute that your output isn't critical to – say – a surgeon?' Now Gillies was looking almost smug. 'Most patients need more plastic during surgery than . . .'

'Pamela Anderson?' Anna suggested.

Which got a laugh from Fiona, but for a moment Richard thought he'd lost Gillies. 'So,' Richard said, desperate now to turn this around for Anna, 'You're only as good as the structure of any given system.' He had it now. 'Which is why plastic injection moulding is no less deserving of the talents of my brilliant wife, than I, a surgeon, am of plastic injection moulding.'

'Right,' Gillies said slowly. Then he got it. 'Absolutely!' He smiled and turned to Anna. 'Which is why we're here – which is why you should start talking and tell me to shut up and listen.'

Now it was Richard's turn to look smug. Seeing the others watching Anna, he raised his glass in a toast. Light sparkled through the pale straw colour of the wine.

'Not at all,' Anna said. 'I'm completely fascinated.'

Owen didn't feel any better now that he was out.

Whatever Dad said, cruising around in a heap that struggled to do over thirty just wasn't the same – even if you were in town and should be going slower.

The truth was, there was only one place he wanted to be. There was one thing he wanted to see: Anna's face; and one thing he wanted to hear: Anna's voice.

Grow up, he told himself. You're acting like a kiddy in a sweetshop who can't have a chocolate bar.

But it didn't help.

Gillies was in full swing in the dining room, but Richard was enjoying the relative peace of the lounge, on the pretext of getting a bottle of Scotch.

He heard the door open, and turned towards it. Anna came in.

'Socrates to plastics in fifty words or under,' he said. 'That's why you married me.'

As she walked past him to the window, she said, 'Twenty words or under would've been clever.'

He smiled at her, knowing she was watching his reflection in the night-darkened glass. 'They're really boring as shit. You'd better get this contract.'

'I was hoping they'd give me an answer tonight.'

Richard put his hands on her shoulders. 'You can have one from me.' He turned her round. She smelled musky.

He dipped his head and kissed her.

Owen cupped his head in his hands, and leaned against the roof of the car.

He was watching Anna's house. Richard kissing Anna and Anna kissing Richard.

The trouble with acting like a big kid was that kids quite often didn't get what they wanted.

Chapter 9

The advantage of behaving like a kid was that you got to sulk like one. The next morning in the scrub room, Owen took full advantage.

'Go anywhere?' John asked.

Owen glowered.

'Do anything?'

Owen glowered.

'See anybody?'

John was clearly getting desperate. Owen was beginning to enjoy sulking. He let his scowl deepen even further.

When Crane walked in whistling, it did so of its own accord.

'Good mood, sir?' Danny said.

Arse-licker, Owen thought. Grudgingly, he let the staff nurse start to gown him up.

'Good reason, Glassman,' Crane said. He was smiling. Smiling!

Owen could just imagine why.

'Sir?' Glassman asked.

Crane gestured expansively around him. 'I'm surrounded by the spirit of youth. It makes me smile,'

'You like the buzz, Sir?'

'From you lot?' Crane said. He was almost laughing. 'You make getting past forty look absolutely essential.' He jerked his head in Owen's direction.

'Look at him!' Owen tried not to scowl, but failed miserably. 'And I'd put a month's salary on me getting better sex than any of you.' With Anna, Owen thought. And then he thought: Crane knows, he knows and he's rubbing it in. The thought was enough to dry his mouth and set his heart pounding triple time – though whether with fury or panic he wasn't sure. 'That's why I'm smiling, Glassman,' Crane said. He turned to Owen. 'Your show.'

Owen couldn't meet his eyes. 'Yes sir,' he said, and realized his jaw had been clenched so tight that it hurt.

Crane moved over to let the nurse gown him. 'Do you know what you're doing?' he asked. Owen nodded. He couldn't bear to speak to the man. Of course I do, Owen thought: I'm wrecking my career and having my heart broken at the same time. Good trick if you can pull it off. Should save a lot of time for my next self-destructive binge.

When they'd finished scrubbing up, they went into theatre. Owen read from his notes, which the theatre sister was holding up for him. Miserable or not, he was determined to out-Crane Crane, so he read precisely and quickly, knowing his notes could not be faulted.

'Fifty-nine-year-old man. Originally thought to have an acutely inflamed gall bladder. Ultrasound scan discounted that so I'm doing a laparotomy. Question – perforated peptic ulcer? Question – acute pancreatitis?

Owen expected Crane to grill him, but all he said was, 'Assisted by?'

'Me, Sir,' John said.

'Fire away,' Crane said.

I'll show you, you bugger, Owen thought. He stepped up to the operating table.

'Your choice of music,' John reminded him.

Owen turned and signalled to the theatre orderly, who slipped the cassette he'd chosen into the player. Usually, Crane chose. Usually, it was something so soothing as to be soporific – Vivaldi or Brahms.

Not this time.

The Manic Street Preachers blared out, loud and raucous.

Crane looked utterly uncomfortable, and just for a second, much older than he actually was. It gave Owen his first real smile of the day.

'Anna, it's me,' said the voice at the end of the phone.

Anna bit her lip. 'Who's me?' she asked, though Owen's Geordie accent was unmistakeable.

'How many me's do you know?' Anna didn't answer. 'It's Owen,' he said eventually.

'I don't like calls at work,' she said. Which was true, but not the point. She stared around the office, wishing someone would rescue her. The last remaining flowers from the bouquet he'd sent her – a few sprigs of gypsum, some daisies, a solitary rose – sat accusingly on the end of one shelf.

'Okay,' he said. 'Give me you mobile then. I'll ring you when you finish. You say when.'

'I don't want you to call,' Anna said. Yet she was flattered, undeniably flattered. 'There's no point.' She loved her husband and he loved her. She had no need of a man fifteen years younger, not even one with a mouth as vulnerable as Owen's, and eyes so blue you could sail away into them...

'I just want to talk to you . . .'

'I have to go.' She hung up.

Damn him, she thought. Damn him.

Owen stared at the phone. All he wanted was to talk

to her. Just to hear her voice. To have a chance to persuade her...

He looked round the corridor. There was no one around. He punched the follow-on call button, and then the redial button.

'Anne Fairley Management Consultancy. Michelle speaking. How may I help you?' said a girl's voice at the end of the line.

'Yes,' Owen said, drawing his voice out into a fair imitation of Crane's southern accent. 'Hello Michelle, Anna Fairley, please'

'I'll see if she's in,' Michelle said. 'Who's speaking, please?'

Owen hesitated. 'It's her husband,' he said. It was wrong, and he knew it. But he had to speak to her.

'Oh, hello,' Michelle said, suddenly friendlier. 'Just a sec.'

Muzak tumpty-tumped at him. Then Anna spoke. 'Hi! Where are you?'

Owen couldn't answer. His mouth was too dry, and his hands were shaking. 'Look, I can't stop thinking about you. What's wrong with talking to me?'

There was a click, and then the dialling tone.

Owen slapped the receiver down. Shit, he thought. She wouldn't talk to him, and that was bad; but now she never would again, and that was far worse.

'Satisfied?'

Owen turned, and saw John watching him. He felt himself go red. He knew he should say something, but he felt like a fool, so he shoved his hands in the pockets of his white coat and walked away.

Richard walked into Anna's offices feeling happier than he had in a long time.

Surprising Anna for lunch was a brilliant idea –

one he'd had as he'd looked at her picture on his desk, the one taken in Greece, three years ago. It had been an idyllic place, one of the smaller islands that the retsina-and-chips brigade never got to. Just white sand, hot sun and each other.

Like last night. He smiled, remembering.

Besides, he thought, forcing himself back to mundane reality. It would make it far easier for him to... break his bad news.

Michelle greeted him when he went up to the desk, then swivelled round to get Anna on the line. He stared around while he waited. The plushness of the place never ceased to amaze him, nor the fact that Anna had built it up from scratch more or less single handed. He stared over at Anna's office door, thinking of how pleased she would be to see him.

All these years, and they were still good together.

Michelle swivelled back to him.

'Yes?' he said.

The girl started to blush. 'She says...' she cleared her throat. 'She says to vanish. And that this is not very adult, is it?'

'Excuse me?' Richard said. He felt his fists clench, and thought that his world was about to collapse around him.

Anna dragged her jacket on as she got ready to go to lunch. She was still furious with Owen, if not a little flattered.

She heard the door open.

He wouldn't, she thought as she turned to face it.

Richard's head appeared round the door. 'What've I done?' he asked.

Oh hell, she thought, and wondered what she could possibly say that wouldn't get Owen into trouble.

Chapter 10

Owen pushed past John to get to the coffee. He'd known coming to the restroom might be a problem, just as he knew what was coming now. He really didn't want to hear it.

'Owen,' John said, 'You seem to me like a guy who can take it on the chin.' Owen ignored him, ostentatiously turning his back and pouring his coffee. 'She doesn't want you.' Owen sipped his coffee. It was foul. 'And you'd better start worrying about her blowing the whistle on you, because if Crane finds out this is the last hospital you to look at standing up.'

It was true – all of it was true. Owen went to the sink and poured his coffee away while he tried to think of a polite way to tell John to shove it. He'd just about given up on the effort when he was saved by his pager going off.

He stepped round the coffee table with its mess of paper plates and stale mugs, and picked up the phone. There was a suspected wound haematoma on Men's Surgical that required urgent attention.

There was a sharp ping. Owen turned round to see John taking a burger out of the microwave.

'Leave that,' he said, 'We're wanted. You can get your ration of grease later.'

John sighed, took a bite of the burger and dumped the rest on the table.

As they walked towards the lifts, he said, 'There's a party tonight. I think you should go.'

Owen knew what he meant. Meet someone else – one-night stand, fling, steady relationship. Anything so long as it wasn't Anna Fairley. 'Look,' he said, trying to sound patient. 'I don't fancy a party.'

They got to the lifts. John punched to go up, and said, 'You've been here a week and nobody knows you. Have you been inside the staff club once? They're very friendly down at the staff club.' He looked round. 'And since the Equal Opportunities Commission leant on the Board, there's been some fantastic tits flying around.'

The lift chimed its arrival, and the doors opened. It was crowded with visitors and a couple of nurses, but they managed to squeeze in.

'Sex, sex, sex – it's classic,' Owen said, making yapping motions with his hand. 'McGinley, you can't have had a shag in the last six months or you wouldn't keep going on about it.' John flushed. Owen realized half the people in the lift were listening openly to him – and the other half were pretending not to. Well good for them. 'Which is understandable,' he said. He caught the eye of a good-looking blonde woman. 'He screwed up his marriage.' The woman smothered a giggle. Owen turned back to John. 'But when she divorced you for a better paid, better qualified and better looking practitioner, did she mention you could bore for England?'

The lift jolted to a halt at their floor. As they got out, John said, 'Ireland. If I bore, I bore for Ireland.' He shot Owen a mock-venomous glance. 'And I divorced her.'

The doors clanged shut behind them. John advanced on Owen.

'You going to shut up now?' Owen asked, walking backwards to keep his eye on the enemy.

There was a murderous glint in John's eye. 'You're completely off your head, Springer,' he said, walking faster.

Owen grinned but John just looked more angry. Owen speeded up to keep out of danger and then stepped sideways into Men's Surgical.

Anna had known there had to be some reason that Richard had turned up to take her out to lunch.

As she allowed the waiter to seat her, she found out what it was: Richard had to go away again.

'Tomorrow?' she said. 'Where?'

'Holland,' Richard answered. 'Philip's had another panic attack.' Bloody Philip, Anna thought. These days, Richard seemed to spend all his time riding off to sort out his screw-ups at the last minute. She was only glad she hadn't recommended him for the job. 'They want me to present the paper,' Richard finished.

'Say no,' Anna said. Surely enough was enough?

She must have sounded more upset than she wanted, because Richard patted her hand and said, 'I know. But the conference has already started. If I say no, there's nobody else.'

Anna forced herself to smile; luckily for her, the waiter presented the menu just then, so she didn't have to try and think of something accommodating to say. Once they'd ordered – chicken Caesar salad for her, grilled trout for him, with half a bottle of a rather more expensive white than either dish deserved – she came back to the subject.

'How long will you be away?' she asked.

'A couple of days. Three at the most.' He filleted his

fish expertly. 'Depends on the reception. At least it's not bloody Birmingham.'

'Do you want me to come?' Anna said. She had, occasionally, when he'd first attained the status to give conference papers.

If she hadn't known him better, she might have missed his slight hesitation. 'Yes, if you want to – and won't feel like a spare part,' he said. 'I'd love you to come.'

Anna grinned. She'd given up going with him because she'd realized she distracted him; and besides, with her own career taking off, it had been harder to take the time. But now, she thought with a great deal of pleasure, she was the boss. 'I could, couldn't I?' She thought about it. 'We've finished the ICI contract, everything else... is nothing Brian couldn't handle.' It really, really was possible. She felt her grin turn into a smile of anticipation.

An expression she couldn't quite read flitted across Richard's face. Was it worry? Maybe he was scared she'd be bored, or distract him.

'And how about Mr Plastics – has he made his mind up yet?' he asked.

Blast, Anna thought. She stabbed at a bit of romaine lettuce with her fork. 'No,' she said. 'I'd forgotten about them.' She tried to think it through. There was no way round it. 'They can't let me know till Tuesday. And if they're floundering, I'll need to push.'

'Oh bugger,' Richard said.

Anna supposed he must have wanted her to distract him after all.

The patient was going to be fine.

Owen hoped the same could be said for John.

As he stood writing up his notes, he murmured, 'If

I'd known whose wife she was, it might never have happened.'

John looked almost irritated. 'Well, now you know, make it not happen.'

He might as well have told Owen to make the sun stop rising in the morning. 'I can't.'

Now John really was irritated. 'Look – there are simple things, and there are complicated things. I think you're looking for complicated things – and I think that's really sad.'

Owen paused. Thought about it. I'll show you sad, he decided. 'What time's your party?'

Owen had to admit that John could pick a good party.

The two of them, plus Danny Glassman, pushed their way through a writhing mass of people – presumably all medics of one kind or another, but so glitzed up as to be unrecognizable, mostly pissed or well on the way, and all determined to have fun in the worst possible way – to the bar, where John got the first round in.

A couple of girls dressed up as fairies – cleavages plunging to *here*, skirts up to *there* and not a hell of a lot of tinsel or anything else in between – shimmied by.

'Told you!' John said.

Danny raised his bottle in a toast. 'The ones who've done the longest shifts are best – sexually repressed and no judgement.'

Owen grinned, thinking to himself that only ones with no judgement would be likely to go for Danny anyway.

John waved at someone across the corner of the bar.

'Who's that?' Owen asked.

'Belinda. Neurological Registrar.' He sipped his beer. 'She can get a pair of jeans off with her teeth.' Owen didn't ask whether John knew by reputation or personal experience. He didn't get the chance. 'And she's a post-post-modern feminist – she likes to buy the drinks and get laid.' He took another swig of beer, and looked at Owen slyly. 'And she's been asking about you.'

So that was what this was about. Owen decided to bite anyway. 'Asking what?'

'How big your neurones are.' John grabbed Owen by the arm and started to pull him round to the other side of the bar. Owen let himself be led.

Five minutes later, he was out on the dance floor with Belinda – and surprising himself by enjoying it. She slid her hands on to his arms, and for a while they danced. When the music changed and slowed, she drew him closer.

All right, Owen thought, I can go with this. Out of the corner of his eye, he saw John dancing. Not touching his partner. Watching him.

Jealous so-and-so, Owen thought.

I can go with this definitely. She nuzzled into his neck. His hands moved across her back. She turned her face up and moved in to kiss him.

He pulled back and her eyes widened with shock.

'Sorry,' he muttered as he left her standing in the middle of the dance floor.

He went to the loo and splashed water on his face as he tried to calm down. Okay, he thought, so she isn't Anna, but you aren't going to have Anna, and you'd better get used to the idea.

When he went back out, John was waiting for him. He grabbed Owen by the arm and propelled him over to the bar.

70

'What was wrong with her?' he demanded once Owen had got the round in and they'd found some seats in a corner booth.

'She used to work in pathology,' Owen said. He sipped his beer, trying to think of a straight answer. 'You don't know where her hands have been.'

He followed the direction of John's gaze and saw Belinda standing talking to a couple of other women. She looked royally pissed off.

'You've upset her,' John said. 'She'll be calling you Doctor No.'

'Well you go over and make her night, John,' Owen suggested.

'I tried once,' John answered. 'She's allergic to divorcees. "Compensatory sexual behaviour," she said, "is a waste of decent laundry".' Owen realized there was nothing fake about the bitterness in his voice. Or about his look of disgust as he surveyed the room. 'Geez, I don't know why I came. I hate these bloody things – and the ugliest part is watching myself need it so much.' Owen tried and failed to think of something to say. 'Doctor No and Doctor Nearly.' John raised his glass to Owen in a mock toast, and laughed shortly.

'From what I've heard, you do all right.'

John's face twisted. 'Yeah, but you heard it from Doctor Never.' He gestured with his glass at Danny, who was bopping around on the dance floor without much sense of style and less sense of rhythm. 'And he heard it from me.' Ah, Owen thought. 'See,' John said, moving in a little closer. 'I still love my wife but I'd like to see her dead or I'd love to see her bankrupt.' His expression changed to something that Owen guessed was supposed to be a smile, but which was actually closer to a grimace. 'But only while she's still with him. So I'm not without sympathy for you.' He chugged back his beer. 'But the tears stop when you make your mind up about someone else's wife.' He glared at Owen belligerently. 'You know?'

'So you've brought me here out of harm's reach?'

'Maybe.'

'John, I didn't look at her and decide to feel like this,' Owen said. John clearly wasn't convinced. Owen tried again. 'I didn't plan it.'

'Plan what?' John looked as if he might explode. 'There's nothing happening for you. And if there's any justice, nothing ever will.'

Nice to know who your friends are, Owen thought. He was about to say something to that effect, when he realized that John was paying more attention to a couple of identically dressed women he'd spotted on the other side of the room. Very nice, Owen thought – if you like pink dresses so tight they look like they've been put on with a paint roller, and so much make up it should be taken off under general anaesthetic.

John got up and started to squeeze through the crowd towards them. He turned and shot Owen a desperate look, obviously hoping for company; or support. Owen raised his glass in salute, but stayed where he was.

'You've got my bag.'

Owen turned. The woman speaking to him was young and dark haired, and if anything she had dressed down for the evening. She was clutching her glass – G&T or vodka and something, by the look of it – as if her life depended on it.

'Sorry,' he said. 'Were you sitting here? I'll move.'

'No, don't worry about it,' she said, taking the seat on the other side of the table. 'Plenty of room.'

Small talk, Owen thought. He was supposed to be good at it. 'You a nurse?'

'Med student. Withington. You?'

'Registrar. St Gregory's.'

She nodded and sipped her drink. Owen stared morosely at his. He couldn't think of a thing to say and worse still, he didn't really want to.

On the other side of the room, John was dancing wildly with one of the pink dresses.

Danny was dancing alone, but didn't seem to have realized.

'You're doing a really bad impression of someone having a good time,' the girl said.

Owen looked at her. To hell with Anna. To hell with everything. 'Was that an offer?' he asked.

'What?'

Owen looked at her quizzically. She smiled, grabbed her bag, touched his hand and led him out.

Chapter 11

Anna had to admit it: she hated Richard going away.

She stared at his things, which were neatly packed in the boot of his car: suitcase, briefcase – surely there was something she'd missed.

She stared up at the looming bulk of St Gregory's while she tried to think. Bloody place – she could come to loathe it, if this went on.

'If you're ringing me from Holland I'll probably be out of the office this week, so be sure you've got the mobile number with you,' she said. Richard nodded. She'd already told him twice. He slammed the boot. Then she realized what was worrying her. 'The tickets! I didn't see you pick up the plane tickets.'

'They're at the reservations desk.' Richard's feet crunched on the wet gravel as he went around to the passenger door.

'I'll be out tonight,' Anna said. As she started towards the driver's door, she spotted Owen coming through the gate. 'So if you try to call me...' He seemed more relaxed than she'd seen him before. Now, why would that be?

'I'll call you,' Richard said. Anna opened the door and slid inside quickly, hoping Owen hadn't spotted her. 'Look, it's three days in Holland – not a South American field-trip.'

Anna smiled. She ducked her head as she fumbled

with the seatbelt and caught a glimpse of Owen going into the building. She was sure he hadn't seen her. A good thing too, she thought.

Owen was on his way to Women's Surgical when he found the corridor blocked by a crowd of men and women in business suits. Viv Richards was with them. Just as he was starting to push his way through, she ushered them into the administration offices.

'What's all that about?' he asked.

'Selling your birthright on monthly installments,' she said. Owen pulled a sour face. 'Oh don't look so sentimental,' Viv snapped. 'If they sign up you all get new white coats and a couple more scalpels to play with.'

She started towards the lift. Owen paced her. 'Who taught you business management, Viv – Robert Maxwell?'

'Viv*ien*,' she said. Fish in a barrel, Owen thought. She punched for the lift. 'Are the rumours about you true?' Depends which ones, sweetheart, Owen thought. 'About last night?' she asked.

'Last night? Dunno what you're talking about.' Or at least I don't know how you got to hear about it – or why you think it's anything to do with you.

Viv grinned. 'I don't know why men call them conquests, because you all look like you've been dragged through a hedge backwards.'

'You're jealous!' It was the best Owen could do at short notice.

'Of a schoolgirl?'

Owen blinked. 'Schoolgirl? She was a med student at Withington.'

Viv's smile turned to a grin of triumph. 'She was the seventeen-year-old sister of a med student from Withington.' Oh bloody hell, Owen thought. Jail bait, or as good as. Viv's grin turned positively vicious. 'You may well think I'm a vacuous mercenary bitch, Mr Springer, but I'm not.' The lift came, and she got in. Owen was too stunned to follow her. 'I'm a vacuous mercenary bitch with *information*.' She pressed the button for her floor. 'Still,' she added pleasantly. 'It's probably helped her get through her A-levels.'

The lift doors banged shut.

Anna hated taking her mother out. The afternoon they'd spent with Owen at the Sanderson hotel had been a revelation. But taking the old lady out on her own was another thing entirely.

She tried, gently but without much success, to angle her mother's arm into the sleeve of her coat.

'I told her it wasn't an issue, but she would insist on going on about it,' Mum said. The staff nurse she was talking about shrugged helplessly. 'And she threatened to lock me in there.'

'No one threatened to lock you anywhere,' the staff nurse said firmly.

'They were just concerned for your health, Mum.' Anna managed to get the coat on at last.

'I mean, if it's that important why call it a "number two"?' Mum said, taking her handbag from the nurse and clutching it primly in front of her. Her voice rose as she got excited. 'Number two is – by definition – secondary. And anyway, why do I need one if all I'm doing is going to the hairdressers?' Her mouth trembled. 'Why keep going on about it?'

There was no point arguing. With a bit of luck she'd have forgotten about it in a minute or two. Anna turned to the nurse. 'We should be back in a couple of hours. Can she have her purse?'

The nurse hurried away to the office. As the door

opened, Anna caught a glimpse of a white-coated back. *No*, she thought. But it was unmistakeably Owen.

She heard him say, 'Do you know when the blood gases are back, on Mrs Hartley?'

'Be half an hour or so,' the staff nurse replied.

Mrs Hartley my eye, Anna thought. Owen had somehow found out she was here. And then she thought, how paranoid can one get?

'I'm not in theatre till twelve,' Owen said. 'I might as well hang on for them. I'll check her over.'

Of course, even paranoid people may have a point, Anna thought.

'Excuse me,' Anna said to her mother. She went out into the corridor. Owen was standing there.

'Oh, hello,' he said, exactly as if he were surprised to see her.

Anna wasn't amused. 'This is getting really ugly.'

'What?' He was all innocence.

'Following me. What the hell are you doing up here?'

'My job,' Owen said. He waved the clipboard as if it were some kind of official authorization. 'My boss's away in the Netherlands, which you don't need telling...' Anna opened her mouth to speak, but he rushed on. 'Why won't you talk to me, Anna?'

Well, that was easy. 'Because I have nothing to say.'

'Okay,' Owen said. Good, Anna thought. At last he's seeing sense. She turned away. 'Give me an hour?' he asked.

She sighed and turned back. 'I've got nothing to say,' she repeated.

'Anna, I'm going round the bend,' Owen said. In truth, he didn't look as if he'd had much sleep. 'I'm just...' If he'd been a stray puppy, she would have had to take him home, he looked so pathetic. 'Half an hour?' She forced herself to keep a poker face. 'Fifteen minutes? Somewhere public? I don't care...'

'Ship-shape and Bristol,' Mum said from behind her. Anna turned. The old lady was coming out of the ward, guided by the staff nurse. 'Oh hello again!'

Amazing, Anna thought. She actually remembers him.

'Hello Myrtle,' Owen said. He turned to Anna. Looked into her eyes. 'Mrs Fairley.'

'This is the man I was telling you about,' Mum said, flapping her hand in Owen's direction. 'The one who sold me these shoes.' She peered at Owen. 'Weren't you meant to be coming back with a size five?'

Owen smiled at her. 'The van broke down in Bradford,' he said. 'The driver went to change the tyre and somebody nicked all the fives out the back. So it'll be a week or two.'

That seemed to satisfy Mum. 'I am sorry! Wish him luck for me, will you?'

'Course I will,' Owen said. He smiled, and walked away.

How does he do that? Anna wondered. Something about the way he accepted her entirely on her own terms. Or maybe it was the way he entered completely into whatever delusion she was currently in. It was really quite... endearing.

'Shall we ask if he's got a six?' Anna asked Mum.

'I don't think they'll fit,' Mum said. Anna felt relief wash through her. 'But he looks like he could do with the money.'

This is stupid, Anna thought. I'm not doing this. She set off down the hall after Owen.

Viv stowed her overnight bag in the luggage compartment of the train. She was travelling first class, so there was plenty of room. Outside, Piccadilly Station bustled with people.

She grinned as she made her way to her seat. Piccadilly, Manchester to Piccadilly, London in under three hours. This was the life.

She came to the seat she'd reserved.

'Excuse me,' she said to the gentleman sitting in the seat next to hers. 'Is anyone sitting here?'

Richard looked up at her and smiled. 'Not that I'm aware of.'

Viv sat down next to him. Oh yes, this was the life.

Irma was vacuuming when Owen got home. He could hear her from outside. He rushed in, through the hall and burst into the living room.

'Dad!' he yelled. 'Irma!' She didn't hear. 'Irma!' he yelled louder. She turned the vacuum cleaner off and turned to him. 'Where's my dad?'

'I think he went for a stroll round Scott Park.' She looked him straight in the eye. 'Feeling a bit chesty, you know...'

'Nice try,' Owen said.

Irma knew when she was beaten. 'He nipped out for a drink...' Owen left at a dead run. 'He promised me, only one,' Irma said behind him.

He shot her a quick look over his shoulder. 'Thanks.'

At least Dad was regular in his drinking habits. Owen tried the Cock and then the Rose and Crown. Dad wasn't in either – but one of the old fellas that propped the Crown's bar up told Owen where he'd gone.

The betting shop was crowded and thick with smoke, but the silence told Owen that a big race was in progress. He spotted Dad watching the television at the front of the shop.

From the set of his shoulders, he'd put everything on one horse. Which was half a neck behind. Come on you bugger, Owen thought. Do it for me, do it.

It was neck and neck and then it was ahead by a nose as it crossed the finish.

'Yes!' Dad yelled. 'Yes!' He spun round, face flushed with triumph and wanting to celebrate.

When he saw Owen the glee went out of his face. 'How much, Dad?' Owen asked.

'At least there's no booze in here,' Dad said sulkily.

Yeah, Owen thought, and you can save money on fags just by standing here and breathing in. 'How much?'

'Three hundred and eighty.'

Add a bit because he was bound to be holding back... call it four hundred and fifty. Owen did a quick calculation. 'Will you just lend us one fifty?' Owen asked. He saw the 'no I bloody won't' form in Dad's face, and hurried on, 'I'm owed back-pay from UCH and my salary's due on the thirtieth.'

It wasn't enough. 'Oh, I like that,' Dad said. 'I'm out of work, on the sick pension. You're a white collar-worker and you're cadging off me.' He looked round to see if he had an audience. Owen was glad the punters were more interested in the next race, but Dad raised his voice anyway. 'I think that's this country in a bloody nutshell.'

'With interest.'

Dad got a canny look on his face. 'What kind of interest?'

'Dad, I'm on my lunch — I've got forty minutes,' Owen said, knowing that losing his temper would only make the old man dig his heels in.

'What kind of interest?'

All right, Owen thought. Give the old man his due,

he drove a hard bargain. But at least he paid up.

It was amazing how fast it was possible to buy a whole new outfit when you were desperate to impress and you were paying cash.

Owen, laden with shopping bags, was back at St Gregory's with ten minutes to spare. He made it up to the restroom in record time, and started going through his purchases. He had a horrible feeling he'd probably bought something dreadful. His shirt, in cream linen, was not bad and the Chinos were good enough.

'I bought a tie,' he muttered. 'I bought a tie!'

He knew he had, if he could just find it... he moved a clutter of newspapers and soft drink cartons, and dumped the rest of his purchases out on the sofa: fresh underwear, not that he expected to get that lucky, a new razor and some other toiletries. A towel, he wondered. He didn't remember buying one but he was sure he had bought a tie.

John wandered in and surveyed the pile of gear. 'Got a date then?'

Owen looked up. 'Yeah,' he said. 'I've got a date.' This was one conversation he wanted to shut down fast.

'Who with?'

'Not with a seventeen-year-old, let's put it that way.' He patted his jacket pocket and found the bag containing the tie.

'What are you blaming me for?' John demanded. 'You picked her.'

'She picked me,' Owen said; it wasn't strictly true, but John need never know. 'And she looked twenty-five.'

John clearly didn't believe him. 'So who's all this for?' he asked. 'The Snow Queen?' Owen didn't answer. 'I don't want to get involved in all this,' John said.

'That's fine by me,' Owen said, though he desperately wanted to discuss tactics.

'It's one extreme to the other with you, Springer,' John said. He leaned forward and tapped Owen's forehead. 'You've got a detonator in there somewhere, mate.'

Owen smiled, though he was feeling anything but amused. 'You'd better not stand too close then, had you?'

He glared at John, trying to stare him down. He might have won, but at that moment Danny came in and he was in a foul temper, by the look of him.

'How long's Crane away for this time?' he asked.

If looks could have killed, John's glare would have murdered Danny on the spot. 'Three days. What's up?'

'I'll tell you what's up,' Danny said. He shoved Owen's gear aside and flopped onto the sofa. 'This is bloody serial abuse – that's what it is. All my time's spent dealing with his private patients while he's at his bloody conference *again*.' There was something odd in his tone, beyond simple anger, but before Owen could figure it out he rushed on. 'They pay him thousands, and I don't even get a bloody tip.'

'Just stop whinging, Glassman,' John said.

'Well, I'm sorry,' Danny said, sounding anything but. 'Have you heard of any surgical conference in the Netherlands?' He looked from John to Owen and back again. 'Actually, I've checked, and I'm telling you now...'

John crossed the room in two strides. 'Shut up.'

Danny did, leaving Owen to wonder where Crane might be if he weren't at a surgical conference in the Netherlands, and what he might be doing if he weren't giving a paper.

Chapter 12

Vivien had a good eye for a hotel. She looked round the crystal and the velvet plushness of the Beresford Royale's reception and was thoroughly pleased with her choice.

Beside her, Richard finished filling in his check-in slip.

'And your credit card, sir?' the receptionist said to him.

Vivien slid her card out of its holder and handed it to him. He looked at her quizzically. His gaze flicked momentarily to Richard.

'Will you be requiring a morning paper?' the receptionist asked.

Vivien glanced sideways at Richard, but spoke to the receptionist. 'What do you think?'

Richard smiled. So did the receptionist. *No morning papers*, he wrote.

Richard led the way upstairs. While Vivien unpacked, he poured drinks: Scotch and soda for him, gin and tonic for her.

'You see,' he said, 'Where do you draw the line? You get a ward sponsored by ICI, one by Ciba Geigy, a couple of National Panasonic operating theatres . . .' If only, Vivien thought as she unfolded one of his shirts and slid it on to a padded hanger. 'Then bugger me, Jim's fish bar wants his name on the cardiology wing.' She smiled. Cost a lot more than some poxy little takeaway could afford. 'He's got the cash, the public spirit,' he said as he sipped his Scotch. 'Do you let him stick posters of stale fish and chips around patients dying from cholesterol?'

Vivien smiled. It was an old argument. Half the time, she thought this was why he wanted her – medical talk bored his wife, and she wasn't much better when it came to the administrative trivia that fascinated Vivien and fuelled Richard to fury. Of course, the other thing was that when he'd talked himself out, she was very good at distracting him. Relaxing him. Oh yes.

But she knew he wasn't ready for that yet. She'd finished with his shirts, and started putting his underwear in a drawer.

'Or do you turn his money down because you can't endorse his product?' Richard demanded. 'In which case, are you then prescribing what all the other multi-nationals can and can't manufacture before you'll take their dosh?' He glared at her, at some imagined dragon of the hospital administration. 'Of course you don't.'

Vivien smiled at him. 'I've booked a taxi for six forty-five.' She took her G&T from the side table and sipped it. 'If we're there by seven, we've time for a couple of drinks before the show.' But the show was the least she wanted from this weekend, and he knew it. 'There's no time after because we need to be at Langhams by half ten – it's the only table I could get.' She sat down on the edge of the bed and crossed her legs, knowing that she was revealing a yard of silky black-clad thigh. 'And I think we should skip the starter – otherwise we'll be rolling back here half stuffed.' She bit her bottom lip and gazed up at him for a moment. 'And we don't want to miss out on this, do we?'

Owen stood outside Gatsby's, waiting for Anna.

She was late but she would come, he thought. She would. He scanned the crowd.

Idiot, he thought. Of course she wasn't coming. Of course . . .

But then she was there, coming out of the crowd towards him, past an old woman hobbling on a stick and a couple of squabbling school kids.

She paused a few feet from him. Then she started forward again. Her gaze darted from Owen to the passersby and back again, as if she were scared they were being observed.

If he reached out, he could have touched her. 'How are you doing?' he said instead. He nodded towards the restaurant door. 'I told them that if that table goes, they're dead.'

She swallowed so hard he could see it. 'I'm sorry,' she said. 'I can't go in.'

Disappointment hit Owen like a punch to the belly. 'We're just going to talk... have a meal . . .'

'I'm sorry,' she said. She started to walk away.

Owen wondered if she had always meant to do it. He hurried after her. 'We're doing nothing wrong,' he said, and hated the note of pleading in his voice.

'You are,' she said. She wouldn't look at him. Speak to me, he thought at her. Say anything – just give me an opening and I'll prove how right I am. 'I just want to know how you can walk up to someone and say you're in love with them.'

'It wasn't like that,' Owen said. Meaning he hadn't intended to hurt her with it.

They came to the monument. She went to the top

step and sat down. A chance! Owen thought as he sat down next to her.

'Okay,' she said. 'Talk me through it.' The dying sun struck copper from her auburn hair. Owen thought, I want to remember her just the way she is this moment – just in case it's the last one I can ever have. 'We meet on a train, we meet in a wine bar.' Her hands rested in her lap. Her fingers were long, perfectly manicured, yet with short nails. Owen liked that. 'Then only again when you decide to pop up and make a nuisance of yourself.'

That hurt. He hadn't thought of it like that. Not at all. 'So,' he said. 'Taking you and your mum to the Lakes was a nuisance?'

'No,' Anna said. 'That was a very kind and well intentioned gesture.' She looked at him. He wondered how it would feel to be touched by those hands, really touched. 'But you weren't in love with me then?' she asked.

'No,' he said, trying to work it out. That moment when he'd known. 'It happened later.'

'It can't have been much later,' Anna said drily. 'You were back on the doorstep within twenty-four hours being embarrassing.'

Yeah, well, he thought. He watched a pigeon peck at crumbs. Nice life, being a pigeon, he thought. Not enough brain to fall in love with. 'I'm sorry,' he said.

'So what happened?' Anna demanded. 'Did you trip and bang your head, or what?'

Owen grinned. He only wished it had been that simple. 'No, it was when I got back to the hospital and you'd gone.' He paused, trying to find just the right words to describe something that was so obvious to him, and yet so difficult to communicate. The feeling that when he was with her, he was home. 'It

86

was just this weird feeling that I should've been there with you.' That didn't quite make it. 'Wherever you were, I should've been there, because I hadn't finished saying what I had to say.' He looked at her, begging her with his eyes to understand. 'And nothing important or epic, you know...' It was useless. 'I just want to be with you.'

She looked at him as if he'd beamed down from another planet. 'So you didn't bang your head then?'

'Look, this isn't easy for me.' He sounded angry. He hadn't meant to.

'Oh well,' she said. 'It's been a doddle for me.' She stared straight ahead without speaking for a moment. Owen wondered if he should go. If that was the only way to make her happy. But he couldn't do it. Literally, couldn't bring himself to leave her. 'I can't believe you're saying all this,' she said. 'I mean, please – what's the attraction about older women, for God's sake?'

That was the least of it. 'Nothing's attractive about older women,' Owen said, exasperation finally taking over from desperation. 'I don't *go* for older women. I'm just in love with *you*.'

He might as well have hit her – the reaction, the pain in her eyes, was about the same.

Owen swallowed hard. One more try. While she was still here to listen. 'I swear to God I've never felt like this about anyone in my life, Anna.' He could feel it starting now, the panic attack, just thinking about it. He forced himself to take a long, calming breath, but his heart still hammered triple time in his chest. 'When I saw you this morning in the car, I nearly died – I couldn't breath, I started sweating, my fingers went numb.' Again, he took a long slow breath. 'I had to go and walk up Oxford Road because the woman standing next to me in the lift said I should see a doctor.' He laughed, wishing he didn't sound so desperate.

'And what about my husband?' Anna asked. 'Your boss?'

That was a low shot. 'I don't want to talk about him.' The thought of Crane made Owen want to put his fist through a pane of glass.

'But you'd have to,' Anna said. 'In the given scenario, you'd have to: the man I love wouldn't evaporate.' Don't say this, Owen thought. Just don't say it. 'The man who loves me isn't just going to step aside for your convenience.'

In the given scenario, Owen thought. So, change the scenario. 'And what if the man you love's not what you thought he was?' he asked.

The pigeon flapped heavily away.

He saw the bewilderment on her face. Suspicion, even. 'In what way?'

Owen took a deep breath. His pulse was steady now. Now that he'd decided what to do. 'What if...' he said, and thought, it'll hurt her so badly and there's no proof so she'll think I'm lying. But most of all, it'll hurt her. He licked his lips. 'Just because he loves you doesn't mean there isn't somebody else who could love you more.'

'But that isn't to be my choice,' she said. It was as if the sky had fallen in on top of him. 'And forgive me, but this is where you come seriously unstuck, Owen. It's not even a respectable fantasy if you can't see past the obstacles.' Owen felt the air being squeezed out of his chest, as if he'd never be able to breath properly again. 'I'm sorry,' she said. 'I don't mean to be cruel, Owen. I'm deeply flattered . . .'

Owen shook his head – nothing in the world made

sense any more. 'No, Anna, I don't want you to be flattered,' he said. 'I'm in love with you.' He searched her face for any sign that there might be something to hope for but he found nothing. 'I want to be with you. I happen to think you're the most fantastic woman I have ever met.'

'I just happen to be very happily married.' Anna stood up and so did Owen. 'For me,' she said. 'Please don't ring.' And she walked away.

It was impossible, Anna thought as she pushed her way through the crowd. He was impossible. She wished Richard were at home.

Change the scenario, Owen thought.

He'd almost done it. In his mind, he kept seeing what might – what *would* – have happened if he had done it. How she would have been hurt and might have cried; how he would have offered her a tissue, then a friendly arm around her shoulder; how they would have walked through the city to . . . his place. Which was Dad's place – not a good idea. Her place, then. But Crane could come home early. No, a hotel was better. He'd pay with the left-overs from the money he'd borrowed from Dad – a cheap hotel then, a small amused voice put in – and they'd go up to their room and . . . By the time he got that far, he was back at St Gregory's.

He barely knew why he'd gone there. Except that if he were going to change the scenario, he had to have proof. He knew exactly who could provide it. He ran up the stairs three at a time. By the time he got to the on-duty Houseman's quarters, he was breathing hard with exertion and adrenaline.

Danny was sleeping like a baby.

Well, that could change.

'Something you said earlier,' Owen said. No response. 'Danny!'

Danny opened one eye and then the other. 'I've had two hours sleep, you inconsiderate bastard.' He glared at Owen, but didn't move. 'What are you doing in work anyway? I thought you were on a date?'

'Where's Crane?'

Fear chased bewilderment off Danny's face. 'Hey, look,' he said soothingly. 'That was me shooting my mouth off...'

Owen grabbed the duvet and yanked it off the bed, revealing a fully dressed Danny. 'He's getting his leg over, isn't he?' He glared down at Danny. 'Isn't he?' No answer. Owen grabbed the water jug from the side of the bed and dumped the contents over Danny's head.

Danny leapt out of the bed and groped for a towel.

As Owen watched him, he began to feel a little calmer. 'I want to know, Danny.'

Danny scrubbed at his face with the towel. 'Viv Reid,' he said. 'Jesus, Owen.'

'Viv*ien*?' Owen said, mimicking her to perfection. 'You're having me on.'

Danny shook his head. 'I only found out because John was off sick once, and nobody could find the standby list. She was away in a hotel.' He ran his hand through his still damp hair. 'So I rang her on the contact number and Crane answered the phone. Just 'hello', but it was definitely his voice. I'd swear it. I just hung up.' He looked at Owen, obviously still bewildered as to what this was about. Owen decided that it was best it stayed that way. 'Now everytime he shoots off on a conference, you don't see her for dust.'

'Which hotel?' Owen had to be sure.

'Why do you want to know?'

'Which hotel?' Owen advanced a couple of steps toward Danny, who was, by now, looking distinctly worried.

'This is...' Owen got another step closer. 'I was talking about months back, and I don't know if I'm right...' Owen advanced another step. 'Okay. Okay. The Beresford Royale. It's in London.'

Owen smiled. 'You look tired,' he said kindly as he left. 'You should get some kip.'

Just as Owen got to the door, Danny's pager bleeped.

'Bastard!' Danny yelled.

Owen smiled, but it didn't last.

Don't do this, he thought to himself. This is stupid. This is madness. This is self-destruction squared and cubed.

But three minutes later he had found a phone, and two minutes after that he'd got the number of the Beresford Royale from Directory Enquiries.

Don't do this, he thought. as he dialed the number of the hotel.

'Beresford Royale, how may I help you?' said a voice with a southern accent.

'Yeah,' Owen said, thinking, I'm not doing this. 'Could you put me through to Vivien Reid's room, please?'

'One moment please.' There was a pause, a click and a ringing tone.

Hang up, Owen thought. You can't do this, boy.

'What?' Viv's voice. She didn't sound pleased. 'Hello?'

Owen hung up. He shoved his hands in his pockets and walked back to the rest room.

Change the scenario, he thought. She loves her

husband, her faithful husband.

The bastard.

A passing nurse looked at him strangely and he glared back.

I love her, he thought and he's hurting her but she just doesn't know it yet. But maybe she never will. If I tell her, she'll hate me. He knew that for definite: the messenger always got shot.

Then he realized what it was he had to do.

He went into the restroom, picked up the phone and dialled the hospital reception.

'Hello,' he said, 'This is Dr Borowitz. We need to get an urgent message to Vivien Reid, Surgical Business Manager. She's at the Beresford Royale Hotel in London.'

He told the receptionist what message to leave. And then he went home and told his dad what a complete bastard he'd been.

Chapter 13

Anna couldn't stand the thought of going into the empty house. So instead, she went next door, to see Phyllis.

'I'm not disturbing you?' she asked. Phyllis was clearly surprised.

'No!' Phyllis said, ushering Anna in. 'Glad to get away from the snooker. He sits there and I swear I couldn't tell if he's alive or dead – if he goes like that, I might not realize for weeks.' They went into the kitchen, and she shut the door on the noise of the television. She looked Anna up and down. 'Nice outfit.'

Oh dear, Anna thought. 'Thanks,' she said. Phyllis smiled. 'What?'

'Never mind "what?",' Phyllis said. 'You "what?" – you never come here at this time.'

'I do.' But Anna knew she didn't.

'Not dressed like that.'

Anna laughed. It was all too ludicrous and too painful. 'I've had the weirdest few days, Phyllis.'

Phyllis pulled a chair out from the table and sat down. 'Oh good.'

'Not good. It's a nightmare.' She sat down opposite Phyllis.

'Even better.' Phyllis poured out a couple of glasses of wine. Anna took one, and drank rather too much of it all in one go. Then she told Phyllis all about it.

Someone was knocking on the door, but it was the rush of cold air against Richard's skin that finally woke him up.

He rolled over in time to see Vivien close the bedroom door. She was holding a note in her hand, and she looked confused – not an expression he was used to seeing on her face.

He sat up. 'What's that?'

She handed him the envelope and the slip of paper. He took it and glanced at the envelope. It had Vivien's name on it. He turned his attention to the note. Read it once, but couldn't take it in so he tried again.

Urgent. Please ask Mr Crane to phone his wife.

He catapulted out of the bed that Anna knew he was sharing with Vivien. He stood shaking and gasping for breath, his pulse hammered at his wrists and temples.

'She knows. Oh Jesus.' He grabbed at his clothes and started to scramble into them. 'She might be here...'

Vivien stared at him coolly. 'If she were here, she wouldn't be asking you to call her.' He tucked his shirt into his trousers and shook his head. Probably she wasn't here, but still... she must know. 'Richard,' Vivien said, 'It could be something else, something innocent.'

He thumped down on to the bed, and started to put his shoes on. 'It's addressed to you, for God's sake. For me! How can it be innocent.' He couldn't get his shoe on. 'If she knows you're here and I'm with you, what other conclusion is there?' He pointed to note, where it lay on the bed. 'That's Anna-in-the-know – it's exactly what she'd do.'

94

'Look . . .'

Richard stared at the wall. He realized he was trembling. 'I can't believe this is happening.' He thought about Anna, about how soft she'd been with him that night after the dinner party. Soft but passionate. 'It's going to destroy her. This is . . .'

'What do you want me to say?' Vivien asked.

Richard looked up at her gratefully. 'I don't know.' Thank God she was going to be reasonable. 'Yes. Would you go in the other room?'

'What?'

'I might need to speak to her.' Vivien didn't move. She isn't going to take this well, Richard thought. Not when she's had a chance to think about it. 'Just go in the other room, Vivien.'

She went and Richard picked up the phone. He got partway through dialling, then stopped. To speak to her now. What would he say? What would he ever say?

He put the phone down.

Vivien sat on the bed. No more Richard. She'd always known it would come to this but she just hadn't expected it to be quite so catastrophic or melodramatic.

She'd thought – roses, a good meal, his painful admission that Anna had found out, and a few awkward silences.

She'd hoped for more, but only secretly, late at night.

She reached for the phone and dialled reception.

'Can I order a morning paper please?' she said. '*The Times* and a *Mirror*.'

'Certainly, madam,' said the receptionist. 'I'll get them delivered with your breakfast for two.'

'One,' Vivien said. 'Breakfast for one.'

No, she thought. She hadn't expected the ending to be so melodramatic, or so painful.

She pulled the duvet up to her chin, switched off the light and lay staring into the half-darkness.

The expression on Phyllis' face was quite comical.

'Of course I said no,' Anna said. She'd just come to the end of the saga of Owen.

Phyllis lowered her glass to the table. 'And he's how old?'

'Thirtyish.' A baby, Anna thought.

'Not a toad.'

'No,' Anna admitted. 'He's very attractive. Footballer – no, boxer – type.'

Phyllis drained her glass. 'What possessed you?'

Anna topped hers up. 'You don't mean that.' Phyllis' expression said she most certainly did. 'Phyllis you don't – there's no way on earth you'd trust a man who made his mind up that quickly.' She poured Phyllis some more wine. 'You'd run a mile.'

'Would I?' She looked uncertain.

'I mean, I can sit in the office and get excited by the remote prospect, but...'

'You see!' Phyllis said triumphantly. She got up and went over to the wine rack. She turned, holding another bottle of red.

'But when he's standing there just coming out with all that stuff...' Anna let her voice trail off. Despite herself, the image of Owen standing in the rain, declaring his love for her came into her head. 'I mean, it's unbalancing. Because he's got me checking myself and wondering what I did to... I mean, I *am* flattered.'

'Oh good,' Phyllis said. She started to open the wine. 'You were beginning to sound dead from the parting down.'

'Do I ever seem vulnerable to you?' Anna asked.

Phyllis yanked at the corkscrew. It didn't budge. 'In your dreams!' she said. She tugged at the cork again, and this time it popped out.

'So why's he picked on me?' Anna asked. Phyllis advanced towards the table with the wine. Anna held her hand up. 'No, I've had enough.'

'It's not for you,' Phyllis said as she poured the wine into her glass.

Richard stood fuming in the empty vastness of the check-in desk at Heathrow.

He didn't care if it was almost midnight. He wanted a flight to Manchester and found it unbelievable that there simply wasn't one.

'Half-past six is no good,' he explained to the clerk. 'It's got to be now. It's an emergency.'

'That's the only Manchester flight after eight p.m.,' the clerk said. Looking at his fixed grin, Richard wondered where he'd come from. Stepford, maybe. 'I can recommend a partnership hotel, if you...'

'I don't want a hotel,' Richard said. The man would have tried the patience of a saint. 'I've just come from a hotel and I need to get home.' The Stepford Clerk just stared at him pleasantly. 'Look, I'm a surgeon...' It wasn't a trick Richard liked pulling, but he'd heard from others that it never failed. 'It's vital that I get back to Manchester...' It didn't work for him, though. For him, it did nothing at all. 'Oh bugger off!' he shouted.

He went outside and got the first cab he saw. Two hundred pounds to Manchester, the cabbie said. Cheap at twice the price, Richard thought.

Anna stared at Phyllis across her wine glass. She'd been right first time: she had had enough to drink. But that hadn't stopped her helping Phyllis to demolish the second bottle.

'Will you see him again?' Phyllis asked.

Anna shrugged. 'Only because of who he is and what he does for a living.' Unbidden, the memory of him gravely telling her mother that his lorry load of size five shoes had been stolen came into her mind. 'Probably...'

'What do you do if he just loses interest?' Phyllis asked. Cheer, Anna thought; but her heart wasn't – quite – in it. 'What if he walks away tonight and that's the end of it?' She slammed her glass down on the stripped deal table. 'And the next time you see him, he cuts you dead because you hurt him? And you have to answer that honestly.'

She took a long swig of wine.

She's jealous, Anna thought. 'I'd miss it,' she said. Phyllis was right. She did need to be honest – for her own sake, if not for his. 'I'd miss the extremes of it all.' She sipped her wine, and when she spoke, she picked her words carefully. 'But I wouldn't regret finishing it.'

Phyllis laughed derisively.

'Look, it's taken me a long time to build what I've got,' Anna said. 'This is the first time we've actually spent time with each other. I wasn't handed this marriage on a plate, Phyllis.' She thought about Richard: about his commitment to his work, about the hours he worked and how it left them so little time for fun – not that she hadn't made the same choices for herself. But he was the bedrock of her life, the base that she had to have so that she could go out and do what she did – as she was for him. 'Would you jeopardize it all for a man fifteen years younger who looks like a boxer? And you have to answer that honestly.'

Before Phyllis could do so, the kitchen door opened and her husband, Frederick, came in. He was bleary eyed and just a bit paunchy.

'I'm off up,' he said. He ambled over to Phyllis and kissed her on the cheek. 'Night Anna.'

'Night Frederick,' Anna said.

He went out. Phyllis craned back to make sure he'd gone upstairs, then she leaned forward. 'Honestly?' she whispered. 'I'd take him somewhere really private, I'd strip us both to the pink and I'd bang the arse off him.'

Anna looked at her friend steadily. 'I'll ask you again when you're sober,' she said.

Phyllis licked her lips. 'Well, be prepared for a shock, because I don't intend to go to my grave wondering what I've missed. I want to try everything at least once.' It's amazing what you'll say with two-thirds of a bottle of wine in you, Anna thought. 'And,' Phyllis went on, staring regretfully at the dregs in her glass, 'If you hadn't thought twice about it, you wouldn't be asking me the question.'

Ridiculous, Anna thought. But it wasn't, and she knew it.

Anna was out. Richard cradled his mobile phone as he listened to her voice on the answering machine message.

He leaned forward in his seat, as if he could force the driver to get a move on that way. She was out, so that just proved something was wrong. What would she be doing, going out without him?

The answering machine beeped at him. 'Anna,' he said. 'Anna, it's me. I'm coming home. I'm in a taxi,

I'm on my way home.' Outside, the actinic lights of the motorway sped past, but not fast enough, never fast enough. 'Darling, please, if you're there, pick up the phone. I can't do it like this. Please pick up the phone.' He waited but nothing happened. He carried on, 'The only thing I can think to say is, I'm sorry. I don't know how to... I'm sorry.' What else? What else could he possibly say? 'Please, don't do anything till I get there.'

It was useless. He hung up and folded the phone away. When he looked up, he saw that the cabbie was watching him in the rearview mirror.

He couldn't take the mixture of pity and contempt he saw in the man's eyes. He looked away and stared out at the motorway lights.

Owen stared out of the living room window. He'd told his Dad everything. That was the thing about Dad: in the end, Owen knew he'd have his unconditional support.

'How much older?' Dad asked.

'She's about forty-odd,' Owen answered, knowing that made her sound younger than she probably was.

'You love her?'

It sounded odd coming from Dad. He'd never been one to ask about Owen's girlfriends. A cloud sailed across the moon. The night got a little darker. Owen nodded.

'I don't know what to say,' Dad said. Not that he'd let that stop him, Owen reckoned. 'I mean, if I was him and you did that to me, I'd kill you.' Owen nodded. 'If I was her and you did that to me, I'd wring your bloody neck.'

I know, Owen thought. I've wrecked my career, she'll never speak to me again... when he was a kid, he'd thought his dad could put any problem right. He wasn't that naive any more, but he wanted it anyhow. 'But would you just turn your back on her, if you loved her that much, Dad?'

The old man didn't say anything. 'Look well on you, by the way,' Dad said at last. 'The new clothes.'

Richard had realized he'd said everything wrong. Maybe, he thought, if he tried again... he redialled.

'Darling, look, if there's any kind of justification – any kind of defense for me... look, I spend about ten hours a day giving orders, being in charge.' He licked his lips. It had sounded right when he said it mentally but now it just sounded feeble. 'All day, everyday, I have to stay above it all. But she's bossy and she takes control...' Useless, it was useless. She'd think he was saying she was weak. 'She's not prettier than you, she's not as bright as you. I swear to you, Anna, there's no question of her overshadowing what you mean to me.'

Anna opened the front door and went in. She flicked on the hall light and heard someone was speaking in the lounge. She hurried into the lounge.

'And obviously I'll do everything I can to put it right,' Richard's voice said. 'Absolutely no question that it's over. You are the last, last, last person in the world I would want to hurt...' He's having, Anna thought, 'I truly hope you can believe that...' An affair. 'I truly hope you can forgive me.'

He's having an affair. Richard's having an affair. She felt as if she'd been dipped in ice-cold water. She was totally numb.

The phone rang. She listened to it, listened to her own voice giving out the message.

Then she heard Richard. 'Anna? We've just passed Keele Services.' I should pick it up, she thought. I should talk to him but she didn't. 'I'll only be another half hour. Please be there.'

Anna pushed past the locksmith.

She'd paid him in advance. It was amazing what you could get done at gone midnight in Manchester, if you were prepared to pay enough.

The cab she'd ordered was sitting by the kerb.

She thought of something, and turned back to the locksmith. 'Put the spare set through the letterbox when you've finished.' Her voice was thick: she'd been crying.

The workman nodded. Anna got into the cab. She stared resolutely at the road ahead as it pulled away.

It had taken Owen hours to get to sleep. The last thing he needed was to be woken up. I'm not on call, he thought. He lay where he was for thirty seconds, then hauled himself up and sprinted downstairs.

'Mr Springer – yeah?' he said. There was no answer. He shivered: it was damned cold standing there in his underpants. 'Mr Springer,' he said again, beginning to get irritated. 'Hello? Am I needed or not?' Still no answer, but the line didn't sound dead. 'Five, four...' if he got to one, he'd hang up. It was probably Danny getting his revenge, anyway.

'It's me,' said a woman's voice.

Anna. It couldn't be.

'What?' he said.

'How many me's do you know?'

Her voice – her phoning him. He tried to say something, but all that came out was a strangled grunt.

'Do you know the Four Feathers in Prestbury?' she sounded strange: slightly distant, but not, he noted gratefully, angry.

'I don't know,' Owen said. He could barely breathe, let alone speak. 'Who's in it?'

'It's a hotel,' Anna said. 'I'll be there in half an hour.'

'No!' Owen said. 'I shouldn't have . . .'

The line went dead.

She doesn't know I did it, Owen thought. How could she? He stared into the darkness, knowing that now he never would have the courage to tell her.

The cab drew up in front of the house at last. Richard pumped frantically at the door until the safety catch unlocked. Then he leaped out.

'Lovely house,' the cabbie called. 'Don't suppose that kettle's going to be hot?'

In answer, Richard slammed the door of the cab.

He ran up to the front door. He hesitated with the key in his hand. Suppose she turned him away? It didn't bear thinking about. He sighed and put the key in the lock. It wouldn't turn.

No! He thought. No!

He stared up at the house. It was in darkness. Please, he thought. Be here for me, Anna.

He went to the front window. The curtains were drawn. He tapped on the glass. 'Anna,' he called, and then again, louder, 'Anna.'

Next door, the dog began to bark.

'Take your clothes off, please,' Anna said. Moonlight trickled in through a crack in the curtains. Like the moon, she seemed cold and distant.

Owen stared at her. This wasn't what he'd imagined, it wasn't at all what he wanted.

'Anna,' he said desperately, 'We don't need to do this. I just want to talk.'

He did want her. He couldn't deny it. But not like this. Not like this at all.

'What if I don't want to listen,' Anna said. 'Take your clothes off, please.'

He did as he was told. Nervously, like a kid, fumbling with buttons and zips while she watched. I could say no, he thought.

But he couldn't.

Later, she kissed him. She was in her underwear – a froth of creamy lace and cotton – but it was a cool touch of the lips to his cheek. A maiden aunt kiss.

Not what he had imagined. Not what he wanted.

But he wanted her. Oh yes.

She kissed him again, brushing her lips over his mouth, his shoulders, his chest...

She stopped. Looked up at him. 'Do I seem vulnerable to you?' she asked.

His mouth was dry with desire. 'I think you've picked a bad time to ask,' he said. He looked at her, at the way the moonlight sculpted her flesh into soft curves. 'You look perfect.'

For a moment there was perfect silence, perfect stillness. And then she smiled, and bent her head to him, and kissed him.

And there was nothing maidenly in it whatever.

Chapter 14

Richard shifted uneasily in his sleep. Almost without waking up, he reached under himself and moved the seatbelt lock to stop it digging into his side. Then he drifted back into the uneasy half-slumber he'd been in for most of the night.

Owen's eyes flicked open. Last night...

There was an empty space beside him in the bed. It was still warm, and there was a note on the pillow. He looked at it: *had to go*.

Owen smiled.

It was strange, going home, knowing what she'd done.

Anna passed Richard's car in the drive. So he'd come back. She wondered where he'd spent the night.

Well, it was none of her business.

Inside, she went straight to the bedroom. She crossed to the *en suite* bathroom without ever looking at the bed.

She ran the shower as hot as she could stand it. She scrubbed at her body as if she could wash away the memory of Owen's touch.

When she was done, and she'd dried her hair, she dressed for work. Downstairs, she'd found the postman had been.

There were a couple of letters for Richard. She hesitated for a second, then wrote *Not Known At This Address* across them.

The sound of a car engine revving startled Richard awake.

What? He thought. Something shiny by his face... car door handle and that smell: the distinctive scent of warm leather and plastic. He was in the car. He'd spent the night in the car because Anna had found out about Vivien.

There was her car, so she was back.

He hauled himself upright and crashed his way out of the car. But she wasn't arriving. She was leaving.

'Anna!' he yelled. She put the car into gear and backed out. 'Anna! Anna, please!'

But she'd gone.

Owen was unreasonably happy that morning when he went into work. He knew John had clocked it, which made him even happier.

In theatre − male, thirty-eight, appendectomy − Owen spotted John giving him the eye.

'Yes,' he said, to save John the bother of asking him the question.

'You should be bloody ashamed of yourself,' John said.

Owen's scalpel traced a line of blood across the patient's skin. 'You can be bloody ashamed for both of us, John,' he said.

Danny's eyes, above his mask, registered bewilderment. 'You know when someone feeds you the punchline first?' he asked.

Owen didn't answer. Danny would just have to work it out for himself − though if he were able to,

Owen realized, the shit would probably hit the fan.

Richard had to talk to Anna: if he could just talk to her, he was sure he could put things right.

He hadn't got anywhere by phoning, but surely she couldn't ignore him if he turned up at her office.

When he got there the receptionist said blandly, 'I tried to tell you, Mr Crane. She went straight out to a confer...'

He wasn't having that. She was his wife, for pity's sake. His *wife*. 'Till when?'

A crack in the girl's armour. 'Well, I don't know...'

She obviously did. 'She can't be out all bloody day. Richard leaned across and grabbed her desk diary. Anna had a three o'clock appointment. 'Right, if she rings in, will you ask her to please switch her mobile on.' He paused. 'Or I'll be here at three o'clock.' It sounded more like a threat than he'd intended.

'Okay,' the girl said. She didn't sound terribly happy about it.

The temptation to settle himself into one of the deep leather sofas and wait for Anna to show up was terrible. But Richard made himself walk away. Even though he felt as if he were leaving the best part of himself behind.

Anna's bleeper went just before she went into the offices of Greenberg Associates for her nine fifteen meeting. She let her assistants go in ahead of her while she switched on her mobile phone.

'Yes?' she said, over the noise of the traffic.

'He's gone,' Michelle said. 'He looked really rough. Where's he been?'

That was not a conversation she was prepared to have, certainly not with Michelle. 'Just tell me what he said.'

'He saw your three o'clock appointment in the diary.' Michelle sounded embarrassed. 'He said he's coming back.'

'Cancel the appointment,' Anna said without hesitation.

'Okay.'

Anna turned her phone off again.

Myrtle really didn't look well. Owen stared down at her. She was pallid and glassy eyed. Danny and a staff nurse were waiting to tell him what was going on.

'Hiya, Myrtle,' he said.

'She started vomiting this morning,' Danny said. 'Her abdomen is distended and rigid and she seems to be in a lot of pain. I've done a rectal examination, but there's nothing there.'

Owen sat on the edge of Myrtle's bed. He examined her abdomen gently, but she still winced. Danny's observations seemed to be on the money.

He stood up again. 'Has anyone contacted Crane?'

'He's in Amsterdam,' Danny pointed out.

'You know he's not.'

'But if he knows I know he's not, I'll be potty training till I'm sixty-five,' Danny murmured. Then he added more loudly, 'Crowther's overseeing her case.'

'Where's he?'

'Liverpool,' Danny said. 'Teaching.'

Decision time. Well, Owen thought, there weren't a lot of choices. He leaned over Myrtle's bed, avoiding the vase of chrysanthemums on her bedside cabinet. 'Myrtle, we're going to take some pictures to see what's going on down there.' She smiled at him vaguely. He squashed the impulse to raise his voice. 'Do you understand?'

'I don't want to be here,' Myrtle said. Her mouth trembled.

Danny turned to the nurse. 'Can we get hold of her daughter?'

'I'll do that,' Owen said quickly. Try and stop me, he thought. He scribbled on Myrtle's notes while he instructed the nurse. 'Give her 10mg of morphine.' Then to Danny – 'Let's get an erect chest and supine abdominal x-ray.' He thought for a second. 'Let's get up a drip and get some fluid into her. And cross match four units of blood.' He turned to Myrtle, who looked utterly bereft. 'I'll try and find Anna.'

As he turned and left, he caught sight of Danny. Poor bloke looked almost as bewildered as Myrtle. Best keep it that way, Owen thought.

Anna took a deep breath. 'Richard told me...' she hesitated. There was no way to put this nicely. 'Richard has announced that he's been having an affair.'

Phyllis paused. She was stacking sandwiches and quiches into a plastic delivery tray. They were sitting in the back of her van, which was parked up outside the Dancing Mermaid, the last stop on Phyllis's round.

'Why didn't you say this last night,' Phyllis spoke carefully. She was a bit the worse for wear – had two more than she should, she said – which was why they hadn't gone into the pub for lunch.

'I didn't know it last night.' Anna hesitated, remembering the shock of hearing Richard's voice when she'd come in. 'Not until I got home.'

'Oh my God,' Phyllis said. 'I can't believe it.' She didn't really sound as if she were having that much trouble. 'Are you sure you've got your facts right?'

Anna stared at the remains of her prawn and avocado sandwich. It was excellent, like all of Phyllis' food. But she just didn't feel like eating. 'There are no facts to cross examine,' she said dully. 'I got these bizarre telephone messages. No lead-up, no preparation, just a down-the-phone, "I'm having an affair".' She put the sandwich back in its plastic triangle. 'I knew absolutely nothing about it. I had no *idea*.'

Phyllis stopped stacking and turned to face her. 'Did he give an explanation?'

'I haven't asked. I haven't seen him. I don't want to.'

'What are you going to do?'

Anna let her gaze fall to the floor of the van. 'I just rang the man I told you about and took it from there.'

'The younger one?' Phyllis sounded shocked.

Anna nodded. She smiled, but it was a smile without joy or even pleasure.

'So you actually had sex?' There was an excited glint in Phyllis's eyes.

'I did exactly what I felt like doing,' Anna said. It made her feel good just to say it, as if she'd taken the initiative. And it made the next thing easier to say. 'And now I'm going to do the next thing I feel like doing, which is filing for a divorce.'

She waited for Phyllis' nod of approval. Not that I need it, she told herself sternly.

Which was just as well, because it wasn't forthcoming. 'Oh don't be silly,' Phyllis snapped. 'Twenty-five years with the same man? You'd wave bye-bye to all that?'

'Richard is the one violating the relationship,' Anna said. Suddenly the van seemed stifling, even though the doors were wide open.

'Anna, he's a man,' Phyllis said as if it weren't the most obvious thing in the world. 'Men do that. They use it like Meccano.' She sat down on the delivery

110

crate next to Anna, and put her arm round her. 'It's not the end of the world, love.'

'Oh for God's sake, Phyllis.' Anna shrugged her off.

Phyllis was affronted. 'Well you can't sneeze at a silver wedding for some jumped up little nobody who just lurches at you.'

'Last night you were telling me to go and bang him senseless,' Anna pointed out. She might be upset, but she still hated illogicality.

Phyllis started counting out samosas. 'I didn't realize you were talking about breaking up a marriage.'

'Phyllis, you're talking absolute crap,' Anna said, and smiled to take the edge off it.

It didn't work. 'Well, we don't want to spoil a pair then, do we?' Phyllis said. She stopped what she was doing and turned to face Anna. 'Can't you even give the poor bloke a chance to apologize for what he's done?'

'I don't want him to bloody apologize,' Anna snapped. Here she'd come looking for support, and Phyllis was more or less taking Richard's side. It was beyond belief. 'He should never have done it in the first place.'

She clambered awkwardly out of the van.

Bloody husband, she thought. Bloody friends.

As she got to her car, her bleeper went off. She phoned the office.

'What're you like, you?' Michelle demanded. 'I've been trying to get through for over an hour.'

Don't you start, Anna thought. 'What is it?'

'A Mr Springer from St Gregory's wants to speak to you urgently.'

No, Anna thought. Not now, not yet, maybe not ever. 'If he calls again, tell him I urgently don't want to speak to him.'

'It's about your mum.' Michelle sounded bewildered.

'What about her?' If this was one of his games...

'He said she needs an operation and they can't find your husband.'

'Oh my God,' she said. 'Why didn't you just say that?'

'I just did,' Michelle pointed out.

Twenty minutes – twenty terrifying minutes – later, she was standing by her mother's bedside.

The ward smelled of antiseptic and flowers, and that special mix of hope and despair peculiar to hospitals.

'Mum?' she said, feeling desperately happy that the old lady was still alive – and desperately guilty that she had enough emotion left over to be glad Owen wasn't there.

'If you needed a new bra, you should've asked me for the money,' Mum said. Her gaze was even glassier than usual. She patted Anna on the hand. 'You know what your Dad's like.'

'She's been sedated,' Danny Glassman said. He looked excruciatingly young to be in charge of her mother.

'She's got a sigmoid volvulous – it's a bowel rupture, like a twisted inner tube.' He lowered his voice, as if he really thought Mum was in a state of mind where she could be offended by something he said. 'It's quite common amongst old people, particularly those with...' he lowered his voice still further '...dementia.'

Anna smiled at him tightly. 'Have you contacted my husband?'

'His pager's off, his mobile's off, and we haven't actually got a number for him,' Owen said from behind Anna. She whirled round and stared at him warily. Even with everything that was going on, she couldn't help but remember how it had been – his hands, moving on her, that mouth... 'Mr Crowther's on his way, called in from Liverpool, but with your permission I'll do the operation with Mr McGinley and Dr Glassman.'

Such a stupid thing to have done. To have slept with him. But those hands...'Absolutely not,' she said. 'Have you done this operation before?' She didn't know whether it came out of fear for her mother or guilt at what she'd done and why.

'I've done a bowel resection, of course I have,' Owen said.

Something Richard had said to her, about heart patients – that they were critical operations, but still just routine. That's what her mother was to Owen: a routine bowel resection.

She saw him looking at her, and realized she was wrong: to him, nothing to do with her was routine.

He wanted to do the operation because he wanted to do anything he could to help her.

She hesitated but before she could make her mind up, John McGinley appeared at her side. 'Mrs Crane...'

'John,' she said. Richard trusted John.

'With respect,' Owen said, 'The longer we wait the sicker she's going to become.' His eyes said, Let *me* help you. Let me help you.

'We're not anticipating any complications,' John said.

Anna nodded. To her horror, Owen moved in on her. 'Let me get you a coffee or something.'

John moved between them. 'I'll see to that.'

And Anna went off, leaving Mum in what she could only hope were Owen's capable hands.

Chapter 15

Owen had chosen Pearl Jam to do the operation by. He doubted Crane would have approved, but that was okay by him.

'This must be like having the Queen Mother on the table,' Danny said.

Owen ignored him. Bowel resection was a simple job. It would be no problem. The staff nurse suctioned for him, and he made the next incision.

'He's going to be looking at every last snip and suture, you know,' Danny said, as if it were good news. 'You're both looking incredibly calm. This is one time I'm definitely happier observing.'

Owen looked round. He glared at Danny over the top of his mask. 'Danny, there's a rumour going around the nursing staff that you suffer from traumatic impotence.'

Danny looked shocked. 'That's gross defamation.'

John got in first. 'Not for long it's not – shut your gob. All right?'

Danny shrugged, all innocence. And the music played.

Vivien would have avoided going up to Private Surgical if she could, but she had to have a word about the way the non-medical staff were filling out their timesheets.

She turned the corner and saw Richard's wife standing by the coffee machine. Luckily, she had her back to the doors.

Vivien bolted. The timesheets could wait.

Out of the corner of his eye, Owen saw Danny talk to one of the theatre nurses.

He came back to the table. 'Crane's on his way in.'

'From Amsterdam?' John said.

Owen smiled bitterly, glad no one could see it under his mask.

Richard almost ran up the corridor to Private Surgical. Michelle had told him that Myrtle had been taken for an emergency operation, but she didn't have any details.

Part of his mind was running through the possibilities, while the rest kept darting to the things he needed to say to Anna.

When he saw Anna in the corridor, he slowed to a walk. She was punching a number on her mobile, and didn't see him at first.

When she looked up, he said, 'Anna,' he said, 'I'm sorry. I am so sorry.' He meant her mother. For a moment, she almost softened. Then he said, 'I'm so sorry...' And he lost her. 'John's in theatre with Owen,' she said.

'Owen?'

'Springer.'

'Oh yes.' Well, she would know him by his first name – she'd recommended him, obviously. He took a step towards the scrub room. 'You will be here when I get out?'

Anna looked away. 'I'll be here when my mother comes out, obviously.'

'Use my office,' he said. She glared at him. 'Please.' Her expression didn't change.

She hates me, Richard thought as he scrubbed up. Jesus, she hates me.

He hurried into theatre. His staff cleared a space for him at the table, and he inspected the site of the surgery.

'Who opened her?' he asked. There was no response. Jesus, what did they think he was – an ogre? 'Who opened her?' he demanded again.

'Me,' Springer said.

Should have known, Richard thought – no one else would have chosen the squawk coming out of the tape deck. He edged Springer out the way. 'Good,' he said. At least the man was more than marginally competent. He looked closer. 'It's good. Well done.'

He took over the operation. It was good to have something outside himself to focus on, and fortunately it turned out to be perfectly routine.

Richard couldn't stand it any longer.

Anna hadn't been outside when he finished cleaning up after the operation. He'd decided he ought to give her some space – let her decide when she was ready to talk.

But he couldn't do it. Not knowing she was only upstairs sitting at her mother's bedside. Besides, he really ought to check on Myrtle.

She was fine – drip working properly, blood pressure, temperature.

All the time he worked, he was aware of Anna as a silent hostile presence in the corner. It was all he could do to take his eyes off her.

Speak to me, he thought. She didn't, and he'd run out of things to do.

116

'Would you come up to the office?' he asked. She looked tired, with bruise-black shadows under her eyes.

'No.' She didn't look at him.

'Another drink...' The wastebin was half full of plastic coffee cups. 'Can I get you... or some food.'

'No.'

He took half a step towards her and then stopped. The words came tumbling out of his mouth. 'This couldn't be a worse time, but I've got to say something first – I swear to you with all my...' But he couldn't think of what to say: clichés and nonsense? 'Firstly, I want you to know that it's absolutely over. Secondly – and this is trite, I know – it meant nothing.' She looked at him. Her face was as rigid as if it had been carved from marble. 'If I've hurt you because you think I went for something better, you couldn't be further from the truth, Anna.' She just stared at him, as pale as marble and as cold as stone. 'I have no answers,' he said. 'I'm embarrassed that I have no answers, but I haven't a bloody clue what went wrong here.' Shit, he thought. It sounded like he was conducting an industrial tribunal. Worse – as if his behaviour might have been her fault. 'Sex?' he added hurriedly. 'Absolutely no. Temptation? What can I say? I knew her two years before the remotest glimmer of anything happened, so it wasn't exactly carnal.' He was losing her or maybe already had. But he couldn't give up. 'But I suppose the only possible mitigation I have – and I'm struggling to avoid cliché here – is age.'

At last Anna spoke. 'She could be an alien with four tits as far as I'm concerned – I'm not interested in her age. I don't want to know anything about her.' And now her eyes were filled with contempt.

117

'I meant my age.' It was all he could think to say.

'Thirdly?' Anna asked.

'Thirdly?' She was giving him a chance. Rope to hang himself on, maybe, but a chance. He chose his words carefully. 'Thirdly, I love you.' Anna closed her eyes. Was that the hint of a tremor at her mouth? He had to hope. 'I do, yes.' What else? There had to be something else he could say. 'You have done nothing – absolutely nothing – to contribute to my disappointing, unforgivable behaviour, and I love you, Anna.'

She looked away. She'll look back, he thought desperately. She'll look back, and she'll smile. She'll have forgiven me.

'Does this lower her life expectancy?' she asked. She was staring at her mother's face.

'What?'

'The operation.'

He swallowed down his disappointment; forced himself to become the complete professional: it was all he had now. 'Well, she certainly couldn't have survived without it.' He had to force himself not to touch her. She hurt so much, and it should be him she turned to. 'With appropriate care, she's probably got as long as ever she had.' Anna turned to him. The merest trace of a smile hovered on her lips and was gone. 'And the colostomy is only temporary.'

'Thank you,' Anna said. She waved her hand at the bed. 'And thank you for that.' She might have been talking to a stranger.

Richard bit his lip. 'I'd really like to clean up and get a change of clothes.'

There was a moment of silence. It stretched out unbearably before Anna delved into her bag and fished out a set of keys.

He took them, watching her face carefully. Was that a hint of compassion there, or forgiveness, even?

'Shall I wait for you there?'

She didn't answer.

Obviously not, he thought. He walked away closing the door softly behind him.

Anna watched her mother for a while. The old lady's skin was parchment coloured in the moonlight. Her breath came in shallow little rasps, and her eyes flickered beneath lids as delicate as rice paper.

And all the while she watched, Richard's face came into her mind. His desperation, his need and his lies.

Then there was Owen, wanting her, wanting to make things right for her. Owen, who had tried to help her even before he was in love with her, out of simple compassion for her mother.

She turned quietly, and began to walk. When she stopped walking, she found she was at the door of the on call Houseman's quarters. She tapped on the door and Owen opened it. She stepped inside and before the door had swung shut, she was in his arms, desperately clinging to him, needing him, wanting him.

His hands moved over her, across her back, through her hair.

She suddenly realized what she was doing and pulled away.

I can't do this, she thought. Just because I'm scared, just because I've never felt so alone. And there he was, looking little-boy bewildered. Don't, she thought.

But he came to her, and held her, and this time there was no passion in it, only compassion.

Owen stroked Anna's shoulder. They were fully clothed and sitting curled up on the bed.

'You're the first man I've slept with since I married Richard,' she said. She was all cried out, and, Owen thought, still beautiful with raw eyes and a red nose. 'He swore this was his first affair. Would you believe that?' She looked up at him, seeking confirmation. He didn't know what to say. What could he say, knowing he'd caused her this pain? And you say you love her, he thought at himself... 'In his position,' Anna said. 'I know, because he's told me − surgeons get propositioned all the time, it comes with the job.' She laughed, but her voice was shaky.

Owen stared straight ahead. The room was almost bare, completely impersonal. Just to be here, holding her, listening to her voice was enough for him. But the cost, he thought; and she was paying it, not him.

'I thought he was only telling me because he'd deflected the attention. It was a household joke how he fought women off.' She bit her lip. 'Well, it was his household joke.' She rubbed the front of his shirt with the back of her hand. 'I don't want to know who she is − not if he's prepared to pick her up and drop her like that.' Thank God for that, Owen thought, if he had to lie to her face... 'Do you know who it is?' he asked.

'No.' He was glad he wasn't facing her.

'She works here − big surprise,' Anna said. 'I know he's known her for three years, but the relationship's quite recent.' She paused. Owen could almost hear her thinking. 'Well − if I can believe that. He'd say anything now, wouldn't he?'

'Will you leave him?' Owen asked, knowing it wasn't what she wanted to hear, and almost desperate not to hear the answer.

'She's younger than me,' Anna said, as if she hadn't even heard him. 'Another big surprise.'

Owen's bleeper went off. He scrambled up, almost glad of the interruption.

'How do I get out of here?' Anna asked as he picked up the phone.

'Cut down the back stairs. Down towards the kitchen, then come back on yourself to the carpark,' Owen said. He turned his attention to the call. 'Mr Springer.' There was a problem on Women's Surgical. 'Give us five minutes,' he said. He hung up. 'I'll walk you down . . .'

Anna shook her head and she left before he could protest.

He ran out after her, and got to the stairs in time to see her disappearing down the stairwell. All he could do was watch her go and wonder what he'd taken from her. And what, if anything, he'd gained.

Richard was still at the house when Anna got there. She hadn't bargained on that. She tried to get upstairs without talking to him, but he pursued her.

She grabbed a pillow from their bed and turned around. He was standing in the doorway. She pushed past him and touched him. *Touched* him. She bolted back downstairs, to the spare room on the mezzanine.

He was just behind her. She slammed the door in his face.

'Anna . . .' he called.

'Don't you bloody dare come in,' she said. She could feel her throat tightening, hear her voice beginning to thicken with tears. 'Don't you dare!'

And then she threw herself on the bed, clutching the pillow. She cried: long, wracking sobs that shook her whole body. Enough tears to wash her away, so that there was nothing left of her at all. But never enough tears to wash away her pain.

Chapter 16

'You're wanted in Crane's office.' Owen opened his eyes. Right. And Anna had...

Danny was staring at him.

Oh shit, Owen thought as he scrambled up.

'You and John,' Danny said. 'Busy night?'

Owen pinched the bridge of his nose. It didn't help. 'Is there any coffee on?'

Danny perched on the edge of the bed. 'I think I've worked something out, and I think it's giving me the heebies.'

Well good for you, Owen thought. He stood up and grabbed his trousers.

'Your friend – this woman,' Danny said. Give him his due, Owen thought – he really did look con-cerned. 'Is she connected in high places?'

Well, that was quick, Owen thought. He put his shirt on. 'Bang on,' he said. 'She's a trapeze artist with vertigo, which is why she went for a doctor.'

'The other night when you asked me who Crane was getting his leg over with?'

'You've no recollection of that.'

'Just tell me and I'll wipe it,' Danny said. He stood up. 'Owen, are you screwing Crane's wife?' Owen hunted around for a way to change the subject, but before he found one, Danny said. 'No. Actually, no – I don't want to know the answer to that.'

122

'Good,' Owen says.

Which, of course, was more of an answer than he'd intended to give or Danny wanted to receive.

'Jeez,' Danny said. 'What have you done?'

'Coffee?' Owen said. 'Can I have some coffee, please?' There didn't seem to be much else to say.

It was embarrassing, Crane thought – having to admit to weakness. Especially in front of a jumped up little so-and-so like Springer.

But surgery was a team game, and he had no place on the team if he couldn't pull his weight.

He steepled his hands in front of him and surveyed McGinley and Springer. 'I don't want to enlarge on the situation, other than to say that Gordon Crowther's covering my list for a few days, which means you could both get seriously busier.' They were up to it, he thought, whatever his personal feelings about Springer. And McGinley was rock solid. 'I'm just not going to be here.'

'That's okay,' McGinley said. 'We've a fairly straightforward fortnight booked.'

'I'll be on call for advice and emergencies, and I'll still be in for the ward rounds.' He looked at Springer. No doubt *Spinetti* never took time off for personal reasons. 'As a newcomer, you must be getting a fairly bad impression?'

'He's fine,' McGinley cut in.

So the little squirt had been complaining behind his back, Richard thought. He raised his eyebrows at Springer, wondering if the man had the guts to say to his face whatever he'd been sounding off about privately.

'Just let us know if there's anything we can do,' Springer said. He seemed sincere enough.

'Thanks,' Richard said, and meant it. 'There's not.

Thank you.'

They left.

My world is falling apart, Richard thought. There's nothing anyone can do.

Owen thought he'd done a reasonable job of being noncommittal. Apparently, John felt differently. He was positively glowering as they walked back towards the surgical wards.

'You're a two-faced shit,' he said at last. 'You're screwing his wife for God's sake.' He did a bad impersonation of Owen's Geordie accent. ' "Let us know if there's anything we can do".'

'So?' Owen said. He hadn't meant to sound so defensive. 'I've nothing against him.' Only against the fact that he was married to Anna. Other than that, he seemed like a good bloke. Good surgeon, too.

'That's big of you!' John's Irish accent became more pronounced as he got more excited. 'You're a maniac, you know that? You're seriously bad news, mate.' After that, he didn't say anything else.

There was just a bit of paperwork to finish before Crane could leave. While he was working at it, the door opened without warning.

He looked up and Vivien was standing in front of his desk. She was carrying a pile of papers, but she obviously wasn't there on business.

He stared at her. She stared back.

She's done nothing, he thought. Like Anna. Two women damaged because of him. If she needed to talk, he owed her that much, at least that much.

'The first thing I remember,' he said, slowly, 'Is having sex in your flat – which is a very vivid memory.' She nodded. It had been late December and there had been mulled wine and a roaring gas fire. He had left at four a.m., in the freezing cold. 'But what I can't remember is – and you have to forgive me for this – did I initiate that, or did you?'

'It was a bit more evolutionary than that!'

He hadn't meant to put her on the defensive. He hadn't meant to sound as if he were looking for an excuse for himself. 'One of us brought it up first,' he said, and realized he was only making it worse.

'Okay, me,' she said. 'I made the first move.'

So it wasn't me, he thought; and hated himself for how grateful he was for that and how close he was to blaming her.

'Was I a pushover?' He hadn't meant to make it so much about him, but he had to know. He had to know how much of a bastard he really was.

'On a scale of one to ten you were about point five,' Vivien answered. Her voice was hard now, like her stare. 'So please, blame me.' She slapped the papers on his desk. 'But you're going to have to tell me how you want to work this one out, because we have to work together somehow.'

He stared at her. Something in the bitterness of her tone, like a gambler who's upped the ante and lost everything made him suspect her. 'You told Anna, didn't you?' he said. She'd been so cool when the note came – so convinced it was nothing to worry about. So determined he shouldn't go, should make it all worse by staying.

'I did not,' she said, and now there was cold fury in her voice.

'Or you contrived for her to find out, somehow.'

'I did not!'

Crane was furious himself, now. He was furious with her conniving, her refusal to at least be honest about it. 'Look, we made a pact when all this started.

We both absolutely agreed there was no future in it.'
He stood up and paced across the office. 'I don't think
I deserve that kind of deceit.' He waved at the door.
'I'm not like this lot – I'm not a compulsive woman-
izer.' He swivelled round to face her. 'You are an
exception in an otherwise blemish-free twenty-five
years. I'm actually a happily married man.'

She looked mortified. For a moment he thought
she was going to admit to what she'd done. It would
be a cleaner ending. Stop this mess becoming something that would eat at both of them for years.

'You conceited sod,' she snarled. 'What the hell do
I gain . . .'

She was shouting. 'Vivien,' Richard said, 'Please
keep your voice down.'

'Bugger off,' she said, even louder. 'What do I gain
from telling your wife? You dump me in a hotel in
the middle of London with a bill for a queen-sized
bed and breakfast . . .'

So that was it, money. He should have known. 'I'll
pay,' he said. 'Obviously, I'll pay for that . . .'

He pulled his cheque book out of his desk drawer.
She flicked it off the desk.

'I am not a sexual sycophant,' she said. 'I do not
sleep with surgeons because I live in awe of their
gifted hands.' She laughed – a short, ugly sound. 'I
lived with a joiner for two years, so I've had it up to
here with gifted hands.' She chopped at the air, then
leaned across the desk to glare at him. 'I do not want
your life, your house, or your marriage, because I
happen to be very happy with my own life, thank you
very much.' There were spots of colour high on her
cheekbones. She wasn't shouting now, but quiet, her
voice sounded even more dangerous. 'I was very
bloody happy with the odd weekend, which is why I

spent six weeks planning this one. I have no reason on earth to want to spoil that by telling your bloody wife. Have I?'

She went for the door.

God, he thought. What have I done now? I'll have no one left at this rate. No one.

'Vivien,' he said. He grabbed her arm. 'I'm sorry.' He pulled her back. She let him. 'I know you haven't. It's me.' He nuzzled the curve of her neck, letting himself drink in the sharp muskiness of her scent. The last time, he told himself, this is the last time. 'I don't want to lose her,' he said.

She pulled away. 'I can't help you with that,' she said, and left.

Owen watched Viv Reid storm down the corridor. She brushed past nurses, visitors, patients on crutches and in wheelchairs as if they were nothing. She was white with anger.

She's been talking to Crane, he thought. And then he thought it was me that hurt her. What I did hurt her, too. Anna, Crane, Viv. But I got what I wanted, so I suppose that makes it all right.

Which was strange, because he felt like shit.

Vivien slammed into her office. John McGinley was outside, making his usual pig's ear of trying to use the fax machine. She yanked her chair out from under her desk. Before she could sit down, there was a light tap on the door.

McGinley popped his head round the door. 'You okay?'

Viv slammed the door shut without answering.

Dammit, she thought. Don't you start being nice to me. I might just cry.

Chapter 17

'Have you been in to see your mum?' Owen asked Anna.

They were sitting in a pub somewhere in the depths of the country. Owen wasn't quite sure where because Anna had driven. She'd phoned him repeatedly, asking him to phone Mary Ellison urgently. He hadn't got it till she'd explained: Mary Ellison – ME.

Their first in-joke, he'd thought, charmed by it.

And now here they were, facing each other across the table, talking as if they'd known each other for years. The way he'd always known it would be. Should be.

He smiled at Anna, happier just to be here with her than he could ever remember.

'She's been asking when she can go home.'

'And what's the Boss saying?' Owen wondered what she'd do if he took her hand.

'I don't really want to discuss it with him,' Anna said. She sipped her half of lager. 'I can discuss it with you, though – you're looking after her.'

Doctor's wife, Owen thought: understands the ethics. 'Well,' he said, 'Physically she'll be fit to leave within six or seven days, but that's only if you're happy about the nursing home taking a post-op. patient back.'

Anna sighed. Her face darkened. To Owen, it was as

if a cloud had passed across the sun. 'They weren't brilliant before, and I'm not banking on any improvements — but if I move into her house, at least I'll be closer.'

Yes, Owen thought. Yes! He struggled to keep the thought off his face. 'You're leaving him.'

'There's not a lot to be gained by staying...'

He reached out and took her hand. It was warm, and he remembered how it had felt travelling down his back, and round to his chest, and down...

'The house feels so weird,' Anna said. Owen forced himself to concentrate on the here-and-now. 'We bought it years ago.' She smiled, but there was more sadness in it than anything else. 'I took the business over from my boss, who shot off to the States. *He* was offered a consultancy at St Gregory's, and I don't think we stopped running from then.' She smiled again, but this time it was all bitterness. 'I thought we were running in the same direction.'

She was looking at Owen's hands. He hoped she liked what she saw.

He was going to say something when a bloke in his forties turned to talk to them from his place at the bar. 'Oh, hello,' he said.

Owen yanked his hands back.

'Hello, Tom,' Anna said.

He turned away as a woman joined him.

'I thought this was somewhere private,' Owen said. 'You know these people?'

'Vaguely,' Anna answered. She looked more than vaguely embarrassed.

'And how vaguely do they know your old fella?' Owen demanded. He felt himself flush with anger. Mug, a voice screamed in his head.

'They play football together sometimes,' Anna

muttered. She looked at her hand.

'Oh for Jesus Christ's sake,' Owen said. If Crane heard about this his career was done for. He hadn't minded when he thought that she cared. Even that, she might, one day, care. He stood up. 'So I'm – what – just a bit of gossip?' Didn't she care what it would do to him? 'Say they filter it back to him...'

'It's nothing to do with him – what you're doing here...' Anna cut in.

'But I'm only here so you can tell him it's none of his business,' Owen snapped, and stalked towards the door, knowing that Tom and his wife were clocking it all.

He could barely breathe. He loved her. He'd trusted her. And she'd done this.

Rage lanced through him. He felt his nails bite into his palms.

He was half-way across the carpark when Anna caught up with him. 'Look,' he said, 'If you want to make him jealous, don't pretend to be subtle.' Give her her due, she refused to look shocked. 'Take somebody home. Have 'em in bed when he gets in from work.' Just not me. Not now that I know the score. '*That's* how you hurt him.'

He'd expected an apology. Something. But Anna snapped, 'What the hell's the matter with you?'

'I can't believe I've done this,' Owen said, meaning, allowing her to use him. Putting his career on the line, just so she could do this to him ...

'Oh for Christ's sake how old are you?' Anna demanded. 'I'm not a child – I knew what I was doing...'

'But what you were doing had nothing to do with me,' Owen said. He felt as if his heart were being torn out.

130

'What's your complaint – you got what you wanted,' she said, and suddenly she sounded as bitter as he felt.

He looked at her, wondering how she could even think that. 'That was nowhere near what I wanted,' he said.

And he walked away.

Owen was still steaming mad when he got home, and in no mood to be jollied along by Irma, so he went straight to his room.

There was no escape. A couple of minutes later, she brought him up a cup of tea. Good old Irma, he thought. The world could be coming to an end – atomic bombs could drop, the Four Horsemen could ride out – but she'd still be there with a cup of tea, making sure everyone was having a good time.

She handed him the mug and the day's post. 'And a few messages,' she said. 'Can you ring Mary Ellison.' She frowned. 'Ellison.' He ignored that, and started opening the post. 'The last one was urgent,' Irma said. 'She's on the mobile,' she added, to prove it.

Fine, Owen thought. He didn't want to know. What could she possibly have to say?

He found a cheque in one of the envelopes. 'I got a pay cheque – back pay!' he said, delighted. At least he could pay Dad back for the clothes.

Irma tried to sneak a look over his shoulder. 'Oh well,' she said, 'If you're rich, it's me birthday.'

Very convenient, Owen thought. 'You're joking.'

'No – I'm having a bit of a do down the Swan. Your dad got us into...' She stopped and peered at him closely. 'Did I iron that shirt?'

'No, I did,' Owen said.

Irma obviously wasn't terribly impressed. 'Your dad

131

got us into the function room for a tenner, with a sherry each paid on.' She grinned, making her plain face suddenly much prettier. 'I don't know anyone who drinks sherry, but it's the thought that counts, isn't it?'

'Happy birthday, Irma,' Owen said.

'You're welcome to come if you're not doing owt.'

Going out and getting pissed was the last thing he felt like doing, though it did have its attractions.

Watch that, boyo, he thought. Last time he'd done that, he'd ended up in bed with a seventeen-year-old. God knows what might happen this time, especially if Irma had anything to do with it.

'Your dad reckons she's a bit older,' Irma said.

'Does he?' And who the hell else has he told about it, Owen wondered.

'Hey hang on – don't get your back up,' Irma said, visibly narked. 'I've made the same mistake you know. Last bloke I had were in his fifties. Builder's merchant from Heaton Mersey. Massive car, he bought me all sorts – a freezer, a stereo.' Owen stared at her. He'd never really thought about her and blokes. 'Then he starts buying me clothes! I looked like Shirley bleeding Temple in half of it,' she said. Owen grinned. Irma was great, but she was built like the side of a house. Well, he thought, in all fairness, half a house. 'I said, "On your way, you sad bastard – nobody tells me what to wear."' She patted him on the shoulder. 'I just don't think there's owt right in relationships like that. I mean, if he were that good at being fifty, what's he want with a thirty-year-old?'

Yeah, Owen thought. But she doesn't want a thirty-year-old, does she?

Before he had to answer, there was the sound of the front door opening.

'Anybody in?' Dad shouted.

'We're up here,' Owen answered.

'Who's we?' Dad sounded suspicious.

Irma went out on to the landing. 'I wish,' she said, and gave Owen a pretend coy grin.

The party was loud and raucous. Owen pushed his way through the crowd surrounding Irma just as they finished singing *Happy Birthday*.

He held out the bottle of Scotch he'd just bought from the bar.

'Oh you shouldn't have,' Irma said, as if he'd put more than thirty seconds thought into it. 'Come here.' He did, and she half smothered him with the wettest kiss this side of a labrador puppy. 'Hey,' she yelled to a gaggle of her female relatives, 'If any of you lot need your veins doing, latch on to this fella, he's a doctor, a surgeon.' They didn't believe her. He could see it on their faces: boxer, more like. Or a binman. 'He is,' Irma protested. 'Owen – take me mam through her hysterectomy.'

Owen laughed and made his excuses, and went off to find his dad. He found him over by the dartboard, nursing half a Guinness.

'This is me first,' he said, wrapping his hand protectively round his glass. 'And I'm on gills, so I'm trying.'

'I know,' Owen said. He didn't want a row – he didn't think he could take one. Not right now.

'I take it you haven't got a deathwish?'

'No.' Don't start about Anna, he thought, just don't.

'So what're you doing chatting up that one?' he jerked his head in the direction of the barmaid.

One joke, Owen thought. Jesus. 'I wasn't.'

'Don't,' Dad said. 'According to half this lot, it's not sex with her, it's like getting mugged.' He grinned.

'Your hands are worth money. Be warned...' Dad went to take his turn at the dartboard, and nodded towards the bar as he went. 'Underdressed and overused.' He chucked his darts. 'So what's the score with overage and underinterested?'

For a second, Owen was going to make a joke of it. But he felt all his anger coiled inside him like an overwound spring, and he just couldn't. 'Mind your own bloody business, Dad.'

'All right, all *right*.' Dad took a long swig of Guinness, and wiped his mouth with the back of his hand. 'I'm only trying to get you on the right track.'

Condescending old – Owen took a deep breath, telling himself there was no need to lose it.

'Look, if I needed counselling I wouldn't be coming to a sick-paid dipso with less sexual history than a tadpole.'

It was out of order and he knew it. But it was too late to take it back, and he wasn't even sure he wanted to.

'Calm down,' Dad said. He sounded anything but calm himself.

'Look, I don't have to be here,' Owen snapped.

He meant the pub, but Dad didn't take it that way. 'Well, you're not flattering anybody by staying,' Dad said. 'If I'm making you feel that out of place, bugger off back to Notting Hill Gate and take your bloody tantrums with you.'

'Who do you think you're talking to?' Owen demanded.

'Hey!' Dad said. He leaned in close and suddenly, Owen saw the father he'd known when he was a kid – big and tough, and as quick with a slap as a smile. 'If you've cocked it up with your bit of skirt, that's not my fault. If you're thinking you've made a mistake coming up to Manchester, it's your own mistake, right?' He looked round at the crowd. 'We all managed well enough without you. All right?'

Owen stared at him. He felt about twelve, no, make that six. And about to get a larrupping.

He bit his lip. Then he turned and left.

Chapter 18

Vivien glared at Owen Springer. Her week just wasn't getting any better. First the argument with Richard, then him wanting to take time off and now this jumped up little oik wanted to resign, when he'd barely been at St Gregory's two weeks.

'Does that get graced with any kind of explanation?' she asked. 'You haven't got any schoolgirls pregnant, have you?'

'I don't have to explain,' Owen snapped. 'I'm telling you, I shouldn't have come.'

'What the hell are you talking about? People's insides are different in Manchester? You're getting altitude sickness?' Attitude sickness, more like, she thought. Springer just stared back at her. 'Have you any idea how much it costs to run interviews for this job, Owen?'

'I'm really sorry,' Springer said.

Maybe he was, she thought. Something in the way he said it... she couldn't put her finger on it. But she thought maybe he had more to feel sorry about than just resigning.

Owen just didn't want to talk to her. Anna hung up on yet another attempt to get through to him – she'd left messages from Mary Ellison everywhere she could think of.

She sighed and went back to the work spread out across the dining room table. She didn't want to be here – most certainly didn't want to be waiting for Richard – but she didn't feel as if she had a choice.

Too soon, she heard him come through the front door. She turned when he came into the dining room. He was carrying a huge bouquet of carnations.

Twenty-five years of marriage, and he hadn't learned that she didn't care for carnations.

'These,' he said hefting them. 'They're not – well – a bribe. The house just feels cold and I thought they might...' She stared at him. What the hell was there to say? 'I'll put them here.'

I ought to pick them up, she thought. Put them in water – but they were tainted.

He walked round the table and sat opposite her. She was grateful for the expanse of polished walnut between them.

'I've started a list,' he said. 'Things, reasons – possible reasons – why I might have...' his voice trailed away. Anna stared at him. He licked his lips. 'I don't know what the word is. Betrayed you.'

He took a piece of paper out of his inside pocket. There were lots of lines of writing on it. Lots of crossings out.

Anna waited for him to speak. She saw no reason to make this easier for him.

'And,' he said at last, 'There's nothing here. You work too hard, but I like you working too hard. You're rude to my colleagues at parties but I like you being rude to my colleagues – it's quite funny.'

A couple of words on the list leapt out at Anna. 'What's "bedroom"?' she demanded. 'Bedroom?' If he were going to say she was no good in bed, she might have a few things to say about his own technique.

He laughed shakily. 'No no,' he said. 'The paper in the bedroom. The wallpaper... I don't like it.' She wondered if he'd just lost his nerve, lost his bottle, Owen would say. 'That's clutching at straws, isn't it?' He looked at her, and there was despair in his eyes. 'I couldn't think of a thing, Anna.'

Maybe he was lying, but she didn't think so. For an instant, she was tempted to soften, but it would only be storing up grief for later on.

'I'm moving into my mother's house,' she said.

'Please don't do that.' He was begging and she hated that. 'How can I try and explain if you're not there to talk to?' She stared at him impassively. Being there for him to talk to was the last thing she wanted. 'How can I redeem this bloody awful mistake if I can't make you listen to me?'

'But you haven't come up with an explanation, Richard.'

'I will.'

The phone started to ring. They ignored it.

'I'm not asking you to invent one,' Anna said. 'You haven't got one, and I'm not satisfied. So I'm moving out.'

'Look,' he said. He glanced at the phone. It jangled away. He leaned over and put the answering machine on.

Anna stared at her hands while her voice on the tape gave the message out.

'I'll move out,' Richard said. 'Why should you move out?' For a second, Anna thought he was trying to make things easier for her. Then he went on, 'I don't want you to move out...' And she realized he just wanted to keep her where he could find her.

'It's Viv Reid,' said a Scottish voice down the phone.

'Oh God,' Richard said. Anna stared at him. He seemed to be reacting a bit strongly, she thought.

But before she had time to work that out, Viv said, 'I'm sorry to have to get you at home, but we've got a situation with Owen Springer...' Owen, Anna thought. What's happened? She could hardly ask. If he'd done something stupid – some prank, like he had when he'd taken Mum out... 'He's just handed his resignation in...'

And she rattled on about strategies for dealing with it.

Anna could barely breathe. How could he do that? Because of her he'd screwed his career up.

Richard looked furious. 'I'm sorry. Forgive me. I'll be five minutes.'

Because of her, because he wanted more with her than just a night of sex. Because she'd used him.

She scooped her mobile phone up, and went upstairs. On the way, she heard Richard starting to deal with the situation. Bloody man.

Owen grabbed his coffee from the machine and started off down the corridor towards the restroom. It was the end of a long, weary day – he hadn't thought there could be so many emergencies in one twelve-hour period – and all he really wanted to do was go home. Start thinking about what he was going to do with the rest of his life.

'You really think she's worth quitting over?' John asked, catching up with him.

I can't win, Owen thought. I'm trouble because I tried to be with Anna, and fool for leaving.

'You could only ever have been a surgeon, McGinley,' Owen said. 'You think straight down the middle and you're only right half the time.'

'I think you're making a huge mistake, Owen,' Danny said. He was still waiting for his drink.

'I think you're making a...' Owen mimicked Danny's London accent to perfection. 'Who asked you, man?'

Danny scowled. He came over to join them, carrying his too-hot coffee carefully. 'While we're on the subject, nobody asked me – you dragged me into this.'

Owen walked away.

'Just a minute,' John said. 'What do you mean, you were dragged into what?'

Owen spun round. 'He knows.'

'He knows what?' John demanded.

'Ask him,' Danny said.

'Don't bother,' Owen said.

He walked off down the corridor, leaving the other two arguing behind him.

Owen walked. He didn't want to be with people. He didn't want to talk.

He had thought of a way to sort things out with his dad without actually stooping to an apology, and that lifted his mood, just a bit.

Dad was eating his tea, still in a strop. Owen got himself something to eat, then did the washing up. As he was drying the last plate, Dad got up and went out.

He came back with a sheet from the phone message pad. *Call Mary Ellison – urgent.*

'Is that good news?' he asked.

'No.' Owen went and got the carrier bag with the stuff he'd bought in it.

'What's this?' Dad asked.

'A present,' he said. Dad looked pleased. Owen produced a box of anti-smoking nicotine patches.

'May God forgive you!' Dad said. 'I preferred you when you were sulking.'

Owen said, 'Just try them for a week.' He reached into his back pocket, and pulled out a Manchester United season ticket. 'Try them for one week, and you get this.'

Dad's face split into a grin. 'Let's see...'

'No.'

'Come on,' Dad cajoled. 'Let's see.'

'No.'

'Just give us a look,' Dad snapped. Owen handed the ticket folder over. 'Bloody hell!'

Owen grabbed the message sheet and skimmed it – *Mary Ellison, Mary Ellison, Mary Ellison* – and crumpled it up. He chucked it into the bin.

There were other things in his life apart from Anna. There would just have to be.

Anna stood in the garden, staring up at the night sky. She had cried again, after she'd failed to contact Owen. And again, when she was sure he wouldn't phone.

But now she was all cried out. For the moment.

She had a plan, too. But she had to be sure of what she wanted. Had to be sure she wouldn't hurt him again.

The only thing she was really sure of was that she didn't want Richard.

'Owen!'

Owen sat up, instantly awake. He leaped out of bed and grabbed his jeans. Then he realized that he was at home and not on duty.

The light came on. Dad stood in the doorway, rumpled and cadaverous with lack of sleep.

'What you doing?' he said. He was carrying a parcel.

'I don't know,' Owen said, zipping his flies. 'What are you doing?'

'Here.' Dad thrust the parcel at him.

Owen stared at it, bewildered. A thank you for the season ticket? He opened the parcel. It contained a mobile phone. Funny kind of present, he thought. Still... 'Thanks Dad.'

'It's not from me, you daft bugger,' Dad said. 'It's two o'clock in the morning.'

Owen glanced at the clock. So it was.

The phone rang.

Owen stared at it, then pressed the answer button. 'Hello?' he said cautiously.

'Why won't you talk to me?' Anna's voice.

What the bloody hell? 'This is mad,' he said. 'This is completely insane!'

'Is it your skirt?' Dad whispered.

Owen gave him a thumbs up. If she wanted to talk to him this badly... if she did... he could barely bring himself even to think about the possibilities.

'Go to the window,' Anna said.

'What?' He was still barely awake – certainly not enough to figure this out.

'Front window.'

Owen left his room and went into Arnold's. He pulled the net curtain aside and looked out. Couldn't see anything, till she gave him directions.

There she was, standing next to her Audi. She looked stunning.

He shot a glance at Dad – who certainly seemed to appreciate what he was seeing – then legged it down-stairs. He wasn't wearing slippers, and he hadn't got as far as a shirt, but he didn't care.

142

He shivered as the cold night air hit him. The pavement was freezing, but he kept walking. He could have been walking on nails, and it wouldn't have stopped him.

He slowed when he got to her and noticed she'd been crying.

She spoke before he could. 'I don't want you to leave.'

'How did you find out?' He didn't care — not as long as she was there. Not as long as she would talk to him.

'How do you think?'

Owen laughed. He couldn't stop it. After all he'd done, she was just as capable of... 'I can't believe you've just done anything like that.'

Anna giggled. He'd never thought of her giggling. 'Me neither.' She stopped abruptly. For a moment he thought she would touch him. 'I'm so sorry if I hurt you.'

'I should be the one who's apologizing,' Owen said. For more than you know, he thought. But he banished it for another time and he was sure there would be another time for his guilt.

'I haven't come here to apologize,' Anna said. He didn't know whether that was good or bad. 'When you walked away from me, I thought, "oh sod him".' He smiled. 'I got to the main road and I just started crying...' If I reach out to touch her now, he thought, she'll let me. She wanted comforting, he could see it in her eyes. Yet it would be taking advantage in some obscure fashion, so he didn't. Besides, he wanted to hear what she had to say. 'I don't know,' she continued. 'You get to this stage and you think the whole world should be sorted and in shape for you, and it's not.' She smiled ruefully. 'Suddenly it's not. And I

143

don't know – I feel I have no one to talk to. And of all the people I don't have to talk to, you're the one who keeps coming into my head.' He moved towards her, just a bit. 'Like I feel I know where you're coming from,' she said. 'You're the most honest man I've ever met, and I trust you for that...' It was like a knife in his heart, that misjudgement, but he wouldn't feel it. 'And I love you.' Loves me, he thought. *Loves* me. 'And I want to say I'm sorry for taking you forgranted...'

And then she didn't say anything else, and neither did Owen, because they were clinging to each other there in the street, just holding on as if there were nothing else in the world.

Anna smiled at Owen. He was so close. She could smell him. She drew him closer still and started pulling at his shirt. She felt his hands sliding over her, tugging at her clothes. His mouth on hers, her hands in his hair.

They went down together, on to the dustsheets that shrouded her mother's lounge.

There was nothing in the world but Owen, nothing in the world but her desire, his hands, her needs...

They made love, and rested, then made love again.

Until at last they slept.

When she woke, it was to feel his arms around her, his face nuzzling the back of her neck.

Later, they made love again, went for a walk in the village. The sky was bluer than she could ever remember it, the swans on the river a purer white and sunlight more golden. She felt young, like a teenager.

Later, when he had to go, that was all right too.

Because she knew he would come back to her.

Richard stumbled downstairs. The sunshine was too bright, the sounds from outside – traffic, a too-bloody-cheery milkman, a couple of kids playing – were too loud.

He supposed a significant fraction of a bottle of Scotch would do that to you, especially when you drank it alone. Especially when you had just begged your wife to come back to you but she left the house instead.

There was post. He picked it up and headed towards the kitchen. He couldn't help noticing that the flowers he'd bought were still on the dining room table, a forlorn little patch of fading colour.

Somehow, he got to the kitchen and got some toast and coffee together. He flicked through the mail, putting anything for Anna to one side. Bills, circulars, a letter congratulating him on opening a new mobile phone account. He didn't remember doing any such thing. He looked again at the envelope, and realized it was addressed to Anna.

What the hell had she been doing, getting a new phone?

People were looking at Owen and he couldn't figure out why, unless they could read his thoughts, which were of Anna and how her face had looked when he...

Then he realized that the ringing he could hear was coming from his jacket pocket. He frowned and then he remembered the phone Anna had given him, only yesterday, but it seemed like a lifetime ago – a very happy lifetime at that.

He got the phone out, and pressed the answer button.

'I'd completely forgotten I had it,' he said, expecting

to hear Anna reply. But there was no answer. 'Hello?' Owen said.

'Hello?' said a male voice.

'Hello?' Owen repeated.

'Who is this?' said the voice.

Owen finally got it.

Crane.

He broke the connection. Oh shit, he thought. Oh shit, oh shit, oh shit.

Chapter 19

The car Owen was test-driving was a real sweet-heart – smooth-running, quiet as a whisper, a darling to handle.

It looked good too. All in all, he was glad he'd brought John along with him to keep his feet on the ground if he were daft enough to imagine he could afford it.

Unfortunately, John was in the mood to give him stick, in the form of a fairy tale about a poor woman whose only son gets knocked down by a car and is saved by a knight in a white coat with a scalpel and a medical diploma; the poor woman is so grateful that – after going out for a couple of drinks with the doctor – she declares undying love.

'Has this got a happy ending?' Owen asked. He hung a left, to start the circle back to the car dealer.

'Would you trust her instinct to fall in love with you? Would you absolutely trust what she's saying, in the shadow of a trauma that size?'

'Would I hell.' Owen could see where this was going, but he didn't care.

'Why not?'

Much greener, John my son, and you'll get mistaken for a bunch of sour grapes, Owen thought. 'Because it's irrational. Because she's in shock.' He took his eyes off the road for a second to glare at

John. He hung another left, and left again, and they were almost back at the dealer.

'Three weeks ago, Anna Crane was serenely devoted to her talented husband. Now she's passionately devoted to you.' He scowled. Owen tried not to grin. 'I mean, that's not a big leap for you?'

'She's in love with me.' Owen knew he sounded smug. He didn't care.

'Can people change that much, and that fast?'

Owen didn't answer till he'd brought the car to a halt on the dealer's forecourt. 'If you'd touched her, you'd know. If you'd kissed her, you'd know.' He waited till he'd got out of the car to add, 'If you'd slept with her, you would know.'

He slammed the car door.

'Okay,' John said. 'Stick us on the list.'

'That's not funny, McGinley.' Owen put just enough edge in his voice to make sure John knew he wasn't joking.

'No, what's not funny is that she wouldn't look at me twice,' John said. Owen wondered if he'd looked at her more than once – if maybe that was why he'd been so down on Owen.

He chucked the keys to the car salesman. 'That dashboard's fantastic,' he said. 'The upholstery's really tactile, and the engine's very sexy.' The salesman looked hopeful. 'But,' Owen added, and paused for effect, 'I'll be absolutely straight with you, mate – I prefer making love to women.'

The salesman looked glum. Owen jerked his thumb at John. 'He's feeling a bit left out,' he said, 'Try selling him one.'

Vivien knocked on Richard's door, but didn't go in till he called her. There had been a time when she

148

wouldn't have needed to do that. Those days were over, though.

He was just putting the phone down when she entered. He looked angry and embarrassed. She wondered if he'd been trying to get through to Anna – and how many times that made.

'Owen Springer's just retracted his resignation,' she said without preamble. 'I've no idea what's going on there.'

'Good.' Richard stared at a point about three inches to the left of Vivien's right ear.

'I spoke to Gordon and he said he's happy about that if you are?'

'Good.' He still wasn't looking her in the eye.

If the atmosphere gets any heavier they'll be using it for ship's ballast, Vivien thought. 'There was a question in there,' she pointed out.

Richard looked at her directly for the first time. 'I'm sorry,' he said. 'Yes of course – I'll talk to him.' He jotted something on his blotter.

I should go, Vivien thought. I've done what I came for. But she couldn't quite bring herself to do it.

'How are you?' he asked softly.

'Lonely.' The word was out before she could stop it. She hadn't wanted to make herself that vulnerable in front of him, but now it was out she couldn't help wondering if it might help her cause. 'Thank you for asking,' she added, and was surprised that it didn't sound at all sarcastic. In truth, she wasn't quite sure herself how she'd meant it.

'Me too,' Richard said, and for a moment Vivien wanted to comfort him. But then he added, 'She's moved out. Gone to her mother's. That won't last long – she can't stand the place.'

Vivien knew she should be angry at him for even

149

mentioning her. And she was, for a split instant. But then she said, 'I'm at home tonight if you want to talk.' He stared at her, and she realized just how desperate that had sounded. 'You don't have to say now.' She'd meant it to sound tough, as if she had plenty of other things to do but she could see from his eyes that she had just sounded weaker than ever.

He nodded. She went to the door. It was okay, she thought. If he couldn't say, that was fine. But it wasn't. She turned back, hoping for something to hope for. But he just looked at her levelly, until she left.

Owen was in a wonderful mood as he prepared to open that morning's operation – a laparotomy. He'd even toned down his choice of music in deference to the others: Crowded House blared out of the tape deck.

He'd phoned Anna. They were meeting after work, and she'd said she loved him, several times. And she'd said, 'we're out of booze'.

We're. He was part of her 'we'. He liked the sound of that.

As he made the first incision, he said to John, 'You're on a couch in the shrink's office. You're there because everything seems to be going right, and you're absolutely sure you've got the numbers up for the lottery.' He glanced slyly at John to see if he were following. Fairy tales? He'd give him fairy tales. 'The shrink's trying to tell you that it's technically a neurosis and that it's his job to take the pain away.' He looked straight at John. 'Do you let him do his job and make you miserable? Or do you get up and walk out happy?'

'I got four numbers once,' Danny grouched. 'Thirteen pounds bloody fifty.'

'I'd walk out,' John admitted.

Point proven, Owen thought.

God, it felt wonderful to have so much to be smug about.

Richard waited nervously for Anna to come out of her meeting. I'll get five seconds if I'm lucky, he thought. That's all I've got to get her to listen to me. He knew her of old: she'd make her mind up that quickly, and he'd never get her to change it.

She came out, followed by the gaggle of management types she'd been addressing.

'They look as if they're buying it,' he said. Get her talking, and she might remember how it used to be.

'It's the truth,' she said. 'Why shouldn't they?'

He shrugged. Nothing he could say would be right, obviously, but he had to try. 'Can I buy you lunch?'

'I really don't think I want to eat with you,' she said.

He swallowed, hard. The truth then. 'Anna, I'm paralysed without you. Please come home.'

She stared at him for a moment longer. Then she turned and left.

Danny Glassman had been avoiding Vivien: he'd bolted when he'd seen her in the canteen, ducked away from the photocopier when he'd spotted her heading towards her office, and positively ran when he'd seen her heading towards Women's Surgical, even though he'd been talking to the parents of a patient at the time.

So, of course, she had to find him. Besides, she thought she knew why. If there was one thing that bugged the hell out of Vivien, it was something she thought she knew but wasn't quite sure of.

She found him in the grounds, eating chocolate.

Typical, she thought as she watched him from behind the corner of a building. She waited till he'd gone past, then stepped out behind him.

'That's the third time you've avoided me,' she said. He swung round and the look on his face could have won prizes for Most Guilty Man of the Year. 'Normally, you're in there, nipping the ankles and taking the piss, because that's what junior doctors do with business affairs people.' He managed to swallow his chocolate. 'What have I suddenly done to deserve your respect, Danny?' she asked.

'I'll need time to think about that.' He tried to step round her.

She blocked him. 'Let's swap secrets.'

'I don't want to swap secrets.'

Rubbish, Vivien thought. She'd never met anyone who didn't relish knowing something no one else did. The only difference was, other people didn't admit it. 'Yes you do,' she said. 'It's a scream.' She measured him up. No contest, she thought. 'My secret is that I've been screwing your boss.' She looked at him even more carefully. 'I don't see your eyes dilating. Wasn't a secret, was it, Danny?' He shook his head, making his mop of floppy red hair bob around. 'How did you find out?'

He looked terrified. Well, at least he knows the difference between a panic attack and a heart attack she thought. He took a deep breath. 'By accident. I rang your emergency contact number once when you were away and he answered the phone.'

Jesus, she thought. 'When was this?' Her blood was like ice-water in her veins.

'November-ish.'

'You've known since November?'

'November twenty-fifth-ish.'

'Why blab now? Why would you want to dump me in the shit now?' she said.

He raised his hands in a gesture of surrender. 'Look, this has nothing to do with me.' He started to back away. She paced him. 'I've got absolutely nothing to say.'

'And you've got absolutely no career if Crane finds out it was you who grassed him to his wife.'

She thought he might cry. 'Yes, but I didn't.'

'I believe you.' All his body language said it was the truth. So if it wasn't him... a hundred little things flicked together in her head. 'I think Owen Springer had something to do with that.' It wasn't much more than a wild guess. But she was good at guessing. '*Now* your pupils are dilating,' she said triumphantly.

'Viv, I've done nothing wrong,' Danny said. He was desperate.

Best he stay that way. 'No,' she said, in a tone that meant she clearly didn't mean it.

'No, yes, no.' He licked his lips. 'Blackmail is an uglier word to have on your file than "gobshite", so let's leave my career out of it.' He turned and left.

She hadn't thought he had it in him. She wasn't sure she had it in her, come to that. Whatever it was that she thought she could do.

In the end, Anna had agreed to let him go for a coffee with her. It was pathetic how grateful he'd been for that small mercy. Something else that was pathetic was the way he'd asked her if he could use her mobile phone. He'd had to fake a reason to call his admin assistant.

Then, to make his embarrassment complete, his own phone – which he claimed to have left in the car

153

– started to ring. He fished it out of his pocket and brusquely told the person on the other end that he'd call back.

'Why did you need my phone?' Anna asked.

Because it's yours, he thought, because you touched it, but he didn't say that; nor did he give her the other answer, the one he'd already acknowledged, that he was checking up on her. He'd found a receipt for a new mobile phone service. Getting a man's voice when he'd dialled the number had been a complete shock. He didn't know what to think – that maybe she was using a new phone, or that the number of the phone would be on the front of this one – or what to do if he had found something suspicious.

'It's a complete aberration,' he said. 'I don't know.'

She clearly didn't believe him. 'Richard, how have you left things with your lover?'

'That it's over,' he said. 'I told you, it's completely over.'

Anna wasn't satisfied. She stirred her coffee absently. 'How did you break it to her?' Before he could answer, she reiterated, 'How, precisely, did you break it to her?'

Maybe, Richard thought. Maybe, a chance... 'I told her that I love you.'

'You told her that you loved me and it's over? Or you just told her that you loved me?'

Love you, he thought, please don't put it in the past like that. 'It was all perfectly clear and very terminal,' he said. Anna stared at him coldly. 'The former,' he added. He didn't want her to be in any doubt.

'Someone's been ringing my mobile on the hour and hanging up,' Anna said.

'Vivien wouldn't do that,' Richard said, and realized what he had said, too late.

Shit!

Anna flushed. 'Vivien Reid? Your Surgical Business Manager? Is that who we're talking about?' Richard couldn't answer. He could barely breathe. 'The woman you invited back to our house for dinner six months back?' After the affair had started, she meant. 'The woman you said was a cross between Virginia Bottomley and Peter Cushing?' Richard could only nod. 'By which time you must have been sleeping with her for – what? – six months.'

Richard could only look at her.

She slapped him hard enough to rock his head. It hurt and people were looking. His face burned with embarrassment as much as pain.

'I deserved that.' She didn't argue the point. He thought she would leave, but she didn't. 'Okay,' he said after a moment. 'That must give me a couple of points in credit. Can I ask you something, Anna?'

She kicked him bruisingly hard on the shin and he grunted. 'No, that gives you credit.' Her eyes blazed. 'Fire away.'

Probably, he didn't want to know, he thought, and probably, he shouldn't ask at all. But he'd taken the punishment for it now. 'Have you done something to hurt me back?'

'Initially, yes.'

Which meant that whatever it was, there was more to it now than revenge. 'You're seeing someone.'

'*Youth will come here and beat at my door and force it's way in,*' she quoted. 'Never ask a question you don't want the answer to. It's what children do.'

He was trembling. He felt a muscle beneath his eye jump.

'I've tasted what you've tasted, Richard,' she said. I deserve this, he thought and he hated it. 'I understand how confused it gets you – so you have my sympathies.' She sounded anything but sympathetic.

Richard moaned. He couldn't look at her. 'Oh my God,' he said. 'I've done this. I've done this.' He forced himself to look her in the eye. 'Who?' She looked like she wished she'd never told him. 'Is it a friend?' he demanded.

'My friend,' she said. 'Not yours.' She got up and headed for the door.

He couldn't let her leave, not like that so he ran after her. 'Anna!' She didn't stop.

He caught up with her outside. 'Anna...' She turned. 'Tell me – *please* – who is it?'

'I'll invite several men round over the next few days.' She was joking, she had to be joking. But she didn't smile. 'And you can work out which.'

'Anna!' Richard said, shocked. 'Anna...' She started to leave but he took her arm. She shook him off. 'Anna this is pathetic...' She walked away. 'It's ridiculous – you're not *like* that.'

She shot him a glance over her shoulder. 'I know,' she said, and smiled.

She started to cross the road. He tried to go with her, but she darted for a gap in the traffic. A bus came along just then. By the time it had gone, so had she.

Chapter 20

Owen sat on the edge of the bed, balancing a tray between him and Anna. Beer. Toast.

Supper in bed, just what she needed, after the way they'd made love. He smiled, just to think about it. Just to see her lying there.

'This is great,' he said. 'Like camping out.'

Anna smiled. She was so soft, now, in the aftermath. 'I've ordered a van to bring some of my things over,' she said.

'Does your mum know you've moved in here?' He levered the cap off one of the bottles.

'Of course, I've told her,' Anna said. She considered that. 'I don't know whether she's taken it in.' She gestured at the tray. 'What's that?'

'Marmite toasties,' Owen said. He opened the other bottle. 'Bite the toast and swig the beer.' He demonstrated. 'It's great – makes it taste malty. Yeasty.'

Anna tried it. She pulled a face. 'Oh, that's disgusting.'

'It's a well-known aphrodisiac,' Owen said. As if they needed it.

'Well known where,' Anna demanded. She laughed, deep and throaty. 'Oh my God, he's an absolute regressive,' she said, putting on an affected accent. 'I'm not going to be able to take him *anywhere*!'

Owen thought about the big house and the dining

room, made for entertaining a dozen guests. He'd never seen it. He didn't need to. 'Would you want to?' Now he was serious.

'I'd want to take you everywhere.' She smiled, as if considering the prospect and liking it.

Owen reached over and scrabbled for his jeans. He pulled a flat box out of his back pocket and gave it to her. He held his breath while she opened it. He'd spent so much time choosing.

She gasped. 'Owen!'

She held the necklace up. The flat links of red gold – they would bring out the lights in her hair, the salesgirl had said – glinted in the lamplight.

'Car boot sale,' Owen said. 'You're blushing.' And she was. He laughed. 'She blushes!' he crowed.

'It must have cost...'

He took it, and moved round behind her. She shivered as he laid it against her throat, swept her hair up, and fumbled for the fastener.

'I've just sold my flat in Notting Hill Gate,' he said. 'What else have I got to spend my money on?'

She reached back and took his hands, just for a moment. Then she twisted round to face him, with the sheet wrapped tight around her.

'Are you tired?' she asked.

He put his hands behind his head and looked at her. He smiled. 'Depends what's on offer.'

She let the sheet drop away, and moved towards him.

Later, they went dancing.

How long is it since I've done this? Anna wondered. She let the beat of the music flow through her, move her, move with it. And he was there. He moved in towards her and said something.

158

'What?' she shouted over the noise.

He moved in closer. 'You're fantastic.'

'What?' she said, though she'd heard him.

He moved in closer, she grabbed him. Pulled him in close and kissed him.

Owen walked down the midnight street with Anna by his side. Another time, he might have put his arm round her, or held her hand. He didn't need to. It was enough that she was there.

'Why do you want to know?' she asked.

He grinned. 'I want to know everything about you.'

'My first boyfriend was an Italian exchange student who came to stay at my house,' she said. 'He was a couple of years older than me, and actually he was supposed to be my sister's exchange student.'

Owen raised his eyebrows at her. 'So you've an early history of infidelity,' he said as if he were taking notes on a patient. She looked taken aback. He smiled to soften it. 'Name.'

'Giovani Degani,' she said, with a perfect Italian accent. Well, Owen supposed it was perfect – after all, it was Anna speaking, so how could it be less than perfect?

'Handsome?'

'Beautiful.'

'I hate him,' Owen said. 'Next.'

Anna moved round in front of him. She fiddled with his shirt button. 'No, it's your turn.'

Owen considered for a moment. 'My first proper girlfriend? Tina Marshall – regular sex, we're talking about here, aren't we?'

'Yes.'

'You had regular sex with Giovanni Degani?' He

159

didn't bother trying for the Italian pronunciation. 'Otherwise it doesn't count.'

Anna grinned. 'Oh yes.'

'Tops, bottoms and belly buttons?' She nodded, and slipped round to the side of him. She pushed her arm through his, and they continued walking. 'I hate Italians,' Owen mused. 'They're really pushy people.'

'Giovanni was not pushy,' Anna protested. 'Tina Marshall,' she added firmly.

'Tina Marshall,' he said, remembering. 'Tina Marshall was taller than me, she was wider than me and stronger than me.' He looked sideways at Anna. 'And she wasn't that beautiful.'

'So you have a history of poor decisions?' She looked at him speculatively. 'What was the attraction?'

'Her dad,' Owen said. 'He was a crowd control policeman, and he got us free tickets for Knebworth.'

Anna's mouth dropped open. 'That's terrible!' She laughed incredulously. 'That's the only reason you went out with her?'

'She got what she wanted,' Owen said, reasonably. 'We had more sex than a pair of chinchillas.'

'Owen, that's completely mercenary,' Anna said. The actinic light of the streetlamps turned her skin milky white.

'Well, I was,' Owen said. 'I am. In the end, she ditched us for a Lou Reed lookalike.'

She laughed. He wondered if she were as shocked as she was making out. He didn't know. There was still so much he didn't know and so much to find out. 'Anna, I don't want to feel like we're cramming all this in,' he said.

'Then don't open up a discussion about it,' she said, just a bit sharply.

'Doesn't it bother you?' he asked. Meaning: what if

we have to cram it in because this is all the time there is? What if we don't say it all, and regret it forever?

Anna sighed. 'Okay, discuss it!' She hesitated and seemed to come to a decision. 'Yes, it bothers me.' They stopped walking. Owen turned to face her. 'I look at how we got here, and I look at the obstacles and...' She looked at the ground. 'It won't always be this easy, will it?'

He didn't have any answers, so instead of speaking, he drew her to him and held her, there in the darkness.

Vivien peered through the spyhole in her front door. She wasn't expecting anyone. Least of all Richard. She opened the door.

'Hello,' he said.

'Thank you for coming.' It sounded ridiculously formal, but what else could she say?

'I'm sorry it's so late,' he said. He took a couple of tentative steps into the hall and she shut the door behind him. 'I'm just...' he faltered. She wondered if he were drunk, but there was no smell of it on him. 'I'm not here to stay the night,' he said by way of an apology.

'I can live with that,' Viv said, but she couldn't manage a smile.

He lurched at her and pulled her towards him. She went, willingly; and when he kissed her, she was more than willing.

Later – much later – they lay together in her bed. She snuggled up to Richard, and tried to pretend nothing was wrong.

'I'd like to ask a favour,' he said. His arm was round her shoulder. He stroked her upper arm, absently. Vivien looked up at him. Here it comes, she thought.

161

She braced herself. 'She's been a bit silly,' he said. 'Because of me, she's seeing someone else.'

That's it, Vivien thought. We're done. There's no point to this at all. She extricated herself from his arm, got out of bed, wrapping herself in her dressing gown. Richard barely seemed to notice.

Next time I want a cuddle, she thought, I'll take a teddy bear to bed. I'd have more chance of keeping its attention.

'Obviously I'm not in a position to complain about that,' he said. 'But I want to try and find some sort of detective – a private detective.'

Oh bloody hell, Vivien thought. 'You want me to...?'

'I wouldn't know where to start,' Richard explained.

'And I do?' she demanded. 'This isn't a bloody hobby, Richard.'

'I'm aware that you're the last person I should be asking but, obviously, I'd be very grateful.' He looked at her: that little boy lost look that showed his need for someone else to take charge. 'I'd be very grateful.'

She wondered, suddenly, whether that gratitude included payment in advance – if that was why he'd screwed her tonight.

All right, if this was the way it was going to be, she could handle it. If he wanted to find out, she would help him – after all, she had her own reasons for wanting to find out who it was. And when she did, revenge was going to be very bloody sweet.

'Are you sure it's a good idea to know who he is?'

'Oh, I'm absolutely bloody *certain* I want to know who it is,' Richard said. His hand twisted into the sheet.

Vivien shrugged. 'Okay.'

Chapter 21

Owen hurled himself out of the cab and into his dad's house. He wasn't late for his shift yet, but he was working on it.

Dad was in the kitchen wrapping sandwiches in foil. 'We're off to Chester Races for the night, with the Buffaloes,' he offered by way of explanation.

'Buffaloes?'

'League of gentlemen dedicated to the public and changing the future.' He snorted. 'Most of our lot are just interfering old gits with chest infections.' He looked appraisingly at Owen, then rubbed his chin with one bony, nicotine-stained finger. 'She's bought you a razor? It'll be a bungalow next.' He stuffed the sandwiches into a bag. 'Is that good news?'

He walked off into the living room and Owen followed. Dad ferreted around down the side of his armchair, and came up with half a pack of cigarettes. 'N reg Audi?' he said, going over to the stereo. 'That's not your welfare state, is it?' He retrieved a hipflask from behind the record collection without the slightest trace of embarrassment. 'How is she?'

'Fine.' He knew Dad was desperate to know more, but wouldn't stoop to asking. But he saw no reason to make it easy for him.

'Well, I didn't get a close look, but from what I could see, you've set a standard,' Dad conceded. He waited but Owen didn't say anything. Dad gave in. 'Will you be introducing us?'

'No.'

Dad looked affronted. 'Why not? You're mine – I seeded you.' He stomped back into the kitchen. 'If she loves you that much, she must be curious about your background.' He shoved the hipflask in the bag with the sandwiches.

Owen wasn't letting him get away with that. 'No, no – you didn't come into the conversation. She's bright enough to fill in the gaps.'

'Well, there's only one problem with women like that.'

'And you'd know,' Owen said. He grinned to take the edge off it. He had no desire to start another row.

A car horn sounded outside.

'If. . .' Dad started. The horn honked again. 'All right – hang on!' he bellowed. Then he said to Owen, 'If you've only taken this long to get this far and she's married to him and used to better – what have you got when the nookie wears off?'

Owen bit back a smart-arsed reply. Dad was obviously serious, but that didn't mean Owen wanted to hear what he had to say. To hell with it. 'Shall I tell you about men like you Dad?' he demanded. Dad's expression hardened. Owen considered backing down. But some things were worth saying. 'Who think foreplay's getting their first name right? The only thing you think's important is the nookie – and that knocks things out of perspective.'

Dad smiled sourly. 'You try laying off the golden poker and see what happens.' He picked up his bag and headed towards the door. 'She'll bloody vaporize, I'm telling you.'

'You don't know her, Dad.'

Dad turned. 'Well like I said – fetch her round. Put me in the picture.' And he left.

Owen stared out the window at him, realizing that he'd been completely outmanouevered.

Owen was preparing to examine a new patient – female, teens, ovarian cyst – when Danny called to him from beyond the curtains surrounding the bed.

Owen stuck his head out.

'We need to talk,' Danny said.

'What about?'

'Global warming and the menstruation cycle of the dragonfly,' Danny said. He glanced down the ward, where Crane was just beginning his round, then shot Owen a panicky look. 'What do you think we need to talk about?'

Owen slid outside, and pulled the curtains round the bed.

'I think Viv Reid's on the case,' Danny whispered.

Now it was Owen's turn to panic. 'And how did that happen, Danny?' he demanded, trying to sound cool. The last thing he needed was for Danny to lose his bottle and start making mistakes.

'No – not me,' Danny answered. He licked his lips. 'She knew before she asked, I've told her nothing and I'm absolutely in the clear.'

Crane was getting closer. Owen watched him introduce himself to the new patient a few beds down. 'Keep it that way, all right?' Owen said. He wondered whether Danny would respond well to threats of physical violence.

'For my sake, definitely,' Danny said. He glanced at Crane. 'For your sake, I might just think twice about that, you ungrateful bastard.'

'I'll buy you a drink,' Owen said soothingly. He'd

never known a strop that a bottle of Scotch couldn't cure.

'Get me a date,' Danny said. 'Then we can discuss it.'

Owen nodded. He slipped back inside the curtains, wondering if Irma's sister, Shirley, would cut it.

On balance, he thought probably not.

Richard dumped his jacket and briefcase in the hallway, then went through into the lounge. He loosened his tie, thinking that there was something to be said for being done with work by noon.

He went to the phone, pulled a piece of paper from his pocket, and dialled the number written on it. It was the number for the new mobile phone Anna had bought. It was switched on – it rang and rang – but no one answered it.

Richard put the phone down. As he turned to go upstairs, he noticed a set of house keys on the table by the phone. He picked them up. Weighed them in his hand. Tucked them into his jacket pocket. She'd left them there. So she wasn't coming back. He went into their bedroom and opened the dressing table drawers: they were empty.

'Stupid, stupid bitch,' he snarled. Then he realized what he'd said. He took a deep, shuddery breath. 'I didn't mean that,' he whispered. 'I didn't mean – oh God, I'm sorry.'

He stared at himself in the dressing table mirror. What had he come to?

Anna carried her burden of magazines, flowers and fruit towards her mother's bed. As she approached, Mum said to no one in particular, 'And if you think that's the end of it, you've another think coming.'

'What?' Anna asked. Mum stared at her vaguely. 'Here are some magazines,' Anna said. She juggled her load till she found what she wanted. 'And remember? You asked for this?'

Mum took it. 'Oh yes,' she said, and suddenly there was a hint of the woman who had stood with Anna outside the Sanderson Hotel, and a merest trace of the girl she'd once been.

A nurse came over. 'Cup of tea?'

'Coffee, please,' Anna said. 'Mum?'

'I'll put the kettle on when I've finished this.'

'And a tea,' Anna said. She smiled at the nurse, and at Mum, who was entranced by the photographs.

'Mum,' Anna said after a while. 'You know I've moved into your house for a bit?' Mum smiled. 'I just wondered if you'd mind me taking some of my bits there?'

Mum frowned. 'What kind of bits?'

'You understand what's happened?' Anna asked, knowing she didn't. 'I'm leaving Richard.'

The name seemed to spark something in Mum. 'That didn't last long,' she said.

Anna smiled sadly. Twenty-five years, vanished into nothing. 'No.'

Mum patted her hand. 'You're being looked after, aren't you, darling?'

Anna smiled without sadness this time. 'I am,' she said. 'I really am.' But something caught at her – that whatever she'd gained, she'd still lost.

Mum held out her arms. Anna leaned into her embrace like a small child needing to be comforted. They stayed like that for a long moment, but then Mum said, 'What's that?'

Anna pulled away. Mum was pointing to a spot on Anna's arm. 'That's your rocking chair,' Anna said. 'I tripped over it this morning, when I was trying to get dressed.'

Mum smiled. 'Only reason I kept that chair was to make your dad think he was more drunk than he was.' She patted Anna's arm. 'Did your man get you drunk?'

'No,' Anna said, grinning at the memory. 'We got drunk together.'

'Oh I love it when that happens,' Mum said. She clapped her hands, like a little child watching a clown. 'Because it doesn't last for long, does it?' She leaned towards Anna. 'Is he good?' she whispered.

'Mum!' Anna felt herself blushing.

The nurse came in with the drinks.

'Well, it matters,' Mum said. 'Sex matters,' she explained, in a voice they might have heard in Liverpool – never mind the nurse. 'If there's no fun, there's no future.'

Anna winced. The nurse seemed amused, but she left without saying anything.

'He's very good,' Anna said when she and Mum were alone. Partly, it was to shut Mum up. But also for the sheer joy of being able to tell someone.

Vivien sat on a stool at her breakfast bar, pretending to take no notice of the conversation taking place around her coffee table on the other side of the room. Find a private detective, Richard had said. So she had. Then he'd needed somewhere to meet, so here they were. Now Richard needed her to keep out of the way, so she was doing that, too.

The detective's name was Penman. He was a grey, weasley looking little man – the sort, Vivien thought, that you could imagine coming up behind you in a crowd. And you'd never know he was there. Richard

168

had just given him all the information he needed to tail Anna. 'And there's three hundred pounds as a down-payment,' he finished.

Penman smiled but it didn't help the way he looked. 'I'm very grateful for the business. Thank you.'

'That's remarkably insensitive,' Richard said, 'But I'm glad you're motivated.'

Coming from him, that was bloody hysterical, Vivien thought.

'The only number I've got for you is a mobile.'

'That's correct.'

Penman stayed seated. 'You've nothing else you could tell me about the man?'

'He's younger than she is,' Richard said.

That was new to Vivien. 'Are you guessing that?' she asked. It would fit with her theory about Springer.

'I don't think so,' Richard said. He turned back to Penman. 'It's a very complex, delicate situation, and I can't afford a single error.' He handed over a wodge of notes and stood up. 'I have to go.' He headed towards the door, but stopped before he got there. He turned back to Penman. 'What I don't want is photographs. Just information.'

'I understand,' Penman said. 'You want a surveillance log discreetly fed back, so you appropriately identify a certain third party. Then you and your daughter...' he looked at Vivien, though whether he'd bought the story was anyone's guess. 'Can make your minds up about the lady of the house.'

Richard smiled, nodded and left.

Penman snapped his case shut and got up to go.

'Mr Penman?' Vivien said. He turned back to her. '*I want photographs*,' she said.

Chapter 22

The wind in his hair, the open road in front of him, and the woman he loved by his side. This, concluded Owen, was the life. Especially considering the deal the garage were offering on the sweet little MG he was driving. He glanced at Anna. Scrap that – especially considering Anna was here to enjoy it with him.

'You want to try driving it?' he asked.

The wind whipped her answer away, but he could see by the glint in her eyes that she did.

They found a lay-by and swapped seats. She was an excellent driver – not overly cautious, not stupidly bold. She took them to the road by the woods and parked.

'Come on,' she said. 'I've got a surprise for you.'

He followed her into the trees. 'What?' he asked, but she just grinned and led him deeper into the woods.

'Here,' she said. 'This'll do nicely.'

'What?' he repeated.

For answer, she came into his arms and kissed him with absolute passion. His fingers tangled into her wind-blown hair. Slid under her blouse. Across her backside.

She shocked him by going for his belt. Then he went for it – lifted her up against him, and went for it.

And went for it.

And went for . . .

There was a sharp pain in his left shin. Owen took a deep, gulping breath and disengaged himself from Anna. He looked down: a little dog had sunk its teeth into him.

He shook his leg. The dog bit harder, and this time Owen knew it had broken the skin. He kicked out at it. The dog skittered away, all snapping teeth and flying saliva.

'Monty!' came a woman's voice. 'Monty!'

Owen tried to fasten his flies. The zip was stuck. The woman came into view – a camel hair coat, a headscarf, a walking stick.

Anna giggled. Owen glared at her and turned his back.

'Here, Monty,' said the woman. Owen succeeded in making himself decent. 'Friendly. He's friendly.'

'I'm bloody not,' Owen said.

Anna stifled a grin. 'I do apologize.'

'I'm bleeding,' Owen said. And he was down one pair of Levis, too – they were never going to be the same now that the Rat Dog from Hell had had its way with them.

The dog ran off to its owner, wagging its tail. She bent down, but not before she'd shot a disgusted look in Owen's direction. '*Good* boy, Monty!' she said.

'Good boy?' Owen was outraged. 'Little bastard wants its teeth pulling.'

The woman walked away. Owen turned to Anna, looking for sympathy. Her grin turned into a burst of laughter. Great, Owen thought, as he limped off.

Owen limped along the row of seats in the lecture theatre, putting a handout on each one. Then he went round to the other side of the desk to make some notes about the transparency that was showing on the overhead projector: Obstructive Jaundice.

The AVA technician came over to ask if there was anything else she could do.

'Are these third or fourth years?' he asked.

'Second,' she answered. He nodded, and she left.

Owen mentally readjusted what he'd decided to say. He quickly amended a couple of the notes on the OHP transparency. He really should have given it more thought, but he'd only just had time to get back to the garage and buy the MG, then dive up to the restroom and clean his leg up and change. He'd need a tetanus jab, but that would have to wait.

The projector suddenly clicked and whirred and its light drowned out that of the overhead projector. Owen frowned. He turned to look at what was up there.

A small, cream coloured envelope; a slip of paper with a crest on it. It took a second for him to grasp it: the writing. *Urgent. Please ask Mr Crane to phone his wife.*

Holy shit, he thought. He felt himself go cold.

'Did you send that message?' It was Viv Reid's voice, coming out of the darkness at him.

'Will you get that off?' If the technician came back in... Nothing happened. 'That note proves bugger all.'

He squinted up into the dark. She was silhouetted by the light from the projector.

'You don't even know me,' Vivien said. 'Why would you want to hurt me?' She started to come down the rake of the lecture theatre towards him. Owen felt like he was in an interrogation from a bad World War II movie. 'I didn't,' he said. He put his arm up to shield him from the light.

172

'You wanted to hurt him?'

'No.' I just wanted Anna, and I didn't stop to think about the consequences for other people.

'You buggered everything up.' He couldn't deny it, and an apology would only make her angrier, so he said nothing. 'You're aware that you've wrecked his marriage?' It was only the truth. 'Was that the objective?'

'I'm not as bad as you think,' he said. At least, if really, truly loving Anna made him less bad.

'Who's standards are we going off there?' She demanded. 'Obviously, I'm off the scale on account of ritual adultery.' She was much closer now. 'Where are you and Anna Crane?'

He couldn't keep the shock off his face. She looked triumphant. Eventually, he managed to say, 'Did Danny Glassman tell you that?'

She came up beside him. 'I've told you, Springer. There are Information-In people, and Information-Out people.' She made a face as if she'd sucked lemons. 'One species lives longer.'

Bluff, he thought. That was the only option he had left. 'You're way off beam, Vivien.'

She smiled sardonically. 'He's having her followed by a private detective.' That did it. He was completely unable to keep up the pretence anymore. 'You don't even know her,' Viv said. But I do, Owen thought, I know her now better than you're ever going to know anyone in your life. It was the only kind of victory he could claim for himself. 'How the hell did it happen?' Vivien asked.

'It's a long story,' Owen said.

She smiled and turned away.

'Are you going to tell him?' he asked her back.

'Piss off!' She didn't even bother to turn round.

Richard stared down at Myrtle. She was sleeping, with a photograph album lying open, precariously balanced on her chest. He moved it, gently and her eyes opened.

'Hello, Myrtle,' Richard said. She tried to sit up. 'No, no – please. If you're tired, you should sleep.' He patted her hand, though he actually wanted her awake.

Myrtle stared at him in her unfocused way. 'I was looking at my eyelids from the inside.' She smiled blearily. 'What time is it?'

'It's about half past one.' He glanced up and saw a nurse fiddling with some flowers just beyond the door. 'I just came to give you a check-up. If that's all right.' He smiled. 'Let's have a look.' Myrtle hoisted her nightie up. Her stitches were fine. He'd expected no less. 'That's all right – there we are,' he said, more for the nurse's benefit than Myrtle's.

The nurse went.

'Anna came in to see you – did she?' Richard asked. 'Was that nice?' He hadn't been comfortable with Myrtle since the dementia took hold.

'I think so.' Myrtle was focused on a point some-where in the top corner of the room, way past Richard's head.

'She brought you the book?'

Myrtle stroked the pictures in the photograph album. 'This? No, I've never let it out of my sight.'

Richard took a quick look at the temperature chart clipped to the end of the bed: all normal. 'Did you talk about anything nice?'

'Yes ...'

'Did she tell you that she's living in your house now?'

Myrtle frowned, that familiar expression she got

when she knew she ought to know something. 'Is she bringing bits in?'

Richard smiled. 'She certainly is.' He licked his lips. Nearly thirty years of medical practice screamed at him that what he was about to do was unethical. But he wasn't listening. 'Did she tell you she's got a new friend?' Myrtle stared at him. 'A young friend.'

She struggled with the idea. Then she giggled, a surprisingly girlish sound. 'Were you there when they got drunk?'

'No.' He couldn't bear it. The thought of her with someone else, drinking with someone else – she'd never been drunk with him – making love with someone else was more than he could stand.

Myrtle stroked his cheek. 'Aah,' she murmured.

Richard licked his lips. 'Her friend – has he got a name?' Myrtle stared at him blankly. 'Has he got a . . .' he repeated, then realized it was simply beyond her. 'What's his name, this friend?'

Myrtle lay propped up on the pillow, thinking about it. She was plainly exhausted. 'Did she say a name?' she muttered. 'I don't think she did.' And then, 'Alan? Alan!'

Anna had implied he knew the man, but Richard didn't know anyone called Alan. While he was thinking about it, Myrtle looked at the photograph album. She put her finger on a picture of Richard – ten years younger and lightyears happier.

'Miladdo turned out to be a bit of a shit, though, didn't he?' she said. She turned to Richard for confirmation.

He had to agree.

Owen braced himself for the jab. He hated injections. 'Knowing your luck, you wouldn't get lockjaw, you'd get a permanent bloody hard-on and the entire female population dropping at your feet like limpets,' Danny said. He swabbed the place where he was about to give Owen the injection. 'You don't deserve friends like me – I've never been this bloody compromised in my life.' Danny prepared the syringe. A few droplets spun in the air. He gave Owen the jab without any warning. Owen winced. 'If you'd been dressed in the first place, this wouldn't have happened.'

Owen rolled his sleeve down and John came in. He walked straight over to Owen and slapped a post-it note down on the table.

'Viv Reid's home number,' he explained. 'She wants you to ring her.' Owen looked at it. Like hell, he thought. 'The least you can do is give her a bit of time,' John said.

Sympathy for the devil? Owen wondered. 'Thanks,' he said.

John left and Owen screwed the post-it up and chucked it in the bin.

Richard felt like an arrow fired from a bow: no more doubts, no more confusions, just one clean purpose to fulfil. He stormed into Crossley's Car Sales, looking for trouble and determined to find it.

Penman was quick, he had to give the man that: he'd phoned Richard that afternoon to tell him he knew who Anna's friend was. Malcolm Crossley, a car mechanic. Her bit on the side. Clearly no real competition.

Nevertheless, he would have to pay.

There was a woman in the showroom. He took her in and dismissed her in a glance – going to fat, greying hair. 'Where's Malcolm Crossley?' he demanded.

'Round the back,' she said, waving at the far door.

Richard marched through. A pair of legs protruded from under a car. Richard kicked them. 'Malcolm Crossley? Do you know who I am?' he shouted. 'Do you? Get up, get out.'

There was a slither of fabric on concrete, and Crossley hauled himself out from under the car and on to his feet. He was fiftyish and blobby, and he glared at Richard pugnaciously. 'What've I done?'

This couldn't be the one. It was beyond the bounds of belief. 'There's been a mistake,' Richard muttered. 'I'm terribly sorry.'

He started for the door. Then he realized that every car in the place was an MG. He turned back. 'Do you own one of these in green?' he asked.

'Not any more,' Crossley said. 'Sold it yesterday.'

'Who to?' Richard couldn't contain his excitement. A minute or two more and he'd know.

'Who wants to know?'

Money does, Richard thought. He pulled his wallet out, and handed over a couple of tenners and a twenty.

Crossley led him to the office. He went through a stack of sales vouchers and credit card slips and handed one over.

Richard stared down at it.

Owen Springer.

Owen *bloody* Springer.

Chapter 23

Richard drove into St Gregory's car park. His eye caught a flash of green: Springer's MG. He grinned wolfishly, and parked his Mercedes so that the smaller car was completely blocked in.

Let Springer try to get away from him now, he thought. Without thinking much about what he was doing, he aimed a kick at one of the MG's headlights. It smashed with a satisfying tinkle.

It was a very small beginning, compared to what he intended for Springer.

He went inside. A couple of people made the mistake of greeting him. He ignored them. All but McGinley.

'Mr McGinley,' he said. 'Where is Owen Springer?'
'I don't know.'

He was lying – they were all in it together, he thought. 'Where is he?' Richard repeated.

'I don't know, sir.'

Very well, Richard thought as he stalked away. He'd do it the hard way.

He went into the restroom, where several doctors were watching TV or otherwise wasting their useless lives.

'Mr Springer?' Richard called out. 'Owen MG Springer?' No response. 'No? Thank you!'

He left. He didn't know where the little shit was.

But he'd find him sooner or later, and then, by God, he'd leave the little so-and-so in need of his so-called friends' services.

Owen made his way from the lecture theatre to the admin offices with his files tucked under one arm, a well-deserved cup of coffee in the other, and a head full of worries about Viv Reid.

His pager bleeped. There was no possible way he could reach it, but he tried anyway. He looked despairingly at the door in front of him. Something was going to have to give. The bleeper sounded insistently. 'Shut up,' he hissed at it. 'Shut up.' It didn't oblige. Owen tried to clamp the files with this elbow, while simultaneously hooking his thumb round the handle.

'Let me.'

Owen looked round. Richard Crane pulled the door open for him.

'Oh ta,' Owen said, and went in.

He turned to dump his stuff. Crane's fist hurtled at him, big as a pile-driver. It slammed into his face and he careened across the room. He tasted salt, knew he was bleeding. He tumbled across the table, smashed into the wall and went down.

'You shit!' Crane screamed at him.

He launched himself forward. Owen scrambled up and went to meet him. Together, they sprawled across the side-bench, sending files and paperwork flying. Crane whacked Owen's face hard. Again. Owen's head snapped back. He got in one punch, then Crane threw him back against the wall.

He went down.

Crane came for him again. But before he got close, John and Danny barrelled through the door. Owen watched them grab Crane through a haze of pain.

'Get your hands off!' Crane snarled. He flailed around, but he was held fast.

'Richard, please!' John said. 'This isn't going to happen, so just calm down.'

'You let go or I'll kill you!' Flecks of spit flew from Crane's mouth.

'Jesus, will you calm down.' John commanded. He twisted round. 'Owen, out of the building – now!'

Owen clambered unsteadily to his feet. I'll kill the bastard, he thought. But he knew he wasn't up to it. He walked past Crane, who threw himself around trying to get free. There was a meaty thump and a yelp from Danny. Apparently Crane had connected with something.

Owen opened the door. A crowd of people had gathered. He slipped out, brushing past Viv Reid on her way in.

As he stormed down the corridor, he heard the glass partition window smash. He didn't care, any more than he cared about the way people were staring at him like he was a zoo animal.

He touched his face. It was tender and smeared with blood. He thought he might have a split lip, but he didn't care about that, either – only about what this might mean for him and Anna.

Vivien stared Richard in the eye. She had her back to the door.

'Move,' he said.

'No.' I'm not scared of him, she thought. But she knew it wasn't strictly true.

'Vivien, move.' His voice was cold, far more frightening than if he had shouted.

But he was flushed and breathing hard.

'No.' As long as she stuck with that one word, she was all right.

'Will you please get out of the way.' He spat the words out like machine-gun bullets and his hands flexed at his sides. It came to Vivien that the only reason he didn't try to move her bodily was that he knew if he touched her, he'd hurt her.

'No.'

'Vivien, please move.'

'No.'

He broke then. 'What are you doing to me?'

She still didn't move.

Owen stormed out of the hospital and across to the carpark. He would kill him, beat him to a bloody pulp, and then see where his middle class, I'm-a-consultant routine got him.

He got to the MG. It was blocked in by Crane's Mercedes. And someone – it didn't take Owen three guesses to figure out who – had kicked one of the headlights in.

Stupid idea, Crane, Owen thought. Putting ideas in my head like this… he kicked in first one of the Mercedes' headlights and then the second. If he could have torched the thing, he would have.

As it was, all he could do was start walking.

The cab turned into the street where Myrtle's house was. Owen spoke into his mobile phone, talking round the handkerchief that he was still holding to his nose. 'I need to speak to Anna.

'I'm sorry,' Michelle said. 'She's in a meeting.'

'You'll have to break in,' Owen said. 'Tell her it's Owen. Tell her it's urgent,' he added.

'Sorry.' She didn't sound it, particularly. 'I'm under

strict instructions not to – she'll only be another half-an-hour or so.'

Owen scowled. It made his face hurt. 'I'm on the mobile.' He broke the connection.

The cab pulled up outside Myrtle's house. Owen got out and paid the driver, then hurried round to the back of the house. The door key was where he was expecting it to be, under a large flowerpot.

He went inside and debated the merits of a pack of cold peas against his nose versus a hot shower to take the ache out of his muscles. The shower won.

Richard looked at his car. The headlights had been stoved in. So Springer wanted to play tit-for-tat.

That was fine by Richard. He went to his car and grabbed a tyre jack out of the boot. He glanced around. There was no one in sight. He roundhoused the jack into the windscreen. It cracked with a sound like a gunshot, and shattered into a thousand pieces.

Richard grinned.

There was a tap on Vivien's door, and then John McGinley came in. He was carrying a couple of Newcastle Browns. He gave her one and opened both. He perched on the edge of the desk. She came round to join him, but then she couldn't think what to say.

'He didn't even like me,' she said at last. 'I pushed and shoved and smiled and preened for six months before I got so much as a handshake.' She laughed, remembering. 'I still feel like he never took his gloves off.'

John gave her a wry smile. 'You won't find Springer agreeing with that one.'

Vivien took a swig of her beer. 'How the hell did

he get mixed up with her anyway?' He could have had just about anyone on the staff, she thought. She hated to admit it, but he was good looking – not her type – funny, and charming when he wanted to be. So why risk everything for a woman half his age again?

'He met her before he got the job.'

Vivien frowned. 'In London?'

'On the train on the way from London.' He looked disbelieving even as he said it. 'Sheer destiny, and would you look at the state of it?'

Vivien stared at the floor for a moment. 'Why did he blow the whistle on us?' She could understand someone doing it for gain, but she couldn't see what Springer got out of it, apart from a quick stall to his career.

'I don't really know,' John said. 'I think Lady Macbeth was too committed to the belief that her old fella was a shining saint, like we all were.' He looked at her sideways. 'Excluding yourself, of course.'

If Vivien hadn't known better, she might have thought there was something close to respect, or even admiration, in that look. But that was ridiculous, of course. She smiled anyway, ditched her empty bottle in the bin, and headed for the door.

'Thank you,' she said, just before she got there.

'My pleasure,' John answered.

That look . . . he really seemed to mean it.

And, she found, she was glad that he did.

Anna escorted her clients to the door, feeling pleased with herself: it looked like they were going to bite. She turned back to Michelle, who asked if she wanted her messages. She seemed worried.

'Owen on his mobile – urgent; your husband on his mobile – urgent,' she said. She hesitated.

183

Anna nodded for her to go on. 'Owen – urgent. Your husband – *very* urgent. And the cleaners saying your suit's ready,' she finished in a rush.

'Oh God,' Anna said. She didn't know what had happened, but she supposed she should have expected it – whatever it was. She went to phone Owen, but there was no answer, which only worried her more.

Richard paced as he punched Anna's work number into his mobile. Come, come on.

'Hello?' Michelle said when he got through.

'She must be out of the bloody meeting by now,' Richard said without preamble. He was sick and tired of the bloody imbecile girl's excuses. 'If she's not, drag her out.'

Michelle didn't sound in the least affronted. 'I think she's just trying to get through to you. Try hanging up.'

Richard did so and the phone started ringing immediately.

'Richard,' Anna said.

He intended to be calm. He intended to talk to her reasonably. Show her what she was missing by going off with that hairless ape, Springer. 'How could you?' he yelled. 'With a jumped-up poxy registrar?'

'What's happened?' she asked.

'How could you, with a grubby, underqualified, charmless little twat like that?' He shivered with anger.

'This is not for discussion on the phone,' Anna said coldly, as if she had any right – any right at all – to set conditions. 'Where are you?'

'I'm at your mother's house,' Richard snapped. Where the hell did she think he would be?

'Go in and wait for me.'

'With an uncultured, pokey-faced bloody drone like that?'

'Richard, I'm putting the phone down now, Okay?'

She'd dare to hang up on him, would she? He tried to protest, but she talked right over him. 'There's a key under the plantpot at the back. Let yourself in. I'll come as quickly as I can. Have a drink or something and I'll be straight over.'

She cut the connection and Richard stared at the phone in disgust. Then he folded it and marched round to the back of the house. Plantpot. Right. That would be it, by the door. He lifted it up. No key.

'Bitch,' he muttered. 'Bitch!'

Still, if she'd lied about the big things, why shouldn't she lie about the small ones? He walked across the flagstones that surrounded the fish pond and sat on the garden bench. Wait for her? Oh yes. He wouldn't miss seeing her for the world.

Owen stepped out of the shower and started to dry himself. As he finished dressing, his phone started ringing. He grabbed it from his jacket pocket.

'Anna?'

'Just tell me what happened.' She sounded frantic, in her understated way.

'He turned up at work and just punched me on the nose,' Owen answered.

'He hit you? In the hospital?' Owen could hear traffic noise in the background, as if she were in her car.

'With half the bloody team watching' Owen said. His fury returned with the memory of them staring at him. 'Anna, how did you manage to get hitched to an arrogant, self-satisfied dickhead like that?'

'Please, don't you start.'

'Me start?' So Crane had been having a go at her, Owen thought. Slagging him off, no doubt. 'What's he said, the jumped-up shit?'

'Look, I'll have to talk to him.'

Oh very grown-up, Owen thought. But he didn't want to be grown-up. 'Talk to him? Anna, I'm gonna kill him.'

He heard her take a deep breath. 'Go down to Casualty, then, or over to your dad's house. I'll catch up with you later.' She paused. 'Just keep away from him. Please, Owen – just leave him alone.'

'Yes,' Owen said. If it would make her happy. He went over to the bathroom cabinet and started looking for something to dress his nose.

'Thank you,' she said. It made it all worthwhile.

'I love you.' It was all the reassurance he could give her. He rummaged in the cabinet. 'Have you got any iodine or anything?'

'Owen, where are you?' Anna said sharply.

'At your mother's house.' He still couldn't find anything useful.

'Oh shit.'

'Why?'

'Oh shit!' There was a sudden blast of car horns.

'Anna?' Owen asked. 'Anna?' Then he glanced out the bathroom window, and understood why she'd been upset. Crane was sitting in the garden.

Owen ran downstairs, taking the steps two at a time. Now, he thought. Now!

He went outside.

Crane stood up.

'Okay, Napoleon,' Owen said. 'You take me now.'

Crane whipped his jacket off and started forward. 'I'm going to break your fingers,' he snarled.

186

'Oh yeah?' Owen said. The fish pond was between them, but he headed straight for Crane.

'I'm going to bust every part of you that touched my wife...'

Owen splashed into the pond. 'You'll have to break lot of it then, Crane.'

'You stubby, pernicious, filthy little shit!' Crane came forward to meet Owen.

Owen grabbed him. He slammed the heel of his hand at Crane's jaw. Crane whacked him in the belly. Owen doubled over but hung on to Crane's shoulders and they both went down. The edge of the pond drove into Owen's back. He grunted – ignored the pain that lanced across his shoulders – and heaved Crane off him.

Crane came back in. Owen lashed out with his foot. Aimed for Crane's groin. Missed, but connected with his thigh.

In the distance, police sirens began to howl.

Owen scrambled out of the pond, forcing Crane to follow him. They squared off against each other. Crane came in early, and met Owen's fist with his face. He whacked the side of Owen's head.

Two police officers belted round the side of the house. Owen lunged at Crane, but one of the officers was in his way. He tried to battle past, but it was useless.

He peered past the policeman. The other officer was restraining Crane.

Sod it, Owen thought. I was bloody winning. 'If she mattered that much to you, how come you were screwing around with Viv?' he yelled.

'None of your business.' Crane tried to break free, but the officer holding him pushed him down and around.

'I didn't take your wife, Crane,' Owen shouted. The officer holding him forced him round. He twisted back to shout over his shoulder, 'You gave her away, you sad, greedy bastard.'

'Bloody hell, it's Alan Bates and Oliver Reed,' said the police officer holding Owen. 'Whose house is this?

'My mother-in-law's,' Crane said triumphantly.

See you and raise you, Owen thought. 'And I'm staying here.'

That got to Crane. 'You're what?' He tried to break free again. 'You are *what?*'

'With his wife,' Owen taunted. 'Anna Crane. Who he cheated on. Who's now cheating on him.' Crane went purple. 'With me,' Owen said as Crane fought free of the officer holding him. The policeman grabbed him. '*We're* staying here,' Owen finished.

The sergeant looked from Owen to Crane, clearly disgusted with both. 'Show 'em your sex aids, Colin,' he said. He pulled a pair of handcuffs off his belt, jerked Owen's hands round and cuffed him.

Anna pulled up in front of Mum's house. The police were already there – two cars. As she got out of the car, Richard and Owen came round from the back of the house. They were handcuffed. The police officers with them seemed mildly amused.

'Anna,' Richard called. 'Anna!'

Anna stared at him. At Owen. 'Oh my God,' she whispered.

They all got in to the police cars and drove away, leaving Anna staring after them. Alone.

Chapter 24

Richard stared at the pinboard behind the police sergeant. The man's voice droned on and on. 'Should you repeat your performance in causing a breach of the peace, your file is automatically handed to the magistrate's court for processing, where it will be made known that you've already been formally cautioned...'

Enough, Richard thought. He wasn't an idiot, and this was all so unnecessary. He grabbed the pen and went to sign his name.

'Not yet,' the sergeant said. 'And that caution will have its bearings on the way the court handles you, so do not treat it lightly.' Richard glared up at him. 'Now,' said the sergeant.

'Is my wife here?' Richard asked. He was suddenly aware of his stained trousers and tattered, bloody shirt.

'She is not,' said the sergeant. 'Been and gone.'

So that was the way of it. 'Is Owen Springer still here?' If he was, there'd still be scores to settle, caution or no caution.

Perhaps the sergeant read Richard's anger in his face. 'I'm under no obligation to tell you that.'

Cretin, Richard thought. 'Well just wiggle a finger or something for yes,' he said. The man stared at him blandly. 'It's an old trick with coma patients.'

The sergeant said nothing, but reached under the desk for a box containing Richard's things. Richard took them – watch, wallet, credit card case, tie. He started to put his tie on, then realized he was in such a mess that it would probably make him look worse. The sergeant looked at him levelly. 'Your wife left shortly after the *much younger gentleman* was released.'

Fine, Richard thought. If that was the way of it – fine.

Anna parked the car, and slammed her hands down on the steering wheel with a mixture of irritation and despair.

'He walloped me first,' Owen said. 'Just remember that.'

And a good job he'd done of it, Anna thought, looking at Owen's bruised and bloody face. 'Oh, I'll try,' she said. 'It'll make all the difference.' Owen didn't say anything. 'You just couldn't resist it, could you?' she demanded. Again, no answer. 'How old are you?'

'It's not an age thing,' Owen said. 'You get stung, you want to sting back.'

'It's completely primaeval,' Anna snapped.

There was silence. Anna stared out of the windscreen, wondering how she had ever got into this in the first place, and what on earth she wanted now.

'Why are we parked here?' Owen ventured.

'Because,' Anna started, and stopped to think about it. 'I don't know where you want to go.'

Owen looked at his hands, with their skinned knuckles and dirty fingers. 'I want to go with you,' he said quietly.

He lifted her hand off the steering wheel, and pulled it towards his lips. Anna pulled it back. 'I'm going home,' she said. 'I think you should go home.'

Hurt flickered across Owen's face as he realized exactly what she meant. 'You don't want me to come with you?'

'I just don't understand what you've done,' Anna answered.

She meant to explain that she needed time to take it all in, but Owen said, 'Okay, fine.' He opened the door and got out.

'I'll drop you off,' Anna said quickly. She didn't want to be at war with him.

He leaned back inside. 'I'm not that primaeval. I can get a taxi.' He slammed the door and walked down the road, where he quickly hailed a cab.

Anna started the car. Fine, she thought. That's the level of childishness you want to bring this down to, that's fine by me.

Owen was getting into his cab as she passed. She soon left him far behind.

Owen rubbed his hair with a towel. The shower he'd just taken hadn't stopped him aching all over, and his face felt like it had been steam-rollered, but he was pretty sure Crane felt worse.

'I know the world's changed,' said his dad. Owen peered out from under the towel at him. 'But whenever I went on a date at your age, I came back looking a lot happier.' He was surveying the torn back pocket of Owen's jeans.

Don't start, Owen thought. Don't you just start. 'If you went on any dates when you were my age, you were still married to my mum, so you didn't deserve to.'

Dad harrumphed and left. Owen put a clean pair of jeans on and followed him downstairs.

Dad was cooking – something with enough calories to feed a gaggle of sumo wrestlers, and enough cholesterol to put the fear of God into any cardiologist Owen had ever known.

Dad turned to him. 'If he looks half as bad as you, he's gaining points by the hour.'

'Dad!' he said.

Dad poked at the mess of minced meat and tomatoes in the frying pan. 'She leaves him for messing about. He finds out you've dodged in there,' he said. He reached for the butter and dropped a good dollop of it in the pan. 'What can a bloke do?' He looked at Owen like he was a fool, then answered his own question. 'He fights for her.'

So much for unconditional support, Owen thought. 'I'm not asking for your opinion, all right?'

Which had never stopped Dad, and didn't now. 'He'll be wearing his bruises like medals.' He chucked some mushrooms into the pan. 'You're playing right into his hands, you daft bugger.'

Owen leaned against the kitchen table. 'Mondays, the furthest you go is the doctors. Wednesdays, the furthest you go is the club. Fridays, the furthest you go is the post office.' He paused for effect. Dad stirred the food serenely. He looked sideways at Owen, then reached for the salt and sprinkled far too much into the pan. 'So how come you think you know so bloody much about the world?' Owen finished.

'I do a lot of crosswords.'

'He walloped me first,' Owen said. He was sick of this.

'You've said,' Dad answered. 'And I'm saying you should have seen it coming.'

The doorbell rang. Owen dived out to answer it. It was Anna. Surely it was...

He opened the door. It was John McGinley.

'What the hell happened to you?' he asked.

Don't you start, Owen thought. He ushered John into the living room and Dad followed them through.

'John, my dad,' Owen said. 'Dad, John McGinley, from work.'

Arnold stuck his hand out. 'Hello, John-McGinley-from-work,' he said.

Owen raised his eyebrows at Dad, who got the message and left the room.

John settled himself in a chair. 'I thought I'd better warn you,' he said. 'There's going to be an inquiry.'

'What?' Owen demanded. 'What's been said?'

'After the fight they went round questioning all the admin staff to find out what happened.' John looked vaguely embarrassed. 'They know it's something between you and Crane because there are rumours of a fight and both your cars were in the carpark looking like a pair of bean tins.' He looked genuinely worried. 'You could get hoofed for this. Crane too.'

'That'd be one tragedy,' Owen said.

'This is gross misconduct,' John pointed out.

So much for lightening the moment, Owen thought. Before he could say anything else, Dad appeared in the doorway.

'There's food in here, if you want it,' he said.

Neither of them did.

Vivien knocked on Richard's front door. The last – and first – time she'd been here, she had had to pretend to be nothing more than a work colleague. She supposed that this time that pretence had once more become a reality. Knowing it didn't make it easy to do, however.

Richard came to the door, dressed just in track-suit-bottoms. His face fell when he saw her. She supposed he'd been hoping she was Anna. No such luck.

'This is not a good idea,' he said.

'They're all I've got nowadays,' she said. He looked reluctant, but at least he did let her in. As she passed him, she noticed that he was much more battered than when she'd last seen him. 'What happened?' she asked.

'I slipped on a dog turd,' he said.

A dog turd called Owen Springer, she guessed. She let Richard show her into the lounge. He excused himself, and she wandered around looking at pictures – Anna, Richard, Anna and Richard together – and ornaments, and wondered who had chosen them. The Wedgwood would be Richard, she thought. Something modern in the style of Giacometti was more likely Anna's choice. Vivien decided she hated it.

Richard came back in. He had dressed. She wasn't disappointed about that. She wasn't.

'You'd better brief me,' he said, very businesslike.

'Ferris called me into his office wanting to know what the hell was going on. I had to say it was a bit of horseplay taken to extremes.' She didn't, and they both knew it, but there wasn't much gratitude on Richard's face, though they both knew that she was putting herself on the line. 'I assured him that you and Springer are actually the best of friends.'

Richard looked sceptical. 'He believed that?'

'No.'

Richard treated her to one of his sardonic grins. She'd found that attractive. Once. 'So he's not as thick as he looks.' He paused, paced up and down and turned back to face her. 'I want Springer sacked.'

'You can't do that,' Vivien said firmly. Any attempt to arrange that would probably get Richard in as much trouble as Springer.

'Oh, I'll do it,' Richard said. His face twisted up. 'I will not have that malevolent little wanker working on my firm.'

He hurt so much, she thought. He wasn't a bad man, nor overly vindictive. He had warned her about the way things were going to be between them. She couldn't deny that.

She moved towards him. 'Your head looks really sore.' She let her fingers drift across the long scratch on his forehead.

He pulled away. 'Don't do that,' he said sharply; and then more gently, 'You mustn't do that.' He smiled. Perhaps he was trying to take the edge off it. 'I couldn't...' he gestured at the house, encompassing Anna's pictures, Anna's things. 'I wouldn't...'

What does he think I am? Vivien wondered. 'Neither would I.'

He was silent for a long moment. Then he said, 'Vivien, you could have phoned with all this.'

It was true. Vivien knew it. She thought she was tough: the ball-breaking superbitch of admin, but when it had come down to it, she'd just wanted to see him one more time. Touch him, one more time.

A horrible thought occurred to her. 'Are you expecting her?'

'Not particularly. But...' he let his voice trail off.

He didn't need to finish: he hoped she would come.

'Let's go to my flat,' Vivien said, already knowing the answer.

'I don't want to go to your flat...' He must have read the hurt on her face, because when he continued, his voice was less sharp. 'Please. I've no wish to hurt you, and I have nothing but regret for the way all this is turning out.' Vivien stared at him, acknowledging her hurt and loss, without trying to disguise it with anger for the first time. 'But I do love Anna,' he finished.

Vivien walked away. She had the front door open before she realized there was one last thing she had to say. She turned back. 'You loved her before. We managed.'

Richard didn't answer. He stood framed in the lounge doorway, with his beautiful big house all around him, and pictures of his beautiful wife.

Vivien went outside. She shut the door softly behind her, and left him there, quite alone.

Chapter 25

Anna parked her Audi outside Owen's house and got out. She went up to the front door, but as she knocked an elderly man turned round and came towards her.

'Anna?' he said.

The resemblance was there: the high cheekbones, the little-boy-lost mouth. 'You're Owen's dad,' she said.

'Arnold,' he said. 'Arnie.' He held out his hand, and she shook it. Same long fingers, but with nicotined nails, bitten to the quick.

'Is he in?' she asked, looking up at the top floor windows.

He shook his head. 'We had a bit of a scrape and he disappeared.' He grinned. 'Sulking.'

Anna made herself smile. 'Join the club.' She wasn't about to admit she'd as good as told him to get lost.

Arnold got his key out and put it in the lock.

'Please don't,' Anna said. 'You were on your way out.'

'Only for a quick drink.' He smiled again, this time with a sly edge to it. 'I'm allowed to, when he's not here.' He started to open the door. 'Unless you fancy a quick drink?' Anna hesitated, wondering what Owen would think about it – whether he'd consider it some kind of betrayal. 'It's walking distance.' Arnold added.

She grinned. To hell with it, she thought. She

might find out how to handle Owen in this current mood of his a bit better. 'How much do you know, Arnold?' she asked.

He offered his arm to her, like an old-fashioned gentleman, and they set off towards the pub. 'Well,' he said, after he'd greeted one of his neighbours. 'I think I'm up to speed on the fisticuffs, but I get a bit foggy on the domestic arrangements.'

Owen stared at the polystyrene cup holding the remains of his coffee. Going out to eat had seemed like a good idea, but the only place they'd been able to find that was still serving was a pizza joint.

John had phoned Danny, and the three of them sat nursing their bottled beers while they compared notes and tried to figure out what to do.

'I got asked three times whether I knew if there was something going on between you and Crane's wife,' Danny said. He poured sugar from a little paper packet to make a pattern on the formica table top. 'They can only be going off gossip.'

'Whose gossip?' John demanded before Owen could ask the same thing.

'Not mine,' Danny said, far too quickly. 'But as I left, Viv was outside the office, waiting to be interviewed.' He scowled deeply. 'She knows I know that she knows I know exactly what the score is . . .' he looked round to see if they were following. Owen, he thought, probably was. He wasn't sure about John. 'So if she tells the truth I'm paddling in the rapids, aren't I?'

'Oh shut your face, you whinging ponce,' John said. He tore a chunk out of the side of his cup.

'I'm a bloody lynch-pin,' Danny snapped back. 'Don't talk to me like that.'

John looked at him as if he were crazy, never mind

a lynch-pin. He turned to Owen. 'We have to know what's been said. If they're talking to us all, we need to make sure we're saying the same thing.'

Owen nodded. He would have liked to think there was friendship involved in all this. He supposed there might be – but not nearly so much as there was self-interest.

Anna smiled at Arnold as he came back to her table with the drinks. The pub was smoky and noisy, and full of people: women with too much make-up or none at all wearing over-elaborate hairstyles, men standing at the bar or around the dartboard, mostly drinking pints of lager or bitter. The blare of the jukebox paradoxically ensured that Anna and Arnold could talk privately.

'I'm trying to work it out here,' Arnold said as he set the drinks on the table: pint of bitter for him, half of lager and lime for Anna. 'If you got wed in 1971 and you'd already got a degree, what age does that make you?' Anna stared at him, wondering what he'd say if she told him to piss off. Not ladylike, that's what he'd think. 'Roughly?' he cajoled.

'Roughly?' She considered and dismissed the honest answer. 'Not forty.'

'Oh right,' Arnold said. He sipped his bitter. 'So when he said forties, he meant top end?'

'He's never asked,' she said, hoping he'd take the hint and change the subject.

'Oh I know,' Arnold said. 'He's useless like that.' He reached into his jacket pocket and pulled out a couple of booklets, which he threw on the table.

Anna looked at them curiously. 'What are these for?' she asked.

Arnold just grinned.

***

Owen leaned over the map Danny had drawn on his napkin. It showed the layout of the administration offices where Owen and Richard had had their first fight.

'Look,' Danny said, 'You came from the lift here, you walked down here...' He stopped to think about it. 'Was Crane with you or behind you?'

Owen felt his face curl into a disgusted expression. 'He's a coward,' he said. 'He came from behind.'

'So the only people who could have witnessed anything were the staff on the ward, here,' Danny said and marked a couple of crosses on his diagram, showing how they could have had a line of sight through the office's internal window.

'No, no, no.' John grabbed the napkin. 'If Crane followed him in and stuck one straight on him...' he paused. 'Was the door open or closed?'

'How the hell should I know,' Owen snapped. All he remembered was Crane's fist driving at him.

'If the door was open,' John said, 'Anyone walking past the admin offices could have seen.'

Owen stared at the formica table top. The whorls of its fake wood grain seemed less labyrinthine than everything that was swirling around him: Anna, Crane, trying to get on with his dad, trying to rescue his career. Figuring out what lies to tell. And Anna had said he was the most honest man she'd ever met. She didn't know the half of it.

Anna stared, bemusedly at the rather stout young woman who was currently the centre of attention in the pub. The jukebox had been turned off, and only a few people were still chattering, although a couple of the loudest were right by the bar. Coloured, numbered balls whirled on jets of air in the transparent dome of the machine next to the woman. One of them popped out of a tube to the side.

'Two and six, twenty-six,' the woman called out.

Arnold reached over and marked the number off on Anna's card.

'Kate Moss, number one,' called the woman. Anna glanced at her card. She had that number as well. She marked it off herself this time. Mark off three more, and she'd have completed a line. She felt ridiculously excited by the idea.

'Three and five, thirty-five.' One of the men talking at the bar said something, and his friend yelped with laughter. 'Shut up!' bellowed the woman, and the whole pub seemed to flinch.

'That's Irma, my home-help,' Arnold whispered.

'You and all,' Irma said, glaring at him.

'As in, "help!"' Anna whispered back, miming a distress call. They laughed like a couple of school kids giggling behind teacher's back.

'Two perfectly normal, well fed women,' Irma said. 'Eighty-eight.'

Anna didn't have that one. She felt a twinge of disappointment.

It was so dreadful, you had to laugh. John was trying to redraw the map – it had become covered with so many crosses that it was useless. Owen caught his eye, and suddenly they were off again. Owen couldn't even remember what had started it.

'Oh this is interesting,' Danny said. He scowled at them. 'This is really interesting – there are five careers on the line here, and there's bugger all that's funny about it.'

But there was, and even the way Danny was taking it all so seriously seemed hysterical to Owen. Danny was right of course, it was very, very dreadful. He took a deep breath and tried to calm down. Then he thought of something.

'Professor Plum did it,' he said. 'With a lead pipe, in the library.'

John howled with laughter. People were staring at them. Let them, Owen thought, and giggled.

Danny's bleeper went off. 'Thank Christ for that,' he said, and got up.

Owen watched him go. Spoilsport, he thought.

Anna watched Irma count out ten pounds in coins: her winnings.

'If you'd got more than a line, we could have gone clubbing,' Arnold said.

Anna grinned. She didn't suppose he'd seen the inside of one since trousers with turnups had been in fashion.

'I'm not allowed to ask,' Irma said, 'But it's usual I get a drink paid on.'

'Oh, right,' Anna said. She pushed two pounds across the table, hoping that was about right. 'Have a drink on me,' she said.

Irma managed to look completely taken by surprise. 'Thank you very much,' she said. She pocketed the money and went across to the next winner.

Anna put the rest of her winnings away. 'At least I did something right today,' she said. She'd managed to put everything out of her mind, but it was back with full force now. If she'd only managed to speak to Owen before Richard. If she'd stuck to her resolution to see Richard only on neutral territory. If . . .

'He's always had a short fuse, you know,' Arnold said, as if that absolved her.

'I don't think it was his fault,' Anna said.

'No,' Arnold said. 'But he could have stopped it.' He looked disgusted. 'If he were half as good with his mouth as he is with his hands, he wouldn't be calling anybody "Sir".'

Anna sipped her drink and thought about that, or rather tried to think about it. She suddenly realized she was really quite tipsy. 'This is going straight to my head,' she said.

Arnold looked at her thoughtfully. 'Haven't you eaten?'

Anna considered that. 'I don't think I have,' she said at last.

'Drink up,' Arnold said. 'I'll treat you.'

Anna grinned. She hadn't known what to expect from Owen's dad, but she certainly hadn't dreamed she'd get on with him this well.

Owen walked down the street with his hands in his pockets. He had definitely had one beer too many, at least. John had offered him a lift home, but Owen hadn't wanted it. In fact, he didn't know what he did want, except that he didn't want to talk about it any more – not to John, and certainly not to his dad.

So he walked, the long way back.

Anna? Of course he wanted her. That was about the only thing he was sure of. But he wanted his normal life back. Wanted things to be easy. Wanted not to have wrecked his career, not to have this impending sense of doom squeezing down on him. Yeah, he thought. Well, he'd wished for Anna and he'd got her. And if wishes were horses, beggars would have an awful lot of shit to shovel.

Anna had never tasted anything quite so delicious as the fish-and-chips she was eating. The bag was a bit hot though. She shifted it round in her hand. It was slow work, trying to spear her chips with the little wooden fork. She looked at Arnold. He was managing to eat his, and juggle the carrier bag of booze they'd bought. He was eating with his fingers. Well, she thought happily, if he can, I can. She pulled a piece of fish off with her fingers. It was wonderfully greasy.

Half a bag of chips later, she was a lot more sober. 'Arnold,' she said, 'What do you actually think of me?'

'I think you're gorgeous,' he said. He paused to eat his chips. 'Very nice lady – done well for yourself. I think our Owen's lucky to have found you.'

That was probably the biggest compliment she was ever going to have from him. Yet something in the way he'd said it – his sly glance, the hesitation – told her not to trust it. 'Thank you,' she said. She didn't want to accuse him of being a liar, yet she was determined to know. 'And that's all you've got to say on it?'

He didn't answer, not for a long time. As they turned the corner into his road, he said, 'No.' She looked at him, wondering how far she could push him. Whether she really wanted to hear what he had to say. He perched against the garden wall. 'This country's still weighted in favour of your type, not his. So he's had to fight to get this far.' He smiled bitterly. 'And I'm very proud of him for that.' He looked at her straight and hard. 'So I wouldn't want to see him messed about with. You know?'

Anna looked at her feet. She supposed she deserved that. 'I'm sorry if you think that's what I'm doing,' she said softly.

She looked up. He was staring at her. 'It's not about what I think, is it?'

204

She couldn't meet his gaze. She looked down again, and was horrified to feel tears burning her eyes.

She felt Arnold put his arm round her, but she still couldn't face him.

'Listen,' he said, 'If it's what you want, don't be sorry.' Anna felt tears cold on her cheeks. 'If it's not what you want, just don't drag it out. That's all I'm saying.'

I do, I do want it she thought. It was just the complication she didn't want. That, and the hurt look in Richard's eyes.

There was a tap at the front door while Vivien was doing her ironing. *Richard*? she thought, without any great pleasure and went to answer it. When she looked through the spy-hole she saw it was John McGinley.

Damn, she thought, and realized she was disappointed. She opened the door.

'I thought you and your party should know what we're planning to say tomorrow,' he said.

Pleased to see you, too, she thought. She really didn't know if she could be bothered with all this, job or not. But it would probably take more energy to get rid of him than to have the discussion. She stepped back to let him in, then went to make some coffee while he found himself a seat among her piles of laundry.

'My party's been called in to see the Execs at ten o'clock,' she said from the kitchen area. She put the kettle on its base and switched it on.

'We're second on. Half ten,' John said. She glanced at him, and had the oddest sensation that he was watching everything she did. She went back to the lounge area to talk to him. Best to get it over with. She sat on the arm of her sofa. 'Obviously, we're tied into what's already been said, but I think we've come up with something convincing.'

'And you couldn't have just phoned?' she asked. A finger of chill ran down her back as she remembered that Richard had said almost exactly that to her.

'Do you want me to go?'

This is stupid, she thought. This is so stupid. 'Can I ask you something, John?' He nodded warily. She hesitated: there was still time to back out. 'If I asked you to go to bed with me now, how would that affect you?'

He stared at his hands.

After a moment, Vivien realized he wasn't going to answer. 'I just failed the test,' she said. Probably a good thing, she thought fiercely.

So why did she feel so hurt, she wondered. The thought of it had come to her the moment before she asked him. It wasn't as if she'd been mooning around after him for months...

'No,' he said. He looked totally embarrassed. 'You know... my divorce isn't absolutely absolute...'

Bloody man, she thought. Bloody excuses. 'Well that's all right,' she snapped, 'Because the bed's not made.' She was not, was *not*, going to let him see how upset she was. 'And it was a hypothetical question.' The kettle clicked off. 'Is instant okay?' she asked.

Damned if she was going to waste the decent stuff on him.

Owen crept upstairs so as not to wake Dad. He wasn't drunk. Not a bit of it. But he was just a bit wobbly.

Up the stairs, into his room and shut the door quietly behind him... mission accomplished, and Dad would never know he'd come in.

He didn't bother to turn the light on. No point, he thought. Definitely a waste of electricity.

The blankets moved.

Owen jerked back. The blankets moved again, and revealed that they'd been hiding Anna.

Owen felt his face split into a grin. 'Anna?' he said, suddenly wishing he'd had a damn sight less to drink.

'Hello,' she slurred. She smiled woozily at him.

He went and put the light on. By comparison with her he was stone cold sober. Still, she was the best thing he'd seen all day.

'I know I'm not completely good news,' she said. 'But come to bed.' She patted the space next to her. Owen stared, wondering how she'd got into that state, and how she'd ended up here. But they were questions for another time. 'You come to bed,' she insisted.

'I think you should go back to sleep,' Owen said.

Anna smiled. She nodded and rolled over on her side. She closed her eyes. Then opened them. 'You're the best thing that's ever happened to me, you know that?'

Owen smiled. He leaned over and kissed her on the cheek, then put the light out.

Chapter 26

Richard stared at Rodney Ferris, forcing himself to meet the man's gaze. He was a jumped up little twerp who'd long since exceeded his level of competence: but he still held Richard's future in his hands, and to treat him with anything less than absolute respect would only provoke him to something Richard would regret afterwards.

'Obviously, it's a very serious matter deserving the best attention I can give it.' Ferris folded his hands together, his perfectly manicured nails gleaming. 'I'd like your version of events relating to – as far as I'm aware – an appalling act of misconduct unbefitting a senior member of staff.'

Conduct unbecoming, Richard thought. Condescending little shit. 'Oh lighten up, Rodney, for God's sake,' he said, and realized how he'd snapped, and how Rodney was staring at him. 'It was a bit of ...' Ferris chimed in and said the rest of the sentence with him. 'Horseplay taken to extremes.'

'Yes, I've been persistently made aware of that,' Ferris finished sounding not in the least convinced.

Richard swallowed hard. He'd believed deep down that this would be a whitewash: they'd want to believe what would get him off the hook; perhaps even give him an opening to get rid of Springer. Now he was unsure.

'You think if I'd got a gripe against a member of my firm, I'd chin him in public?' he asked, trying to sound as reasonable as possible.

'I've seen your temper,' Ferris said. He stared levelly at Richard. 'Yes. How's your car?'

'Fine thank you,' Richard answered. He was rapidly losing patience. 'How's yours?'

Ferris wasn't to be deflected. 'It had smashed headlights when I last saw it. Owen Springer's car had a smashed windscreen.'

'We had a prang.' The big lie, Richard thought. He looked at Ferris without blinking, and made sure he didn't fidget. Vivien had gone over the whole body-language thing with him that morning. At the time, he thought she was just making excuses to be in his company. Now he was glad she had.

'What kind of prang?'

Richard swallowed and started to explain.

Owen swallowed. 'Well, a prang,' he said. 'Pure physics – irresistable force meets immovable object.'

Ferris never cracked a smile. 'At right angles?'

'Right angles?' Owen repeated.

'Sources say neither car was actually moving at the time,' Ferris said.

Don't get smart, Owen thought. He'd promised Anna that morning: no jokes, no piss taking, no over-the-top behaviour. 'Well,' he said, desperately trying to think of something reasonable. Nothing came to mind. 'That's not physics, that para-physics. And I'm not genned up on that.'

Ferris's icy glare dropped thirty degrees in a split instant.

'You know violence on the premises carries an automatic suspension?' Ferris asked.

Richard's heart flip-flopped. 'Of course I do,' he said as steadily as he could. 'Of course I do.'

'Tell me about the joke,' Ferris said. 'Some of your colleagues say it started with one. 'What do you say?'

'How can you tell when a Wigan prop forward has an orgasm?' Owen tried to look properly aggrieved. It wasn't hard.

'He drops his chips,' Richard said. As a punchline, it wasn't a lot of use. Ferris certainly wasn't smiling. 'That's all I said. He took offence. It was a class thing.'

Owen flicked his finger and thumb. 'I just flicked a bit of water at him. Like that.'

'How?' Ferris asked.

Owen demonstrated again. 'Like that.'

'It landed on my face, round here,' Richard said. He lifted his chin up. God, this was so undignified.

'Water or yogurt?' Ferris asked.

'Water,' Owen said firmly.

'Yogurt.' Richard was quite sure of it: just as long as Springer stuck to the story, if his pea-brain was up to the task.

Vivien stared at Ferris. She was beginning to feel outclassed, and she hated it.

'They were laughing as they went through the door and Owen must have tripped,' she said. She waited for a response, but didn't get one. 'I'm not sure what happened, but Springer went forward and and banged his face on the corner of the desk.'

'Desk or filing cabinet?' Ferris asked.

That's not in the script, Richard thought. He was sure he was right. If it were a trick question...

'It was the door,' he said, then qualified it hurriedly. 'I think.'

'Filing cabinet,' Owen said, feeling grateful to the others that they'd taken time to organize a consistent story.

Ferris looked at Viv.

'Desk,' she repeated.

Surely it would be over soon?

Ferris paced the room. Up from the window, turn. He was coming round the back. Owen resisted the impulse to twist round to keep him in his sights.

'You don't like him, do you?' Ferris asked.

Bright lad, Owen thought. That was worrying. 'I don't dislike him,' he said cautiously. He'd never had the chance to figure out what he might have thought if it hadn't been for Anna.

'It's all right,' Ferris said. 'I do.'

That was a mousetrap so big it could have caught an elephant. 'He's my boss,' Owen said. 'I can go either way.'

Ferris steepled his hands in front of him. 'But you resent him, don't you?'

'Resent him?' When in doubt, Richard thought, buy time.

'Is there something going on between you?'

'You'd have to elaborate,' Richard answered, wondering what he could possibly say to satisfy the man.

'Domestic?' Ferris said.

Richard feigned bewilderment. 'How are you defining that?'

'Your wife.'

'I beg your pardon?' Richard said, knowing he couldn't keep this up for much longer. He stared past Ferris's shoulder and out of the window. There were so many more things he could be doing with his time.

Perhaps Ferris felt the same way, because he snapped, 'Is there or is there not romantic interest between Owen Springer and your wife?'

'You need to see a bloody shrink, Ferris,' Richard snapped back. 'I think she'd rather sleep with a drone like you than a drone like Springer.'

If only it were true, he thought.

'Who's wife?' Owen asked, trying to sound innocent.

'Mr Crane's wife,' Ferris said. 'Are you or are you not seeing her?' He had clearly run out of patience.

Owen managed to sound shocked. 'Do you know how old she is?' he demanded.

'Do you?' Ferris countered.

'No,' Owen snapped.

And at least that was true.

Richard stared straight ahead, at the lift doors. Surely the damn thing couldn't take much longer to go five floors?

'Thank you,' Springer said.

The damn impudent puppy was in the other corner of the lift, safely on the other side of Vivien. Richard could feel his presence, even though he wouldn't look at the man.

212

But he wouldn't be outdone – certainly not when it came to civility. He jerked his head round just enough to make eye contact with Vivien. 'Thank you,' he said.

'My pleasure,' Vivien said dryly.

Then Richard realized he had this one opportunity to make things clear to Springer. 'I can't sack you without going to more trouble than you're worth,' he said. 'So you'll suddenly apply for a new surgical post about ten thousand bloody miles away – for which you'll receive a totally disproportionate reference...'

'I decide when I'm moving on,' Springer said.

Of all the insolent little... 'So long as you do it in the next three days,' Richard said.

Springer glared at him with a gaze that was pure venom. Before he could speak, the doors pinged. He went. The doors shut behind him.

'Is that wise?' Vivien asked.

It felt very bloody wise to Richard, but he supposed it might just set Ferris off again.

'Bernard Beecham's picked up the rumours,' Vivien continued. 'He asked me this morning if Springer was unhappy in your firm – he said he'd be willing to take him into Casualty on an internal transfer, if that didn't seem predatory.'

Well more fool him, Richard thought. Then again, Beecham was a widower. 'Fine,' he said stiffly.

There was a moment of silence, then Vivien said, 'If he's still in the building but not under your authority, you'll have no power to separate them.' The lift pinged again, and the doors open. Vivien went out. As the doors shut, she said, 'Will you?'

Richard considered she was probably right. Then again, she might want him to keep Owen around to increase the chances of him stealing Anna away – thus leaving herself for Richard.

But all she'd actually done was give him an idea for a plan. He grinned. By the time he'd finished, Owen Springer wasn't going to be able to tell one end of a stethoscope from another.

Richard was just finishing the last in a large stack of reports when there was a knock at his door. He glanced at his watch: eight-thirty. There was one thing about no longer having a home-life – he no longer resented staying back to do paperwork the way he once had.

'Come in,' he called. He already knew who it was. The downfall of Owen Springer was about to commence.

John McGinley came in. 'You wanted me?' He looked about as enthusiastic as a schoolboy facing a sticky interview with a sadistic headmaster.

'Sure,' Richard said. 'Sit down.' McGinley did so. The fearful look on his face had, if anything, intensified. 'Drink?' Richard asked. After all, McGinley was about to become his righthand man. Like it or not.

'I'm fine.'

Richard got himself one – Scotch, single malt, large measure. Neat. The only way to drink it.

He went and stood in front of the desk, near McGinley's chair. He sipped his drink. Let McGinley worry, he thought. Let him get good and scared, and then let him do what he was told.

Richard smiled. Time to cut the crap. 'I want you to take Danny Glassman off nights. He's been working too hard and I worry that his judgement may become impaired.'

McGinley bit his lip. 'I can't do that, sir.'

'Of course you can,' Richard said. He'll bloody well do a whole lot more if I need him too and it's time he was made to realized that. 'Glassman's completely overworked. His brain's fried – half the time he barely makes sense.' It was even true, Richard thought. Exactly the sort of decision a concerned team-leader ought to be making.

'If I release Glassman from night cover, that means Springer has to do it,' McGinley said. His face and tone were both equally neutral.

'If that's the only option you've got, so be it,' Richard said. 'I'll leave it completely up to you.' He smiled.

'I can't do that,' McGinley said. There was a stubborn set to his chin that bothered Richard. Obviously, he needed to learn what the chain of command really meant.

'Can't or won't?' Richard said. 'And be very careful.'

'With all respect, sir, this is your private life, and I don't want dragging into that.'

So that was it: traitors all around him. 'It was my bloody private life when you kept it from me, John,' Richard said, and was startled both by the depth of bitterness in his voice and his inability to disguise it. 'How long had you known?' He kicked the leg of McGinley's chair. Didn't want another incident, oh no – but if he could have wrung the other man's neck, he might have. 'How long had you known?'

McGinley looked at his hands. 'I tried to stop it,' he said after a time.

'So you were in at the start?' It sickened Richard.

'I tried talking him out of it.'

'You've known him how long? Long as I have, slightly less?' Richard demanded. McGinley looked

215

uncomfortable. So he bloody should, Richard thought. 'How long have you known me, John? Five years? Six?'

'Six.' McGinley met his gaze now. His expression was unreadable.

'Six,' Crane said. And it counted for nothing.

'I just work with the guy,' McGinley said. 'It was privileged information.' He stared up at Richard as if begging to be let off the hook. To hell with that. 'I did nothing wrong.'

He would say that. As if ethics and morality counted for nothing? Friendship, nothing. Loyalty, nothing. 'What you did wrong was to leave me in total bloody darkness about an event that was about to destroy my marriage.' It made him so angry that he couldn't contain himself. He began to pace the office. 'I gave you this job, John. I transformed you from being a highly strung, fitful experimentalist into a surgeon.' He was back near McGinley's chair. 'Where's your bloody loyalty, you miserable shit?'

McGinley took a deep breath. He looked as if he were trying to come to a decision. 'With respect, sir, my discretion cut both ways.'

That startled Richard more than almost anything McGinley could have said. 'It did what?'

McGinley stood up. 'I also knew about you and Vivien Reid. I said nothing to anyone about that, so I'm comfortable about my loyalty – and you've no right pushing me to distort Springer's work schedule for your benefit.' He headed to the door. 'I won't do it, and if you ask me again, I'll have to go to the BMA.'

Traitorous, smug... Richard let McGinley get to the door before he said, 'You know you were third choice for this post?' McGinley turned. It was clear from the wounded look on his face that he hadn't, as Richard had expected. 'Third,' Richard said. 'Not very impressive, is it?'

'Thank you for sharing that with me,' McGinley said levelly.

'You've applied for a consultant post,' Richard said. He went round to his desk drawer and pulled a wodge of papers out. 'I'm not actually going to have time to do your reference for a day or two – or three or four.' He pushed the papers to the bottom of a large stack of reports. 'You'll appreciate that my wife means substantially more to me than your progress, McGinley – so don't think about this for too long, will you?'

Owen smiled at Anna, he couldn't help it. Here they were at midnight, outside in the freezing cold, drinking red wine, all warm and toasty despite the weather because of the fantastic way they'd just made love.

The lights of Manchester were spread out below them, glowing like a handful of gemstones scattered on velvet. Owen wanted to shout to the world, to tell them all why he was luckier than them, than anyone.

But what he did was put his arm round Anna. She leaned against him as they perched against the Audi. Some passion-wagon, he thought. Bit more class than the old Beetle he'd played his first games in.

'He wasn't like anyone I'd ever met,' he said. 'He knew about all kinds of things I'd never experienced before, like cheese and jam sandwiches, like beer and marmite, like having a jump in the back of an Audi.' He glanced back at the rear seat. Even the thought of it was enough to get him going again.

Anna grinned. 'Wrong,' she said. She punched him lightly in the ribs. He was still sore from the fight, but he managed not to wince. 'You think I've never had sex in the back of a car?'

Well, yes, Owen thought. There were lots of things like that that he thought she had too much class for. Like playing bingo down at the pub, say, or getting drunk on cans of lager, both of which she'd done with his dad. 'You weren't as clever with your legs as you could have been.' He kissed her quickly on the cheek to show it wasn't really a criticism.

'They fit headrests as standard nowadays,' she said. 'The geometry got lost somewhere.'

Owen giggled. 'You nearly kicked my bloody head off.' Which wasn't to say he didn't appreciate those wonderfully long legs of hers.

'Might knock some sense into you,' she said tartly.

He kissed her again, this time full on the mouth and lasting for an extraordinarily long time.

When they broke, she said, 'Did Arnold tell you what we'd talked about?'

'Nope.' Owen grinned. 'I've even offered him money but he said it's classified.' He waited. Of course, Anna wouldn't have secrets from him, they weren't ever going to have secrets from each other. But she didn't say anything. 'Well,' he said when he couldn't stand it any more.

She looked at him slyly. 'That's classified,' she said.

Chapter 27

Owen stormed into the scrub room, the new shift roster in his hand. Apparently, he wasn't the only one with things to say, because Danny was talking to John. But where Owen was furious, Danny seemed pleased in a bewildered kind of way. Which was hardly surprising.

'What's all this crap?' Owen demanded. He shoved the roster in John's face. 'He gets a month off night cover – how come?'

John didn't answer, just carried on checking his paperwork, but Danny said, 'Look at the state of me.'

It was true – he looked like three day old cadaver. But what did he think junior doctors were for, if not to be abused?

'And you're asking me to cover for him for a month?' Owen demanded. Still no answer from John. 'In house?' Owen persisted.

John swivelled round. 'Obviously not. I'll cover on the odd occasion, or we'll get a locum in, though that might take a while to set up.' His face hardened. Guilt, Owen reckoned. Nothing like guilt to make a bloke take the hard line. 'But yes, when you cover you stay on the premises.'

He went to walk past Owen, who caught him by the arm. 'So what's your schedule tonight, John?'

'I'm busy.' He went back to checking the operation list.

'This week?'

'Busy, all week.' This time, John didn't even look up.

Owen's fists clenched at his side. 'Great,' he said.

John slammed his clipboard down. 'That was the deal when you took the job. If you've got a problem with the way I'm handling this, you go to my boss...' He glared at Owen. 'Your boss. But get off my back, all right?' And he stalked off.

Go to Crane, he meant. Fat chance. Owen watched him go. He looked over at Danny. Even he seemed to have figured it out.

Lunch alone was no fun. Anna ate the last piece of pasta on her plate and signalled to the waiter. She didn't mind Owen not showing up – emergencies came with the job. But she hated the fact that she'd told the waiter that she was meeting someone. That look on his face when she finally ordered and ate alone.

She paid and went out, and only then did she think to check her voice-mail. Sure enough, there was a message from Owen saying he couldn't make it. Fair enough, she thought. There was always tonight.

By mid-afternoon, he'd left another message while she was in a meeting: he had to do night cover, and wouldn't be able to see her that evening.

By the time she got home, there was another message for her. She listened to it as she went up to the house.

It was more of the same. '...so try us on the mobile then,' Owen finished. 'Love you.'

The message ended. Anna spotted a huge bouquet of flowers on the doorstep. She smiled and scooped them up. It was so typical of him to send something to make up for her disappointment. She took them inside and prepared a vase for them.

It was only then that she found the card. It said: *I love you. Richard.*

Richard felt wonderful when he walked into St Gregory's the next morning.

'Morning,' he said to McGinley when he saw him in the corridor.

But McGinley walked straight passed him. No understanding of the realities, that was his problem.

Owen staggered into the restroom feeling like a zombie and looking worse. He'd had maybe four hours sleep the night before, and not all of that in one piece.

Danny was there, looking bright eyed and bushy tailed. Owen didn't want to talk to him, so he went and got a can of Coke from the machine. He needed the caffeine boost, but he was sick of the taste of bad coffee.

Danny came over. He sniggered. 'Now you know what it feels like.'

Owen shook the coke and opened it in Danny's face. It sprayed him with foam. Worth the fifty pence, Owen decided. Definitely.

Anna was opening a pack of ready-made chicken casserole – there was no point cooking for one that she could see – when her phone went. It was Owen. She smiled, just to hear his voice.

'What are you doing,' he asked, making it sound like a seduction.

'Nothing special.' She speared the plastic cover of the carton with a fork, as per the instructions.

'Tell me what?'

For a second, she fantasized about telling him she was doing something extremely rude and interesting. But instead she said, 'Making supper.'

'What time are you going to bed?'

'I've a couple of reports to finish.' She popped the casserole in the microwave.

'What are you going to be wearing?' he murmured.

Anna laughed, almost embarrassed. 'What do you think?' she asked.

'Tell me.'

Maybe her first idea hadn't been so far off the mark, she decided. 'Nothing,' she said. She was beginning to enjoy this.

'For me?'

'If you like.' She pulled a chair out and sat down.

Owen laughed, that laugh she loved to hear. 'Okay,' he said. 'You're half asleep in bed. I'm coming back late. You've had a hard day, I've had a hard day,' he paused. 'And you look like heaven. Peaceful. Dreamy. So I'm not going to dive on you. I slip my kit off and come to the bottom of the bed.' Interesting idea, Anna thought. He was speaking so quietly she was sure other people must be around. The thought excited her. That tinge of danger... 'I lift the duvet,' Owen went on, 'And find your feet. Kiss your feet. Lick your feet. Find your knees. Kiss your knees... I can't see your face but I know you know I'm there.' He paused. Anna licked her lips. 'Everything's perfect. We both smell perfect. By the time I get to your lips, you really know I'm there, and you're smiling and kissing me and licking me, and...' A sharp beep drowned out his next few words: Owen's pager. 'Oh shit,' he said. 'I've got to go. I love you.'

And that was the most interesting thing that happened to Anna all night.

Richard paced up and down. The house wasn't a home anymore – it wasn't a dwelling, even. It was a mausoleum, a place where the dead corpse of the marriage he'd killed, lived. Moonlight filtered round the edges of the closed curtains. It showed him the bed where Anna had slept, had loved him. The stool where she had sat and brushed her hair, where she had smiled and sometimes cried. It glittered on a pair of crystal earrings dangling on their jewelery tree. An anniversary present. She had left them behind. He flicked them. They rang out, the pure sound of his pain.

Anna's eyes snapped open.
She knew. She knew why she was alone.

Owen palmed sleep out of his eyes. He'd just performed his first operation of the day, and all he wanted was to get changed so he could have a coffee. He opened his locker and changed. There ought to be a law against burst appendixes at three a.m., he thought. Never mind. Another beautiful day was beginning, and this time he was determined to do more than practice his telephone seduction skills on Anna. Not that she needed much seducing.

As he left the room, he passed Crane's locker. One of the messages was written in red ink, and it leaped out at Owen: *Your wife's waiting in the office.*

What the hell? Owen thought.

Crane came in, grabbed the note and left, all without saying a word or wasting a second.

A cold knot formed in the pit of Owen's stomach. If she'd found out that he was the one who'd forced Crane's hand... but no, he thought. There were a million – okay, a hundred. All right then, he thought.

Maybe ten. There were maybe ten good reasons apart from Myrtle why Anna should need to talk to Crane.

Owen just couldn't think of one.

Crane couldn't remember when he'd felt so happy. Anna. His Anna coming here to talk to him. The world was going to be put right. He could feel it all through him, the way that he knew his heart was beating and his lungs were taking air. He went into his office and she was staring out of the window, with her back to the door.

'Anna,' he said. She would turn to him, come to him, let him hold her.

She spun round. She was incandescent with rage. 'How bloody petty can you get?' she demanded. Richard forced his smile to stay on his face. Whatever it was, as long as she was talking to him, there was hope. That was more than he'd had in a long while. 'You put him on call for a month?'

Richard waved his hand. 'Nothing to do with me,' he said. 'That was McGinley's decision.'

'You can't sack him,' she said. 'So you just punish him till he gets bored and I get frustrated.' The contempt in her eyes was too much for Richard to bear. He looked away. 'And you send me flowers every other day.' She made it sound like something shameful.

'The flowers have nothing to do with him,' Richard protested, but he still couldn't meet her gaze.

'You're a bloody coward, Richard,' she said. She was flushed with anger now. He couldn't remember her ever looking this beautiful: she glowed. 'You're a devious, self-centred, bloody coward.' She stepped towards him. For a moment he thought she would hit him. She had before. He moved back, matching her step

224

for step. 'I've got an appointment at one o'clock,' she said. For a moment it seemed like an irrelevance. Then she went on, 'I'm filing for divorce.' She moved round him to the door. He stared after her, stricken, but she wasn't done yet. She turned at the door. 'When you get those papers, I hope you realize you've done all you can as far as this marriage is concerned.' She paused. He would have said something, but he didn't dare. Besides, nothing he could possibly say would be appropriate to the moment. 'You did it all by yourself, Richard.'

She left. The door slammed after her. There was nothing, Richard realized, nothing he could say, nothing he could do. Nothing left in his world at all.

Chapter 28

Anna came out of the office to make her ten thirty appointment. She felt more content than she had for a long time – more in control.

Then she saw Richard. If she could have got away with it, she would have walked straight past him, but she knew she couldn't. 'Hello,' she said, and kept walking, so that he had to keep pace with her.

'The decorators came this morning,' he said. He sounded puzzled. Hopeful, even.

'Good,' she said. She really didn't want to get into a major discussion in the middle of the street.

'Obviously, I didn't know what you want doing, and obviously they need to, so ...'

Used it as an excuse to come and annoy me, Anna thought. She'd been most precise in her instructions. 'I'm putting the house on the market.'

Richard looked as if he'd been hit. 'You've no right to do that.'

'Yes I have,' Anna said. How much of a fool did he think she was? 'You took a stake in my business, and I took over the mortgage on the house. October 1993.'

Richard nodded. She was sure he hadn't forgotten, he was just being difficult. 'Doesn't that leave your business open to reprisals?'

If you want war, she thought. 'Absolutely,' she said. 'But I think I can live with that, if you want to start playing games.' She smiled, but made sure her tone told him exactly what she would think of him if he did. She hurried across the road, making sure Richard got stuck where he was.

Richard walked in on the first operation of the day. He took one look at the incision and decided he was working in an abattoir, not an operating theatre.

'Who opened the patient?' he demanded.

No response, which told him everything he needed to know.

'Who opened the patient, please?' he repeated. He'd be damned before he'd put up with insolence. 'Retractors!' he called to the nurse.

Springer and McGinley exchanged what they obviously believed was a furtive glance.

'I did,' McGinley said.

'Then I suggest you get your eyesight tested,' Richard snapped, 'Because you obviously couldn't carve a joint, McGinley. Swab!'

He could see from the look in Springer's eyes that he'd hit home. Good.

Owen was examining x-rays of one of the night's first emergencies when his bleeper went off. He phoned in and told them he'd be a quarter of an hour. He'd no sooner put the phone down when his bleeper went again. Again, he put them off.

Owen held the x-rays up to the light box. They were about as bad as they could get, and Mr Roberts' physical condition meant any treatment would present great danger. He decided he needed more information, so he had the patient sent down to theatre.

On the way down, one of the nurses happened to mention that she'd seen Danny going off duty and being full of himself over it. Owen thought for a second, then asked her to go and find him. It was unfair, but they were so understaffed that it was the only thing he could think of to do.

Down in theatre, he performed an endoscopy on Mr Roberts. It confirmed his worst fears. The veins in the man's throat were swollen and twisted.

Danny came in just as he was considering his options. 'This is you worried about how much I'm doing?' he asked.

'That was never my impression,' Owen said. He indicated Mr Roberts. 'This guy's got oesophageal varices...'

Danny looked at him impatiently. 'What's he doing here? Don't we just operate?'

Owen replaced the endoscope on the trolley. 'He's got cirrhosis and his blood clotting's way off. An operation's the last thing he needs.'

'So what do you want me to do?' Danny asked.

Good man, Owen thought. 'I'm thinking.'

'Have you phoned Crane?'

Owen was taken aback: it was like suggesting that Churchill take military advice from Hitler, as far as he was concerned. 'No,' he said shortly. 'Anyway, he's not on tonight.'

'Phone Crane.'

'No.' Owen turned to a nurse. 'Can we get hold of Mr Crowther, please?' Danny stared at him as if he were crazy. Well, it wasn't the first time someone had thought that of him. He turned to the anaesthetist. 'Give him another couple of units of blood, and cross match six more. And get some plasma into him.' He turned to the other theatre nurse. 'Ring the pharmacist on call and see if we can get some Somatostatin – it might stop the bleeding.' And finally, back to Danny.

'Call the Intensive Care Unit and see if there's a bed free.'

A frantic hour later, the patient was stabilized and they were prepped and ready to go with the operation; but Owen still wasn't sure. He badly needed a backstop, and Crane was his only choice – Crowther had been called away on emergency surgery himself.

But he didn't want to call Crane. Tell that to the patient's wife, he said to himself, and punched Crane's number.

It took several rings, but eventually he got through. 'What?' Crane demanded. He sounded pissed.

'It's me,' Owen said. Silence. 'I've got a forty-year-old man with cirrhosis and bleeding varices,' Owen said at last. Crane was obviously going to make him work for this.

'And what's the question?' Crane had obviously decided he could be magnanimous, now that Owen had come crawling.

'I think he might need an operation.'

Crane sighed heavily. 'I'm not even on call,' he pointed out. 'Is this a favour?'

Owen looked through the office doorway into the theatre, where Roberts was lying on his trolley, hooked up to saline and plasma drips. 'This isn't about us,' he said. 'Don't make this about us.'

'Look,' Crane said, 'I'm not really in a state to advise you.' He was speaking precisely, presumably because otherwise he'd slur. 'Where's Gordon Crowther?'

'He had to go to St Mary's to do a vascular emergency.'

Crane sighed again. 'Hold on,' he said. 'I won't be a moment.'

Owen waited but he didn't know how long the

patient could. Crane came back quite quickly, and he sounded a bit more together. 'How much blood has he had?'

'Twenty units.'

'What have you done for him?'

'I've injected them, put a balloon down and he's had Somatostatin.' It was the right treatment, Owen had no doubt about that. It was what to do next he was frantic about.

'And he's still bleeding?'

'Yes.'

'Then he needs an operation.' There was no doubt in Crane's voice. Owen wished he could find such certainty in himself.

'But if I do, he might die on the table,' Owen said. It was his worst nightmare, every surgeon's worst nightmare.

'He's going to bleed to death if you don't,' Crane said bluntly.

Owen bit his lip. 'So you think I should just get on with it?'

'Yes,' Crane said. Again, his certainty was comforting. 'And let Gordon Crowther know what you're doing.'

A nightmare. That was what Owen was in. A nightmare of blood that just kept flowing, and decisions that were the right decisions but just didn't do any good, and blood pressure that dropped and dropped and dropped.

And a patient who died under his hands, despite everything he could do.

Owen cleaned himself up. He had never felt so bleak; there was a numbness in him, a sense of failure that was like nothing else he'd ever experienced. Not that Roberts was the first patient he'd lost, but there was the nagging feeling that he'd been too tired, let his argument with Crane distort his judgement, somehow missed a trick somewhere along the line. None of it was true: he knew that but nevertheless, he couldn't shake the feeling.

He went to phone Crane. He owed him that much.

'He died,' he said when Crane answered.

There was a long silence. One smart-arsed retort and I'll kill him, Owen thought.

But Crane said, 'I'm very sorry.' He sounded as if he meant it.

'So am I,' Owen said. 'So am I.'

Chapter 29

Richard was waiting for Anna again as she left her office. She supposed it was her fault: she wouldn't see him, so the only time he could find her was when she went to her early morning appointments.

He was sitting on the stairs.

'Richard?' she said.

He looked wrung out. 'I've got this, and this, and this,' he said, laying out a selection of letters: divorce application, building society, bank, estate agent. 'Telling me why you're divorcing me. But I've heard nothing from you.' He stood up, leaving the letters where they lay on the plush carpet, as if they were completely unimportant. 'I cheated, you cheated back. So why am I relying on total strangers...' he waved at the letters. 'To finish things off?'

Anna stared at him. She had nothing to say that hadn't been said, now that her anger had been lanced.

'I'm moving out of the house,' he said. 'It feels as if someone died in there.'

And he went.

Poor Richard, Anna thought, and was surprised to find she really meant it.

Owen was excited when he got home. He had an evening off – John was covering for him. A whole evening to spend with Anna. He'd left her a message to ring him, but she hadn't. That was okay though. She'd probably left a message with Dad. Or he could phone her.

In the event, there was an envelope with her company logo on it lying on the kitchen table.

'Has Anna been round?' he asked. Seemed a bit strange, but she'd certainly taken a liking to Dad.

'She must've come while I were out,' Dad said. 'That was behind the door.'

Owen scanned the letter. Not good news. 'Oh for Christ's sake, that's exactly what he wants.' Dad looked at him questioningly. 'She's gone round to see him.'

'Oh,' Dad said.

'That's exactly what he wants,' Owen repeated.

'So what's the big deal?' Dad asked. He went and put the kettle on. His answer to any crisis, Owen thought.

Owen read the note out. ' "He's just confused about things and I'd just like to set the record straight." ' Owen pulled a disgusted face. How could she be so naive? 'Like shit he's confused,' he snarled. 'He knows exactly what he's doing.'

Dad filled the teapot. 'I don't know what you're panicking about,' he said. 'She's divorcing him, isn't she?'

Owen nodded. He knew when he was being stupid. Tea, that was what he needed, a nice cup of tea. He sat down. But she was going to talk to him. Which meant he was going to talk to her, which meant he could say anything. Bloody charmer.

Owen leapt up again. It was no good. He had to stop this nonsense before it started.

Anna followed Richard into the lounge of their house. It smelled of gloss paint and dust, and the decorators had covered everything in dustsheets. They'd left a couple of stepladders, with a plank stretched between them, in the middle of the floor.

'I've checked into the Midland,' Richard said. Anna had seen his suitcases in the hall. 'I'll go tonight. You belong here – you shouldn't be holed up in the house you grew up in...' His voice trailed off. He was staring at her. She'd dressed for the occasion – heels, hair and make-up as perfect as she knew how to make them. She wanted him to know what he was losing. 'I just want to know if you think you actually love him,' he said at last.

'Which isn't a loaded question?' Anna asked. 'If I say yes, you think I don't know my own mind. I've been duped by some ingenious little scally.' He didn't answer. She decided it was time to go on the attack. 'What made you sleep with the woman who wears more than she earns?'

Richard shrugged. 'She makes decisions. She's...'

And I don't, Anna wondered. And then she realized what he was trying to say. 'About you?'

'Yes.' He looked away.

'She seduced you?'

He flushed. 'Yes.'

Like hell she did, Anna thought. 'She knew where you were both going to have sex on your first big date?'

He didn't answer for a moment. Then he said, 'Yes.'

'Balls!' Anna snapped. 'You'd never have been pulled into that. "She's bossy." That's absolute crap. You've always thought of yourself first.' She could feel her throat go tight, but anger was surging through her, giving her strength and she knew she wasn't going to cry. 'Did you think about me?' she demanded. 'Did I vanish from the equation?'

Richard looked chagrined. 'Of course you didn't.'

So that made it everything all right? 'So you went off with her to some hotel, you had sex with her, you orgasmed – and all the while with a picture of me looking wronged hanging there?'

'Why are you doing this?' Richard asked. 'Why are we painfully discussing the sex I had?' Because you owe me, Anna thought. And nothing you can say, no hurt look in your eyes can repay that debt. 'Do we discuss yours?' he asked.

Your choice, Anna thought. She crossed the room and pulled aside the dustsheet covering the cocktail cupboard. Liqueurs no; Scotch no – that was Richard's drink; gin no, it made her a sloppy drunk. Brandy. That would do. She grabbed the decanter and a glass, and poured herself a large one.

She sipped it. It sent fire burning through her. Just the thing, she thought, and sipped again. When she was good and ready, she turned back to Richard. 'I've spent nearly two decades waiting for you to become available. I went through university knowing I'd have to sit back and wait for you to reach your full potential before we could actually start a life.' She took another sip of brandy. 'That wasn't a few years, or five years...' she thought about it, all the wasted time, especially before she'd taken over the Consultancy, the jobs that were never careers, that always came second best, the moving around the country when he needed to change hospitals so he could move up. 'I've waited twenty bloody years for you stop looking at your self-important little doctor's badge and look at me.' She glared at him. She should have said this long ago, long before Owen came into her life. But the next part was new. 'And when that time comes, I discover you're sharing your success with a young piece of middle management.'

Richard stood a little straighter. 'I've apologized,' he said, as if that meant something deeper.

'That's just not bloody good enough, Richard,' she snapped. 'All I did was what you wanted me to do, what you asked me to do, which was to wait.' Again, the images came flooding back in. They fuelled her. 'I spent the first ten years of our marriage living like a widow because you were climbing the ladder.' She took a good big sip of brandy this time. 'I viewed houses without you, I moved in without you, I decorated without you, I had dinner parties without you.'

Richard nodded at the brandy. 'Could I have some of that?'

'Get it yourself,' Anna snapped.

She turned to keep him in her sight as he went to the cupboard. 'I stifled everything I was ever good at for you, without you. All I'd done was make myself so boring and sycophantic you felt compelled to find something more interesting.'

'Yes.'

'What?' She'd expected protests, she'd expected him to say that Vivien had offered him nothing apart from a change of scene and here he was admitting he found her boring.

'If you say so,' Richard said.

Anna slammed her glass down so hard on the top of the television that brandy slopped out and stained the dustsheet. She headed toward the door. 'I don't know why I bothered.' She glared at him, challenging him to stop her.

It was obvious from his expression that he had something to say. She was almost out of the door before he got it out. 'Oh for Christ's sake, if you go off believing all that shit you deserve all you get.'

Anna whirled round.

'I didn't make you cook dinner,' Richard said. 'I didn't send you to view houses. You had a brain. We both had degrees, ambitions.' He knocked back the remains of his brandy in one gulp. 'Well, I wanted to be a surgeon and you wanted – what?' Anna didn't answer. 'What?' he demanded again. 'You didn't bloody know, did you?'

Anna felt her eyes go wide. She hadn't known where her own arguments had come from – all that repressed resentment and anger – but she certainly didn't know where he was finding his.

'I offered you a deal and you leapt at it,' Richard continued. When did you say, 'no more dinner parties'? When did you say, 'stop moving house'? You didn't – you couldn't, because it handed you a role that suited you to a tee, Anna.' He poured himself another brandy. 'You weren't waiting for me, you liar. You were waiting for yourself to get your finger out.' He swigged his drink. 'And the longer you waited, the harder it got, the further I went and the more jealous you got.'

Anna felt like she'd been slapped. How he could twist it all – his need for her to play the good little wife, the homemaker, the hostess; his desire to grab every promotion, till they'd crossed the country half a dozen times... 'What? What? You conceited *bastard*!'

'I didn't marry a cook, an estate agent or a decorator,' Richard said. No, but you were damn glad you got one, Anna thought. 'I married an ambitious, intelligent woman who just bottled out because she just couldn't face the bloody competition.' He waved his glass at her as if he were holding forth to an audience. 'So bollocks to your Lady In Waiting – that's a gross untruth, Anna.'

He stopped talking – the silence was dreadful. Anna

didn't know who was more shocked – her, or him. All she understood was that there was a complete numbness in her. Was there any truth in what he was saying? She didn't even know that much.

'Look,' he said, more quietly, 'When your time came and you talked about taking over the business, I was sitting there thinking, "what took her so long".'

'You were not,' Anna protested. 'You hated that.' She supposed she ought to point out that she could hardly have started any kind of business while he was still haring around the country going for promotions.

'All that waiting and you picked then to strike out – when there was this much of a gap...' He held his thumb and forefinger a quarter inch apart. 'For a family.'

'A what?' Anna said. She genuinely didn't understand.

'A baby, a child, a son, a daughter – family.'

'Is that what this is about?' Anna asked. She could barely believe it. He didn't reply. 'Richard, don't you dare do this to me,' she said. 'You contrived not to have a family for ten bloody years, by which time I was over thirty-five and feeling very nervous about that.' There were more downsides to being married to a doctor than the obvious ones.

'By which time,' Richard said pointedly, 'You were applying to the bank for another loan on the business.'

'Is that what this is all about?' She said it quietly. She needed to know. To go past it and go on.

'I asked you a direct question. "Anna, what do you think about children?" March, 1987.'

It was so like him to keep score. But she did recall him asking. 'A direct question,' she said. 'Which usually meant I knew exactly what answer you were looking for – which on that occasion was no.'

'You were wrong.' Richard swirled his brandy in its glass.

'You only asked once,' she said. She remembered thinking that if ever he asked again, she would try at least to open the conversation up a bit more.

'I wasn't qualified to push it because "I'd made you wait so long,"' Richard said. She wondered if that meant he was admitting he had expected her to wait; but it was too complicated to disentangle, and even trying would probably be counter-productive. 'Which was why I never asked again.'

So he might have, she thought. She might have... she pictured herself with a baby, a toddler, a teenager. The idea was unsettling. But they might have... And then a terrible thought struck her. 'Richard, have you...' she let her voice trail off while she worked out how to phrase it. 'When you slept with Vivien Reid, did you have unprotected sex?' He didn't answer. Oh God, Anna thought, not that, please, not that one thing. 'Was she protected?' He still didn't answer. She was surprised he could even look at her, so perhaps she needed to ask the direct question. 'Is she pregnant?'

There was a long, long, silence.

'No,' he said. His voice was heavy with regret.

And at that precise moment, the doorbell rang. Neither of them moved. It rang again.

Richard went to get it. Whoever it was, she didn't want to see them. They could play good neighbours another time...

She heard Owen's voice. No, she thought. Not now. She felt tears stab at her eyes. She dabbed at them with a tissue. There was no way he'd go without talking to her, she knew him well enough to know that.

She went out into the hall. Owen was standing on the doorstep. 'What are you doing here?' she demanded.

'Are you all right?'

'Just dandy,' Richard cut in.

'You shouldn't be here,' Anna said. She didn't want them to fight, didn't want an argument. 'I'm fine.' Owen stared at her. 'Go home,' she said.

'Come with me.' He took a step forward. Richard moved to block him.

'No.'

'Come with me.'

'No!' She was crying again, great big gulping sobs that she couldn't stop. She turned away and went back to the lounge.

'Wipe your feet,' Crane said sharply. She heard both of them follow her through, which wasn't what she wanted at all.

'Please Owen,' Anna said, as he came through the lounge door. He nodded at Richard, who had perched himself on the step of one of the ladders. 'How come he's allowed to discuss me, but I'm not allowed to mention him?'

'You barely entered the conversation,' Richard said quietly.

Please don't let them fight, don't let them argue, Anna thought.

'All he wants you here for is to persuade you to take him back.'

Richard looked at Anna. He obviously expected her to say something, but she didn't know what. She didn't want him, that was for sure; but right at that moment she didn't want to be with Owen either – she wanted time alone to think things through.

'I didn't walk into your life to wreck it,' Owen said.

He was talking to Richard, not Anna, and she was glad of that. 'I fell in love with her long before I knew who she was married to.' And then he did turn to her. 'Come on.'

'You knew she was married to someone,' Richard pointed out.

'No.'

Richard thought about that. 'Ahh... the ring. Maybe not.' It was the fairest thing Anna had heard him say since all this started. 'Anna took it off when she started her business as an independent management consultant.'

Oh yes, Anna thought. She'd been so proud of that decision. But it seemed all she'd done was to give Richard something to smile about behind her back – his good little wifey, going off into the big bad world alone at last.

Well, she'd been damn good at it once she did get started.

Something must have shown on her face, because Owen said, 'If he's upsetting you, why are you taking it?'

Richard positively smirked. 'Million dollar question, isn't it, Anna?'

'I love you,' Owen said. He did. She could see it in his eyes in all the little things he'd done and said while they were together. And she couldn't deny that she had had more pleasure – more *joy* – in those weeks than at any time in... well, in the last twenty years, if not the last twenty-five. 'Just tell him you love me – tell him you're going through with the divorce, and come with me.' He was so earnest, it was charming.

'How old are you, Springer?' Richard demanded. He, quite obviously, was less than charmed.

'Young enough to know she deserves better,' Owen

241

snapped back. His jaw worked, and she saw the muscles in his shoulders tense.

'If you start fighting, I'm phoning the police,' Anna warned.

'Wouldn't waste the energy,' Owen said.

'Wouldn't, couldn't,' Richard sneered. Anna couldn't take much more. She took a long, shuddery breath. 'Some more tissues over there,' Richard said.

'Thank you.' She got a handful.

'Tell him you're in love with me, Anna,' Owen begged.

Richard smiled. 'He's asked you twice.'

Anna glared at him. Didn't he know which way he was pushing her? He wasn't stupid.

'I love him,' she confirmed.

Richard got up. Paced. 'But you only went that way because I made that much of a mistake in twenty-five years.' He held his thumb and finger a half inch apart. So that was how he viewed adultery, Anna thought. That was how he viewed her hurt. And he seemed to have forgotten all the things they'd just said, all the admissions of accumulated resentment and poor communication, all the stored anger and hurt. 'I was wrong,' Richard said. 'You were hurt and then this Jacobean Tin Tin starts waving his genitals at you.'

'Listen to him,' Owen said. 'He only wants you now because he knows how much you mean to me.' Don't make me a pawn in your game, Owen, Anna thought. You love me, fine. Maybe we can have something together. But you and Richard have turned this into a grudge match. Well, you can sort that one out between yourselves. I won't be used. But Owen spoke to Richard before she could say any of it. 'I wasn't around to blame when you started slipping Viv Reid one.'

'Indeed you weren't,' Richard said. 'But you were there when the news broke, weren't you?'

He stared at Owen, who didn't answer back, and didn't meet his gaze either. Anna stared at him. What didn't she know about? What...

'Tell her,' Richard said.

'What do you gain by that?' Owen asked. He looked terribly uncomfortable.

'Let's see,' Richard said. He was clearly enjoying this. 'Tell her who made the phone call.'

'What phone call?' Anna demanded.

'To me,' Richard said. 'To me and my mistake, Vivien Reid at the hotel in London.' He swivelled back to confront Owen. 'You left a message for us, didn't you, Springer? Addressed to her, but for me – *Urgent. Please ask Mr Crane to phone his wife.*'

Owen flushed. Anna couldn't believe it. He'd done that. He'd arranged for her to be hurt, just so that he could – what, seduce her? Have his fifteen minutes of fame?

'Which I did. I rang my wife and told her everything.' Richard turned back to Anna. 'He made me tell you everything.'

But Anna wasn't interested in Richard. She turned to Owen. 'Did you do that?'

'Look...' Owen said.

But Richard cut in. 'If he loves you so much, how does he justify all this pain?'

Anna ignored him. 'Did you do that?'

At last Owen answered. 'I couldn't think about anything but you.' He looked at her. She glared back till he looked down at the dustsheet covered carpet again. 'You told me you were happily married. I knew you weren't.' He sounded utterly miserable, but Anna didn't care. 'Can you blame me for that? I loved you.'

'Get out,' Anna said flatly. She'd had enough.

'I couldn't think about anything but you.'

'Get out,' Anna said again. She turned to Richard, who was doing a bad job of trying not to look self-satisfied. 'You too.'

'Obviously, you need some space to breathe,' Richard said. 'So I'll leave you with that. I'm at the Midland.'

He walked out. Owen stared at Anna. She wouldn't look at him. Couldn't. The thought of what he'd done to her life made her feel sick, and three weeks in paradise couldn't make up for it. Eventually, he followed Richard out.

Owen sat in his MG and watched Crane pull away in his Merc. He wished he'd totalled the thing when he'd had the chance, instead of just doing in its headlights.

And now the bastard had screwed things up between him and Anna. Just because he hadn't known how to treat her. She didn't love him any more and he couldn't bear to see her happy.

Well, Owen would show him something, anyway.

He gunned the MG and roared off after Crane's Mercedes.

Crane was well ahead, but Owen caught him at the next set of lights. Crane revved his engine. Owen matched him. The lights turned amber. Owen took his foot of the clutch and let the MG go. She roared forward. So did Crane in the Merc.

A van swung across their path. Close. Too damn close. There was nowhere for Owen to go. He slammed the brakes on. Too late. The MG carried on into the van. The impact rocked Owen, but his seatbelt took the brunt of it.

He was winded, not hurt.

He climbed out in time to see Crane – who'd evidently swerved – cruising away.

Richard leaned out of the window and waved a goodbye, leaving Owen standing in the middle of incipient chaos.

'Bastard,' Owen muttered. He stared at the MG. The front end was a mess of twisted metal and glass.

In the far distance, he heard a police siren howl.

Chapter 30

Richard was scrubbing up for an emergency operation – a bleeding ulcer – when McGinley accosted him.

'You could have let the switchboard know you were in a hotel,' he said.

Richard didn't want to talk about it. It was bad enough being called out after midnight. 'You found me,' he pointed out.

'Yes,' McGinley said. He hesitated. 'Anna told me.' He glanced around, but the theatre sister was busy checking the instrument trays. 'Is she all right?'

Bloody stupid question, Richard thought. 'Did she sound all right?'

'No.'

'Then she's not all right,' Richard said.

There was an odd kind of satisfaction in that. He elbowed off the scrub tap and thought about it. What kind of man was he – what kind of human being – if he derived pleasure from the person he loved most in all the world hurting? Even if it did mean he was coming closer to winning her back?

His inner voice offered no answers.

A bell was ringing. Anna struggled awake. The radio was playing. Vivaldi: Richard's wake up music. She looked around at the debris on the bed and by it and on the bedside cabinet: an empty wine bottle, a glass with a drop of red wine still in the bottom, her photograph album – her younger self, naive and hopeful, beamed up at her, and on the opposite page, Richard as an up-and-coming young surgeon.

'Oh God,' Anna muttered. Her voice was thick with tears – hardly surprising since she'd cried herself to sleep.

The doorbell shrilled again. Anna got out of bed, grabbed her dressing gown and put it on as she hurried downstairs. The decorators had arrived. They were the last people she wanted to see – next to last, she corrected herself: Richard would be worse, Owen would be worse. She let them in, dressed hurriedly, and went to make coffee.

She came back out with it on a tray, and plonked it down on a dustsheet shrouded coffee table.

'Eddie, by the way,' the decorator said. 'We've only talked on the phone, haven't we?'

He stuck his hand out for her to shake. She ignored it. 'That's right,' she said.

He looked at his assistant, a young lad who smiled shyly at her. 'we were starting to think you were a figment.'

He laughed. She didn't join in: her head hurt too much. She hunted in her bag and found a spare set of keys, which she handed to him. 'If I'm in bed when you come, it's because I want to be.'

She started for the lounge door.

'You still haven't said which,' the lad blurted out.

Bloody hell, Anna thought. 'Which what?' she snapped.

He tapped a wallpaper book, and flipped through it. 'This one...' He found another page. 'Or that one, but you didn't know which yet.'

What do I care? Anna thought. I won't be living here. 'You choose,' she said.

She turned away. At the last minute, she realized this was just one more thing to lose control of. She turned back. The lad had clearly chosen the first of the two samples. She looked at them again briefly. 'The other,' she said. Again, she headed for the door.

She hadn't got there when she heard Phyllis call out, 'Are you there?'

Anna went into the hallway. Phyllis was there, holding a bag of laundry and a foil-covered casserole dish. They hadn't spoken since they'd argued. Anna didn't want to speak now.

Phyllis had the good grace to look embarrassed. 'I was looking for Richard,' she said.

'Clearly,' Anna said. 'He's not here.' She eyed the shirts. 'If you're taking in laundry, I've a coat and a couple of dresses that need cleaning.'

'I'm not.'

'You just do it for Richard?' Anna asked. 'And what was that,' she added tartly, 'Some kind of investment?'

'I beg your bloody pardon?' Phyllis snapped.

She flounced off. Anna went into the kitchen.

Her head hurt. She dumped her coffee mug into the sink and considered making another one, but decided against it. Time to get real, she decided. She rang Michelle on her portable phone; while it was ringing, she tucked it under her chin and started to empty out the fridge. She hadn't expected Richard to be good at looking after himself, but there was enough gone-off food in the fridge to poison a small army.

Michelle answered while Anna was still dumping it in a black plastic bin bag. Anna checked how things were going, and said she wouldn't be in. She closed the phone, and finished clearing the fridge. Nestling behind an open tin of peaches gone fuzzy with age, she found a casserole dish that matched the one that Phyllis had been carrying.

She glared at it, then took it out and put it on the worktop. She finished clearing the fridge, then started the washing up. Eventually, she got to Phyllis' casserole dish. She scrubbed off the remains of lamb cassoulet, then faced the fact that she probably ought to take it back.

In her current mood, to think a thing was to do it. She marched round to Phyllis' house with the dish. Phyllis answered to her knock, and she held it out.

'I think this is yours,' she said.

Phyllis took it, and started to shut the door without a word. Something crystalized in Anna's mind in that moment. I'm losing people, she thought. Richard, Owen, now Phyllis. She felt as if the world were falling away from her and there was nowhere to stand, no safe place to be.

'Phyllis,' Anna said. Phyllis turned back. Anna tried a smile, and was horrified at how hard it was. 'I'm sorry. I had no right to ask you to take sides.'

Phyllis shrugged. 'I didn't offer to do his shirts,' she said. She looked sheepish. 'I couldn't say no.' Anna could believe it. Richard always had been so very good at getting what he wanted. 'Do you want to come in?' Phyllis asked.

Anna stepped inside. Phyllis looked at her for a second. The next second, they were hugging each other, and Anna knew she hadn't lost quite *everything*.

After the MG Dad's car was a pig to drive and a sty to sit in. Still, it got Owen to work all right. He parked up and got out. As he was crossing the carpark, Danny caught him up. Danny looked back at the car and grinned. 'When I was a kid, I had a treehouse that looked something like that,' he said.

Owen wasn't in the mood for it. Not by a long way. 'When I was a kid, I had a dick your size,' he said.

Danny gaped at him. He grinned and left him standing there.

Anna was just finishing off clearing out the kitchen when the phone went. She didn't want to talk to anyone, with the possible exception of Michelle or Brian from work – and then only if it were a genuine emergency. She picked up a double handful of milk bottles – why Richard couldn't even have put them out on the doorstep was beyond her – and took them out.

She paused by the phone. Her outgoing message was just ending. The machine bleeped. She waited for the caller to speak, but the line went dead instead.

'I should bloody well think so,' she muttered, and carried on outside.

Crane was back on full duty. That one fact was enough to wreck Owen's morning, his day and his month. Still, he thought as he collected his things from his locker, at least John had had the sense to schedule them in different theatres: Owen and Danny, with possible assistance from another surgeon in Theatre 6; John and Crane in 7. Now, if only Theatre 7 just happened to be in, say, Alice Springs, he'd be getting somewhere; better yet, make that the dark side of the moon.

The down side – there was always a down side – was that he had to put up with Danny. He was taking off his shoes slowly, because he was reading the British Medical Journal while he did so. God forbid, Owen thought, that he should give any one thing his full attention.

'Here we go,' Danny said. 'It's perfect – Senior Surgical Officer at the Queen Elizabeth Hospital in Botswana.' He rolled his eyes theatrically. 'God, this is amazing. Accommodation, relocation expenses, living expenses... tennis courts!' Owen ignored him. 'It's you!' Danny insisted. Owen carried right on ignoring him. Danny flopped the paper shut. 'Well, if she knows you sent the note, there'll be no redemption.' He chucked his street shoes into his locker. 'I'd book my ticket, matey.' Just ignore him, Owen thought. Just ig... 'You're dead in the water.'

Owen felt his jaw clench. If he'd thought there was any chance at all he could get away with thumping him, he would have. As it was, he turned and walked away. Small victories, he thought. They were the only ones he ever seemed to win, these days.

Crane wasn't a fool. He knew when he'd made a mistake, and he prided himself on being man enough to admit it to himself and to others. Not that apologies came easily to him. Besides, he needed to be able to function in his job – more now than ever – and to do that he needed McGinley on his side. And having allies never did any harm.

He waited till he and McGinley were alone in the scrub room, gowning up. The nurse assisting them went out for a moment. Richard took the opportunity to say, 'I'd like to unreservedly apologize for my recent behaviour.' McGinley shot him a sharp look. 'I'm not like that,' Richard said. 'Forgive me.' McGinley didn't answer. After a moment, Richard said, 'Goes without saying I'll write you a reference for that consultant post.'

But McGinley said, 'Don't bother. I withdrew my application yesterday.' He looked ruefully at Richard.

'If I can still get shafted by the likes of you, I'm nowhere near ready.'

Richard didn't know what to say. It seemed his apologies cut no ice with anyone. All he could presume was that he'd made another enemy.

But to his surprise McGinley went on, 'I think you've done the right thing moving out, by the way?'

'Really?' Richard was as startled by the idea that he'd done something right as he was that McGinley was willing to give him advice – he'd assumed the man was on Owen's side, and an enemy, after Richard's last *faux pas*.

But McGinley was talking, and Richard was determined to learn everything he could.

'You stand more chance of looking like a victim than rolling about in the family silver,' McGinley explained. Richard was beginning to realize that the man liked Springer very little more – perhaps even less – than he did himself.

Light dawned. 'Of course,' Richard said. 'You've been through all this.' He sighed. 'If she wants him that badly, there's bugger all else I can do.'

McGinley raised his eyebrows. 'She's said she wants him?' he asked.

She said she loved him, Richard thought. But I pushed and pushed till she had to say something. He shook his head, hoping it didn't count. 'It's different for you – you divorced her.' He thought of nights spent alone, awake, wine bottles drunk dry. And Scotch. 'But I've lost all bloody sense of reason.' That was too simple, didn't begin to cover it. 'I've just never felt this...' He couldn't find the words for his constant restlessness, his fear that he'd screwed up, worse this time than last; his desire and dread that she might be standing round every corner he turned. 'I daren't relax. I can't relax.'

'I only divorced her to show her how much she'd hurt me,' McGinley said softly.

'Well that was arse about face wasn't it,' Richard said, and then realized how harsh that sounded. There was genuine pain in McGinley's eyes. 'If you loved her,' he added, trying to soften it.

'By the time I'd picked myself up off the floor the *decree nisi* was through.' He paused, clearly remembering things too painful to think about. 'He was a consultant,' he said at last.

'Do I know him?' Richard asked, letting curiosity get the better of any attempt to be sensitive.

'Hussein from St Barney's.' McGinley spat the words out.

'Hussein...' Richard pondered. He'd heard the name. 'Hussein – oh! She was *your* wife?' McGinley nodded. 'Why haven't we discussed this before?' Richard asked.

'Because *you've* never needed to, sir,' McGinley said with more than a hint of edge.

The nurse came back then, so the conversation had to stop. Richard thought that was probably a good thing, though he resolved to pick McGinley's brains again later on.

Anna was a great fan of lists. They kept her sane, she reckoned. She was sitting in the early morning sun in the lounge, trying to ignore the regular husking sound of the decorators sanding down the gloss paint in the dining room, while she wrote a list of things she had to attend to so that the divorce could proceed – estate agents, solicitor, accountant, on and on.

The phone rang again. Well, let it ring, she thought. This time though, there was a message. It was Richard's mother, Muriel, wishing him happy birthday.

Damn, Anna thought. She'd forgotten. She was flicking through her diary when she heard her name mentioned.

'Have you told her what I told you to tell her,' Muriel said, her voice slightly distorted by the phone line. 'Don't let me down will you? I'd be very disappointed if you let her go. Show her the pictures. Bordeaux, 1991. You both looked so happy then.' She paused. Anna realized she couldn't hear the sounds of the decorators working any more. 'Things can't have changed that much,' Muriel added.

Yes they can, Anna thought. But Muriel was going on about one particular set of photos. Anna didn't want to think about it. I don't have to listen. Muriel sounded far more upset than she'd expected. 'I've written to her at her mother's,' Muriel said, 'but I haven't heard anything back.' Again, she paused. 'Your father's more upset than I am. Please don't let her start talking about a divorce, Richard. Promise me that.'

God, Anna thought. It wouldn't just be losing Richard. It would be his family, too. She liked them. Loved them, even. And his friends. The fabric of her life pulling apart, like a jumper with a pulled thread.

'I love you lots,' Muriel said. 'Ring me, won't you?' She rang off.

Anna sat in the sudden silence for a moment. Then the rhythmic sound of the decorators' sanding began again.

Canteen food was never wonderful, and that night it was particularly bad. Richard picked at his shrivelled lamb chop and string beans that had been boiled to a pulp. On the other side of his desk, McGinley did the same.

254

Richard scanned the list McGinley was helping him make. It was divided into two columns, passive and active, depending on whether Crane could take the initiative or not.

'House sale?' he asked.

'She'll go through the motions whatever you do,' McGinley said. 'It's obligatory.'

Richard put his fork down and wrote *House* in the passive column on the list.

'Has she made an offer?' McGinley asked round a mouthful of instant mashed potato.

'Sixty-forty split in her favour,' Richard said. It seemed fair enough to him.

'You've agreed?'

'Not yet,' Richard said. He fully expected McGinley to say he should hold out for fifty-fifty.

'Agree,' McGinley said. 'Stand your ground briefly, then concede the lot.'

Richard frowned. 'Did that do you any good?'

McGinley looked just a bit sheepish. 'Well no – I lost the house.' He pushed his plate away. 'But the gesture was crucial.'

'Flowers?' Richard asked.

'Did you buy her flowers before?' McGinley asked.

'Frequently.' It had been a matter of pride that he never forgot.

'No flowers,' McGinley said firmly. Richard stared at him, startled. He was beginning to suspect this wasn't so much a case of the blind leading the blind as a half-wit leading a dimwit. After all, no one but a half-wit would have divorced the woman he loved, and none but a dimwit would have let a woman like Anna slip away from him. 'You haven't changed if all you do is what you did before,' McGinley pointed out.

It made a kind of sense, but Richard hated the idea. 'It's the only communication I'm being allowed,' he protested.

'Write,' McGinley advised. 'She'll cope with a letter a lot better than a phone call.'

Richard jotted that down. Before he'd finished writing, McGinley said, 'Viv Reid?' Richard glowered at him. Who the hell did he think he was, anyway? 'Have you discussed her?' McGinley persisted.

'Not in any depth,' Richard snapped. And he wasn't about to, either, no matter what McGinley suggested.

But McGinley was quite mild about it. 'Don't you think you should?' he asked.

'With her or you?' Richard spat.

McGinley shrugged. 'I'm not a gossip – I'm trying to help. But if you're not comfortable with it...'

Next he'll be suggesting I seek therapy, Richard thought. He studied McGinley carefully. He seemed genuine enough. And so he, haltingly, began to explain how he'd wrecked his marriage.

'I'd been called in for an emergency – some cock-up by a registrar.' He couldn't even recall what it had been, now. 'I don't actually know where the moment turned, but as I walked back to my office, Vivien was standing there. Working late, presumably.' He paused, remembering the moment. How the light had caught her hair. Her stance. 'She came in the first batch of Thatcher's number crunchers and I couldn't stand the sight of her.' He knew it was a common feeling among the rest of the medical staff – that it was partly on general principles, partly personal: Vivien did sometimes seem to go out of her way to be abrasive. 'But...' he tried to find the right words. He'd tried and failed to explain it to Anna, but he'd had layer upon layer of motives then, most of which he didn't understand himself. 'She knew how to make things better. I don't know how she did it, but it worked.' He paused again. This was hard, harder than he'd ever imagined it could be. 'She made me feel better.'

McGinley was staring at him as if he'd just grown horns.

'I offered her a lift home that night,' he said. 'We parked outside her flat and she was . . .' Again, he really couldn't find the words for it: outside the hospital, she'd been softer, somehow. Less guarded. 'She smiled.' It was the best he could do. 'Totally confidential?' he demanded. If this went round the doctors' restroom, he'd be a laughing stock.

McGinley nodded.

'She didn't even offer me coffee. She didn't say it. I just got the impression that if I got out of the car at that moment, coffee was certain.' He sighed, remembering. 'Before I knew it, I was in strange shops, buying expensive dresses for a woman who didn't really . . . we have very little in common.' But those legs, those breasts, the intensity of her . . . 'It's extraordinary,' he said at last.

McGinley just stared at him.

Chapter 31

Anna didn't understand it. She read the letter through a second time, just to be sure, then stared up at her solicitor, Mr Callahan.

'Well, this is a first for me,' he said.

'It's ridiculous,' Anna protested. 'Why's he doing this?'

'I don't think we should pause for breath or he might change his mind,' Callahan said. 'I'm just having an acceptance letter signed.'

Anna stared at the letter again. It gave her the entire house. 'I haven't asked for his share of the house – why's he doing it?'

The door opened, and Callahan's secretary came in with the acceptance letter. While Callahan checked it through, Anna read the other papers – the petition for divorce, the suggested split of their other property and Anna's business. Her eye lit on the divorce papers: so final and so black and white.

'Good, good,' Callahan said. 'Fastest money I've ever earned – fax it now, won't you?'

The secretary started to leave. As she got to the door, Anna said, 'Don't send that.'

A hint of exasperation flickered across Callahan's face. 'What's wrong?'

Anna stood up and grabbed her jacket. 'I just...' She couldn't find the words. 'Everything.'

Danny didn't learn, that was his trouble, Owen reckoned. They were in the pub having dinner, and Owen had almost shoved the British Medical Journal down his throat sideways before he'd stopped reading out job ads in ridiculous places. Then he wanted to know which of the several lone women in the bar Owen fancied.

'Her?' he demanded.

'Yes,' Owen said, though she was too blonde.

'Her?'

'Yes.' Too young, but pretty with it.

'Her?'

She was okay, Owen thought, but a bit dim looking. Besides, she was being joined by a bloke who looked like he wrestled polar bears for fun.

'With a couple of painkillers if he found out,' Owen answered, and then admitted, 'But yes.'

'You're normal!' Danny said, as if it were a discovery to rate with Fleming finding penicillin. 'So where's the block? Get out there and pump some pheromones.' He slurped his lager. 'Lick somebody's neck, or whatever you do when the blood starts going.'

Owen laughed. 'If you took her and her and her and put them altogether, they wouldn't come anywhere *near* Anna Crane,' he said.

Danny looked at him as if he was nuts. Which definitely made two of them, if he couldn't see what made Anna so special, Owen reckoned.

'All right, all right,' Danny said. 'Somebody's thirtieth. And it's full of people the same age-ish.' Owen could see where this was going. He just thought it was trivial. Trivial, immature and shortsighted. He'd have told Danny as much, if he could have got a word in edgeways. 'She trots along with you. For a start, what's she wearing?' Something devastatingly sexy in pure silk, Owen thought. That little black number with the red jacket, maybe. 'Does she feel comfortable? Do you?' He'd feel wonderful, Owen thought. Who wouldn't, with the sexiest woman in the room on his arm? 'You came for a laugh with your buddies,' Danny continued. 'What can you do with your mother in the room?' Owen stared at him. What would he want to do? Sink fifteen pints of lager and pass out in the street? Hook up with some little bit of fluff who didn't know what her interesting bits were *for*? But Danny obviously didn't see it like that. 'Face it, Owen,' he said. 'You just got off the Titanic at Southampton.' He drained his glass. 'Move *on*.'

Richard stared at Anna. How many nights had he dreamed of this? How many sleepless nights had he prayed for it. Yet here he was watching her by candlelight, getting his chance to prove things could be mended. And if he'd wanted a sign, she'd bought him a birthday present. He unwrapped it and opened the box. A heavy-braceleted gold watch lay inside, swaddled in a mass of tissue paper. He picked it up. The reverse was engraved, *Richard, Love Anna*.

Then however bad things looked, it wasn't all over yet.

'That's stunning,' he said. 'Am I allowed to say thank you?'

She didn't say no, so he leaned across the table and kissed her delicately on the cheek. Bliss.

When he'd pulled, regretfully, away again, she said, 'I bought that in Paris.' He stared at her, feeling hope die within him just a little. 'In January.'

He stared at her, and realized that perhaps whatever this was, it wasn't a reconcilliation.

'Why have you given me everything?' she asked. 'In the divorce?'

He wanted to say, to win you back. If money can win you back, or the possibility that I'm not a complete prick and I do care about your well-being. But he couldn't say any of it. 'You deserve it,' was all he could manage.

'To feel guilty,' she said. Candlelight glittered in her eyes, made her look soft. But there was nothing soft in her tone.

'A little bit,' Richard admitted. 'I'm trying to make things look as they really are.' And even that wasn't the truth. He stared across the table at her. It might as well have been a million miles. 'Please stop the divorce.'

She shook her head. 'We've only told the truth since the divorce started. You want to *stop* telling the truth.'

It hurt. He supposed he deserved it. But made everything sound so hopeless. All their adult lives, based on lies and deceptions and evasions. 'The truth was out of context,' he said, and wondered if that, too, were an evasion of responsibility.

'How badly did you want children?'

The question, coming now, took him by surprise. 'Quite,' he said. It had been an assumption he'd always made: he'd only noticed he'd failed in it when the time was almost gone, and then it was too late to say how much it mattered to him.

'But you couldn't tell me that very important thing,' Anna said softly. 'Is that the kind of marriage you want to hold on to, Richard?'

He felt his throat tighten. But he would not cry. Not. 'Worth repairing, surely,' he said.

There was sadness in her eyes, but her voice was

implacable. 'All you want is what someone took from you. That's all.' He wanted to protest, but he had nothing left. No words, nothing he could do. 'You needed things to change.'

He swallowed hard. He wasn't crying. Was *not*.

'Well, they've changed,' she said. 'We go back to the original agreement of a sixty-forty split.' She hesitated, clearly considering something. Hope rose in him, just for a split instant of frozen time. 'No,' she went on, 'Fifty-fifty. Then we're only as guilty as each other.' He stared at her. She waved at passing waiter. 'I'll have a glass of wine now,' she said, almost cheerfully.

Vivien stared at herself in the bathroom mirror. She would never have admitted it to anyone, but she was terrified.

She opened the pregnancy test kit and followed the instructions. Wait five minutes, it said. She set the kitchen timer she'd brought in with her and went to wait.

She wasn't at all sure what was a good result or if there were any such thing as a good result.

Owen stared at Danny across the clutter of glasses that separated them. 'You know what's tragic about you?'

He was slightly pissed. Danny was even more pissed and he said, 'We're not talking about my problems.' He was slurring his words, just slightly. '*Your* problem is, you can't face the truth.'

There was no point, absolutely no point trying to reason with him. 'There are six million sperm in a single shot,' Owen said. 'Which means five million, nine-hundred and ninety-nine thousand of 'em were

262

bright enough to avoid being you.' Something wrong there. Something complicated and mathematical. Not to worry. 'I'm an optimist, Glassman. I'm a positive person.'

Danny looked hurt. You'd think he'd be used to having the piss taken out of him, Owen thought. Apparently not. Maybe this was the first time he'd noticed?

'Fine,' Danny said, 'But your other problem is that she's having dinner with him tonight.'

Owen looked at him suspiciously thinking: could be a wind-up? If he were lucky. Yeah. 'Where'd you get that?' he asked.

'I dropped some files into Crane's office.' He produced a yellow post-it note. 'This was stuck on the computer.'

Owen looked at it: *Anna, seven thirty, Cafe Alto.*

'I'm really sorry,' Danny said.

But Owen was already half-way to the door. He made the trip in record time – Dad's old car would never forgive him – but by the time he got there, they had gone.

Vivien poured herself a glass of wine. A large one. She took a single sip, and then her kitchen timer went off.

She breathed in, deep and hard, and headed for the bathroom. The pregnancy test kit was on the bathroom shelf. She took the wand out of the phial of chemicals.

And began to cry.

Chapter 32

Owen tapped nervously at Anna's front door, but when she opened it he managed to smile and say, 'Nice evening?'

'Lovely,' she answered coolly. 'You?'

She let him follow her inside, which was much more than he'd hoped for. Much more. He only hoped it wasn't just that she was trying to keep him and Crane even.

They went into the kitchen.

'What have you been talking about?' he asked.

He expected her to demand where he'd found out she'd seen Crane – or why he thought it was his business. But she said, 'Not you.'

She put the kettle on its base. He tried to take her hand. She pulled away. 'Excuse me,' she said.

He realized that just because she'd let him in didn't mean he wasn't in big trouble. 'What have you been talking about?' he asked again.

'You don't need to know.'

That was more what he'd expected. 'I love you,' he said. It was all he could think of.

'I don't need you to make me feel good or bad about myself.' She got the coffee out. 'I manage both adequately.'

'I love you.'

She rounded on him. 'You sent a note pretending to be me?'

'I love you.'

'How could you? If he's off in a hotel boosting the morale of some bimbo that's his problem. I didn't want to know about that.' Behind her, the kettle clicked off. She ignored it. 'But you're there making decisions about what you wanted.'

'I love you.'

She flushed. Took a deep breath. Then raged at him anyway. 'You wanted something you'd been told you couldn't have, and I had to suffer the consequences.' Her eyes were brimming with tears. 'You selfish bastard.'

'I love you.'

She slapped his face, hard. Fury lashed through him, but he stood there and took it. Took it again when she hit him again. But the third time, he reached up and grabbed her wrist when she raised her hand.

'I didn't mean to hurt you.' He said it as calmly as he could, which was not very calmly at all. He kept hold of her wrist.

'People keep saying that.' She was shaking. He could feel it in her wrist, the tension. 'It means sod all.'

The tension went out of her. He let her wrist go. Took a single tentative step toward her. 'Nothing I do or say or breathe or think happens without you.' He was close enough to kiss her, but he didn't dare. Not yet. He hadn't said everything yet, and he was terrified he'd never get another chance. 'I'll pay any price for any mistakes, but I can't lose you.' She was glaring at him, rage so bright, so pure, it almost burned. 'Please, Anna – just tell me you love me.'

There was silence. For a moment, he thought she would hit him again. Then she kissed him tentatively.

And then there was nothing tentative about it as they grabbed at each other, holding and needing. There was nothing in the world but Anna's eyes and Anna's mouth and Anna's damn clothing that kept getting in the way...

Next thing, they were on the floor, passion spent. The real world intruded – the decorators working, cars outside, someone on the phone leaving a message.

Owen didn't want the real world. It might not include this. He decided to chase it away, and leaned in to kiss her. She tilted her head away, just enough to stop him.

'In all honesty, I don't see any other explanation,' Anna said. 'I agree with Man A, because he's absolutely right – I dipped out of that marriage the minute I knew how fast he was travelling. I was jealous.' Her fingers knotted in her bit of soggy tissue. She squinted into the sun, at her mother who was sitting propped up in bed near the window. 'If he wanted children and he couldn't just say that to me, what kind of a smell was I giving off?' She thought about that, and it made the tears come again. She got a fresh tissue. 'Man B just lit the bloody touchpaper, didn't he? I'd only known him days, and he worked that out...' She let her voice trail off, as she tried to gather her thoughts. 'I think he only kept coming because he knew I was really looking for something else. I *was*.' She hesitated. She didn't mean to imply that Man B – she couldn't bring herself to call either of them by name – wasn't truly in love with her. She knew he was. The question was, how it had got that far. But the next part was the hard, the important part. 'What I'm finding very sad is that they're both right. What I'm finding very, very sad is that Man A and Man B are so similar.' Stop me, she thought. Say something, because I don't want to hear myself say the next thing. But Mum was off in her own little dreamworld. So there was nothing for it but to continue dissecting it. 'What is it about me that means I attract these people? I wish to God I knew what I'd done.' And with that, she'd run out of words.

Mum ran her fingers up and down the crotched edge of her cardigan. 'Have you told me this before?' she asked.

Anna nodded, and realized that mum, too, was crying.

Owen was in a foul mood. He'd been round to Anna's and she wasn't there.

He stared at the door of his locker and started pulling the post-it notes off it. All the messages were either out-dated or trivial, and besides none of them were from Anna so they really didn't matter.

But one of them puzzled him. He stared down at it: *Ring Viv Reid.*

Now, what the bloody hell could she want? John's hand appeared in front of his face. 'That's mine,' he said. He swapped it for one from his locker. 'Here.'

Owen read the new note: *Your car is not repairable.*

It was amazing how even the worst day could get worse.

Richard stared at Phyllis. She'd always been Anna's friend, not his, and he didn't know how trustworthy she was.

'Day before yesterday,' she said.

'Has the car been here?' he demanded. He really

couldn't be bothered to be polite, not considering she might be lying – at least if Anna asked her to.

'Just the decorator's van.' She was clearly running out of patience. Tough.

'Did she say anything?'

Phyllis pursed her lips. 'Well, yes.'

'Like?' Phyllis didn't answer. 'Look, don't bugger about,' Richard snapped.

'She came in for a drink. We had fifteen minutes and a cup of tea, then she went.' Her expression said he was never going to find out what had been said. 'All right?'

It wasn't all right. Not at all. But, since he clearly wasn't going to get the bloody woman to behave reasonably, Richard left. He went back to his house – his half a house, he thought wryly, and found the decorator. The man was obviously well practised in being obstreperous, because he refused to give a straight answer till Richard lost his temper.

'How the hell did you get in if you haven't seen her?' he demanded.

The man slapped on a piece of wallpaper. 'She gave us a set of keys,' he said without looking up.

'Her car's not been here since yesterday?'

'No, and the milk was on the step this morning.' Now he did look up. 'The other fella came again, though.' Richard glared at him. 'You know, the *other* fella. He's been looking for her and all.'

Springer. Damn him.

Richard went over to the phone. There were a dozen messages on the answering machine. But when he'd heard them all, it wasn't Springer whose heart he wanted to tear out. It was Vivien's.

Owen watched his dad cooking up another one of his messes. No doubt he'd call it stew.

268

'Ring her on the noddy phone,' Dad said.

'She's turned it off.' Owen sipped his tea.

'Right. You're stuck then.' A thoughtful look flickered across his face and was gone.

'What?' Owen demanded.

'What?' Dad was useless at playing the innocent but it didn't stop him trying, though.

'Has she said anything to you?' He watched Dad carefully.

'Me?' He said, too quickly. 'Why would she want to talk to me?'

'She did before.'

'Only because she came to talk to you and you weren't here.' He ladled out some grey looking stew. 'Do you want chips with this?'

Vivien opened the door to Richard's pounding. and as soon as she did so, he stormed inside. 'What the hell are you trying to do?' he demanded. She looked at him blankly. 'The message. To Anna.'

Vivien shut the door behind him. 'What harm could it do?' she asked. She told him what had happened — all that had happened.

She had met up with Anna and given her the photographs she'd got from Penman, the detective Richard had hired. She'd intended to use them as amunition, but there seemed little point now.

Anna had looked at them and said, 'You can tell him from me, you make a bloody good pair.' The contempt in her voice was enough to make Vivien squirm, even now.

'Why should I believe that?' Richard demanded. He moved up close to her.

She thought he would touch her, and found the notion repellent. 'Don't,' she said, and moved away.

'Don't you feel pathetic?' he asked. There was a sneer in his voice that made him loathsome to her.

'I do now,' she said. She smiled sourly. 'I'm pregnant.'

He stared at her. Said nothing for the longest time. 'I don't believe you.' he said finally. She stared him down. 'When?' he asked. 'Since when?'

'Two months,' she said.

'Oh my God,' Richard said. He reached behind him for support. Found none and he sat down instead. 'Look . . .' he began.

'No,' Vivien said gently. 'You mustn't say anything.' 'I'll . . .'

'No.' Vivien was determined about this. 'I don't want to know what you're going to do. You have to wait to hear what I'm going to do.' She let that sink in before she added, 'And I haven't decided.'

She opened the front door for him. 'I've got a friend coming round,' she said. 'If you don't want to be seen here, I'd vanish.'

He nodded and left. She closed the door and wept. Again.

Chapter 33

Owen clutched the letter he'd found in his pigeon-hole nervously. It was from Anna, saying she needed some time to be alone, and please not to contact her.

He was nervous because he'd seen Crane collect an identical letter. It was probably stupid, but he had to know whether it said the same as his.

He tapped on Crane's door, and went in without waiting for an answer. Crane looked up from his paperwork. 'I'm not in the mood for games,' he said. Fine by me, Owen thought. He wasn't looking for a fight, but he wasn't going to play the doormat, either. 'May I see what's in your letter, please.'

The letters were identical: Wedgwood blue, tissue-lined envelopes, deckle cut paper. The notes, to all intents and purposes, were the same.

As he put Crane's note back in the envelope, Owen checked the postmark. He noticed Crane doing the same to his envelope.

'Derbyshire,' Crane said.

'Is that somewhere you go often?' Owen asked, trying to sound innocent.

'She asks to be left alone,' Crane said. 'You instantly want to know where she might be.' As if, Owen thought, he hadn't checked the postmark himself. 'You're completely bloody untrustworthy. That's why this isn't going to work.'

'What's not?'

'A gentleman's agreement not to pursue her,' Crane said.

Owen laughed. It was that or knock the arrogant bastard's teeth down his throat. 'Don't crack on you know where she is and you're restraining yourself,' he said. 'If you had the faintest idea, you'd be out that door like a gun dog.'

Crane actually managed to look offended. 'I would not,' he said. 'I respect her.'

'You're panicking because you know I'd be better at it than you.'

'Whatever you think.' Crane went back to his paperwork.

Time to wind the bugger up and see if he ran, Owen decided. 'Okay,' he said, 'I'll agree to a gentleman's agreement.'

Crane looked up. 'She's left alone, without prejudice, to make her own decisions?'

'Fine,' Owen said, and stuck his hand out. Crane shook it.

Owen wondered if Crane actually intended to stick to it. He knew for sure he didn't.

It was a wet day and Richard was cold and miserable as he waited outside Anna's office. That was okay, he thought as he saw the receptionist – what *was* her name? – approach. It meant he'd got to her before Springer did, and that was all that mattered.

'I know you've got the number,' he said without preamble. 'She told me in the letter...' he waved it at her. ' "In the event of an emergency, my office has a contact number."'

'Yeah,' the girl said, 'But this isn't an emergency, is it – or you'd have rung.'

Crane schooled himself to patience. 'Her mother's in trouble – we're all concerned,' he said. She stared at him, obviously not buying it. 'Ring.'

'No.' She'd obviously taken lessons in stubbornness from Anna.

'You'll take that risk?' Crane was surprised. The girl looked like she had all the initiative of a goldfish. Well, even goldfish could be persuaded, one way or another. 'Her mother dies during the night, and I say, "I did what you asked. I told Lorraine." How's she feel about you then, Lorraine?'

'It's Michelle,' she said. She stared at him impassively. She obviously had the conscience of a block of wood, or she'd see what she was doing to him.

He lost his temper. 'You've worked for her for less than six months. I've been married to her for twenty-five years. Why in God's name should you decide when I speak to my wife?'

'Because she told me to.'

Quite obviously, that was the limit of her understanding of the situation. Richard turned to go. Then he had a thought. He spun back round and pulled out a wad of twenties from his wallet.

'You're blocking my doorway,' the girl said.

'No, I think your parents did that for you, actually,' Richard snarled.

He slammed off down the street. Bloody girl. bloody, bloody woman.

Owen waited for Michelle to come out of the building, then matched her pace.

'Hiya, Michelle,' he said. 'How you doing.'

'No,' she said.

So Crane had tried to get it out of her already. Owen had thought as much – the man had been useless in surgery, and hadn't managed to meet his eyes once.

Michelle crossed the road. Owen paced her. 'I bet she's great to work for, because...' He searched around for a reason. 'When you first meet her, you'd never guess in a million years she could be a real laugh.'

'I'm not listening,' Michelle said. She headed for the bus stop.

'Did she talk about us?' Owen asked. 'I bet there were rumours.' Michelle didn't answer. Her expression didn't even flicker. Owen would have hated to play her at poker. 'Office gossip – you all knew about me, didn't you?' Bingo! Michelle nodded. 'Did she tell you me and her old fella ended up scrapping?'

'When?' Michelle looked delighted. It had been odds on she couldn't stand Crane.

Owen grinned. 'I didn't think she'd shout about that one. We both got arrested...'

'You're kidding.' She eyed him up and down. 'Who won?'

He gave her a look that suggested she was crazy to even think it might have been Crane. 'Do I look like an honest bloke to you, Michelle?'

She was instantly wary. Well good for her. At least it meant Crane probably hadn't got anywhere. 'If I told you I loved you more times in a week than you could count, would you believe me?' Michelle looked dubious so Owen did an instant rethink. 'She doesn't either, but it's true.'

'I didn't say I wouldn't,' Michelle countered.

'She'd believe me if I told her I nicked that phone number out of your office drawer, or out of your bag.' He paused. 'I could make her believe that. And she'd expect it of me.' Which was sadly true, though he hoped to get the chance to make her revise that opinion.

Michelle grinned. 'You'd have a job – it's not written down anywhere.'

There was a rumble of a diesel engine and Michelle moved forward a bit. Running out of time, boy, Owen told himself.

'Okay, Michelle,' he said. 'Answer us one more question – in all the time you've worked for her, did she seem more happy or less happy since the rumours started?'

Michelle put her hand out to stop the bus. 'Yeah,' she said. 'But she's not so cheerful now, is she?'

The bus stopped and the doors clattered open.

'Yeah but...' Owen said. Last chance... 'Come on, Michelle – I'm not a liar.' She went to get on the bus. He grabbed her arm. 'She knows I love her. I swear to God, I wouldn't let you down.'

Michelle pulled away and got on the bus. At the last moment she turned. 'Once,' she said, and rattled off a number. The doors shut and the bus left.

'Oh shit,' Owen said, and scrabbled for a pen. He didn't have one. He went for his phone instead. The battery was low.

'Shit,' he said again, and ran for the nearest phone box. Made it. And he still knew the number. Punched it in.

'Yes,' Anna said.

'Where are you?' Owen asked. Stupid place to start, but...

Anna hung up. Owen dialled again and she hung up again.

He was still trying to get her to speak to him that evening. He nearly caused a fight in the pub over the way he was hogging the phone. And when Dad broke it up, he stormed off.

He went down the road. He felt like he couldn't live in his skin any more. He had to do something, anything. But there was nothing he could do. He suddenly realized his Dad was walking along behind him.

'I always knew you were going to be like this,' Dad said. 'I knew from when you were three. We were getting you out of nappies and every time we took the nappy off, you'd wait about ten minutes and then shit on the carpet.'

Owen ignored him.

'Only reason we never got new carpet was because it gave me great pleasure watching you eat your crisps off the floor.'

Owen laughed. He couldn't help himself. He waited for his Dad to catch up.

'You're as clueless now as you were then,' Dad said. 'You remember Willy Tattersall?' Owen frowned. 'Lived next door to your grandad in Exmoor Street? Worked for the old GPO. Had a telephone in the toilet – that's why he got sacked. He had phones all over his house. Whenever somebody rang him up, the bloody roof shook.'

Owen nodded.

'I bet he could get you an address for that number.'

Owen stopped dead. 'Now?'

'No, not now. Calm down. He's a businessman. He does things like a businessman.' Crook, Dad meant. 'And you're a surgeon. So stop doing things like a dick.'

It cost, but the next day at the pub, Willy Tattersall had an address for Owen. He didn't even complain when he cottoned on that Dad had added a couple of notes to the price for himself.

276

Owen drove through the afternoon to get to Derbyshire, while the bunch of flowers he'd bought for Anna wilted on the seat beside him. At least Dad had a cassette player in the car, but he only had a Vince Hill tape in it. Still, Owen began to enjoy the drive. After all, he was going to the best place in the world.

The trouble started once he came off the motorway. By the time he'd seen the same pub three times, he knew he was lost. To cap it all, it started to rain.

He pulled up outside the pub and dived inside, leaving the engine running. The barman knew the village he needed. Owen was memorizing the directions when the sound of Vince Hill's singing blared out.

He froze. Legged it to the door just in time to see Dad's car disappearing down the road. 'You bastards!' he screamed at the unknown thieves.

A splodge of colour on the road caught his eye: Anna's flowers. He scooped them up.

'I'll ring the police,' the barman said.

'I don't want the police,' Owen said. I want to kill the little so-and-sos. But he said, 'I want a taxi.'

'I'll ring for a taxi, then.'

A horrible thought dawned on Owen. 'My wallet was in my jacket,' he said.

'You're knackered then, aren't you?' The barman seemed quite cheerful about it.

Owen walked. Three hours later, he was still walking, and soaked through to the skin, but he'd found Anna's cottage.

He walked up to the door. Now it came to it, he couldn't bring himself to knock. He realized it was that or turn round and go back. So he knocked.

No reply. He was about to knock again when Anna

finally opened the door. He had never seen her look so beautiful or so shocked. He held out his ragged bunch of flowers like a flag of surrender. 'Can I come in?'

She just stared at him. Love me, he thought. Love me. Let me love you. For one delirious moment he thought she would take him in her arms but she stood back to let him come in, and the moment was gone.

He followed her into the living room. It was like a nest – all comfy chairs and cushions, with a roaring coal fire and books and magazines scattered everywhere. Anna asked if he wanted a bath. It sounded divine, even if she wasn't going to share it – not that he dared say that.

'The hot water's from an immersion,' Anna said. 'It'll take about half an hour.'

Owen started to strip off. She was watching him. He liked that. Tried not to read too much into it. He started to undo his flies.

He grinned. 'So long as you don't mind staring at the wettest willy since Waldegrave.' She just looked at him. Suddenly, it was all wrong. He fastened his jeans again. 'Oh God,' he said. 'Anna, please don't make any decisions.' She just stared at him, as if she were weighing his worth. Finding him wanting. 'I haven't come to rush any decisions.'

She shook her head, any minute now it would be all over. 'Don't shake your head,' he begged. 'Don't... I'm going to go away again, and you can just think.'

'It's not going to work, Owen.'

The world ended. 'I won't even ring...' But she was shaking her head, reaching to pat him on the shoulder as if she'd never touched him anywhere more intimately. 'Why?' he said. 'Why?'

'Because it should never have happened in the first

place,' she said. She was almost crying. 'And the only reason it did was my problem.'

It was ludicrous. How could the world still be existing when she was saying something so ridiculous? 'It's not a problem to want to change your life.' She stared at him blankly. 'You want what he gave you? I don't believe that.'

Anna sighed. 'I don't want what anybody gave me,' she said. 'I'm selling the house, I'll get the divorce and think about things properly from there.'

'You're wrong,' Owen said. He knew it, as surely as he knew it would be wrong if rain started falling upwards, or the sun rose in the west.

'It's the only way I can go on.' A look of intense loneliness crossed her face. 'I don't believe anything anybody says.'

'We'd never have managed to keep this up. Not in the real world.'

They would. Once Crane was out of the way, they would have. 'You're wrong.'

'I'm sorry,' Anna said. The terrible thing about it was, she even sounded it.

Owen couldn't look at her. He started fastening his shirt. It was still sopping wet.

'Don't do that,' Anna said. 'You can't go out like that.' She put her hand on his. He jerked away as if he'd been burnt. 'Owen, please.' He headed for the door. 'Take my car,' she said. She tried to push her keys into his hand. He refused them. 'Owen!'

But he was through the door and into the cold and the rain. He headed down the path.

'That's just bloody stupid,' Anna said from behind him.

He heard the door slam. Heard her sobbing inside the cottage, and kept walking.

Chapter 34

Owen lugged his cases downstairs.

It was for the best. Really it was. Dad was waiting for him at the bottom.

'Bye Dad,' he said. He hugged the old man, feeling less awkward than he had expected. 'Take care of yourself.'

'You and all,' Dad said.

Irma came over to him. She was all choked up, so he gave her a hug, too. 'See you soon, Irma.'

He took his cases outside. There was a cab waiting for him next to the shiny new car that had arrived that morning.

Dad nodded towards the car. 'Do you trust me with this?'

Owen had bought it when he realized the MG was a write-off, but he'd decided he'd had enough of car-ownership for a while. Besides, they were a liability in London, and he owed Dad for the car that had been stolen, among other things.

He grinned. 'So long as it stops you drinking.' He got into the cab and wound the window down. 'I'll see you.'

The cab pulled away.

Richard stuck his head round Vivien's office door.

She looked up.

'I don't know... yet,' she said.

Richard just had to accept that.

It was painful, going to Crane for his reference, but not nearly so painful as a lot of other things in Owen's life. Crane handed him the envelope. 'It's glowing, obviously,' he said. Owen reckoned there was nothing obvious about it, but he wasn't about to say that. 'Can't fault you as a surgeon, and I'd be a fool if I tried to.'

Fair enough, Owen thought. He put his hand out for Crane to shake, but the older man didn't take him up on it. Owen shrugged and started to walk away.

'Ever operated on a long term coma patient?' Crane asked.

Owen turned round. He shook his head wearily, wondering where this was leading.

'Weirdest feeling. He's been spark out for three months. Not a peep. Suddenly he's got us lot buggering about like flies round a jampot.' Owen stared at him, bemused. 'He's damaged,' Crane went on. 'We decide we can help. But who asked?'

There was a metaphor in there somewhere, Owen decided. He left the room feeling vaguely got-at.

He went down the corridor to the restroom. He had just a few things to pick up, and then he was done with St Gregory's, done with Manchester, done with Anna, and he hated it.

He opened the door, and realized the place was packed. A cheer went up, and he saw there was a banner across the room: *So long, Springer.*

Someone had got some beer in. He took a can and did the round of the room, making his farewells. Then someone demanded a speech, and then several people did, and after that, there was no getting out of it. They gathered round to listen.

'I've worked with some of the best in my time, and some of the worst.' He gazed round at the crowd, biding his time. 'I'd just like to say to all the staff at St Gregory's – you're *crap.*' That drew a big laugh. He waited for it to die down. 'No,' he went on. 'Seriously – Danny Glassman, John McGinley...' He hunted them down with his eyes and found Viv standing close to John, surprisingly close. He couldn't really leave her out; and found that he didn't actually want to. 'Viv Reid. Brilliant surgical team...'

'What about Richard Crane?' someone yelled back.

That got a big laugh.

'Yeah,' Owen said. 'Well...'

He stopped speaking. How come he was going to miss this lot so much, when he'd only been here a month?

Anna showed the third couple of the day through the house.

'Has it been a happy house,' the woman of the pair asked as they came back into the hall.

'Yes,' Anna said. Well, it was mostly true.

The woman looked at her husband. 'You get a sense of it when you come through the front door, don't you?'

'Good,' Anna said. The sooner she got rid of the place the better. She opened the front door. Owen's dad was standing there, looking all spruced up.

'You're early or we're late,' the woman said. She turned to Anna. 'Thanks Mrs Crane.' They left.

Arnold pulled a jiffy bag out of his pocket. 'I never gave him this.' He held it out to her. 'I'm sorry. You were wrong to ask me to, in all fairness.'

Anna nodded: he was right. She'd timed the visit so

carefully, to be sure Owen would be on duty. Then when she'd got there, she'd feigned disappointment, but Arnold had see straight through her. 'Come in,' she said.

Arnold shook his head. 'No – I've got a couple of errands.' He smiled awkwardly, seeming a million miles away from the man she'd got sloppy drunk on lager and red wine with. 'He's gone off for the knees up.' He thought about it. 'Hardly that though – if he's still planning to get the half-past.' He patted her on the arm. 'You look after yourself, won't you? And if you fancy your chances on the bingo, give us a ring.'

He turned and left before Anna could say anything. She watched him go, then went back inside.

She picked up a pile of things that needed taking upstairs and headed for her bedroom.

She got half way up the stairs before she couldn't take it any more. She sat down and opened the jiffy bag. It contained the necklace Owen had given her, as she'd known it did. The red-gold links slipped coldly through her fingers.

She thought of something, and rooted through the things she'd picked up. The envelope she was looking for was there – the one containing the photographs of her and Owen. They were in black and white, grainy and unsharp.

Owen laughing and her worried, Owen sad and her laughing. The pair of them, making messy, dangerous love up against that tree, in the back of the Audi... so different from the posed formality of the pictures of her and Richard that surrounded her in this house: sharp and technicolour, with all the doubt removed.

She sorted the photos out, found the one she liked best. Owen smiling. She traced the line of his mouth.

And knew what she'd done. She raced outside, sending the photos flying and into the car.

To the station, but which platform? Which goddamned platform?

But it didn't matter, because the train had gone. He had gone.

'No!' Anna wailed. 'You stupid, bloody cow.'

She trudged back to her car. Drove slowly home. It had to be slowly, because she could barely see for tears. She parked the car in the drive – she couldn't have negotiated the garage to save her life. The house loomed in front of her, cold and empty.

She took a deep breath. She had chosen this. She got out of the car, and fumbled for her key.

'You're wrong.' a voice said.

Anna spun round. Owen was standing on the far side of the garage, surrounded by his bags.

'Give me a chance to prove it.' She ran to him. He grabbed her. She held him. And knew they would never let each other go again.